BEGIN THE
WORLD OVER

BEGIN THE WORLD OVER

KUNG LI SUN

EMERGENT STRATEGY SERIES

Begin the World Over
Emergent Strategy Series No. 5
© 2022 Kung Li Sun

ISBN: 9781849354721
E-ISBN: 9781849354738
Library of Congress Control Number: 2021944656

AK Press   AK Press
370 Ryan Avenue #100   33 Tower St.
Chico, CA 95973   Edinburgh EH6 7BN
USA   Scotland
www.akpress.org   www.akuk.com
akpress@akpress.org   akuk@akpress.org

Please contact us to request the latest AK Press distribution catalog, which features books, pamphlets, zines, and stylish apparel published and/or distributed by AK Press. Alternatively, visit our websites for the complete catalog, latest news, and secure ordering.

Cover design by Herb Thornby

Printed in the United States of America on acid-free paper

One of the ways we can understand our current state is as the outcome of millions of choices made by preceding generations. In this alternate history, Kung Li helps us imagine what would have happened if the Haitian revolution had spread throughout the United States. The first work of fiction in our Emergent Strategy Series is a queer, multicultural, adventurous, and revolutionary text that shows how the subtle, bombastic, and often intimate work of organizing can have a large scale impact. Readers should expect to be delighted by the time travel experience of deeply researched historical fiction, and inspired by the strategic invitation to use our lives for liberation.

adrienne maree brown, EMERGENT STRATEGY SERIES

Author's Note

In addition to the better known revolts—Stono, Gabriel's Conspiracy, the 1811 German Coast uprising, Denmark Vesey in Charleston, and Nat Turner's rebellion—there were hundreds of organized uprisings by enslaved people in the United States and prior colonies. These uprisings happened in clusters, when conditions appeared that increased the chance of success. One such cluster occurred in the 1790s.

This is a work of counterfactual fiction of that historical moment. Characters are, by and large, real people, acting within the bounds of available evidence. Any resemblance to actual persons, living or dead, or actual events is intentional.

Chapter 1

James Hemings was doing well, thank you very much, when he first met Denmark Vesey in the sailmaker's loft. James's task: deliver a dinner invitation to Edmond-Charles Genet, ambassador from the newly declared République Française. The invitation was in James's right coat pocket, laid neatly alongside a perfect slice of plum cake.

James took the steps down to Water Street and found Philadelphia's famous taverns already open for business, though it was not yet nine in the morning. The street was filled with men pushing drays from the wharfs to the store-houses. The river gleamed as if polished. James wove his way around the carts teetering with crates stacked atop crates. The flow of traffic was halted by a boy struggling with a pig, the lead rope stretched taut between the two. James stepped around the pair and into the sailmaker's loft.

This was no musty warehouse—the loft was tall as a ship's mast, the roof punched through with skylights. The space was filled with a bright, golden light. Sails spilled over the tables and collected in puddles on the floor. Three posts along the center of the loft were rigged like masts. On each, a sail was stretched to full majesty, as if a strong, steady wind was blowing through the loft.

Dozens of men sat and sewed, bent over their work in quiet concentration. One pointed James to a path roughed out along the floor, winding through the benches and piles of cloth. The path led to a steep ramp up to an open platform overlooking the loft. There James spotted a white man in a ruffled blue waistcoat with the face of a noble, eager squirrel. Ambassador Genet.

James hurried up the ramp and introduced himself as maître d'hôtel to Thomas Jefferson.

"Our friend Mr. Jefferson!" The pinched set of Genet's face opened into a smile. "Has he good news for France?"

James presented the small ivory envelope containing the invitation to dinner alongside the slice of plum cake.

"Secretary Jefferson would be honored to host you tonight, monsieur," James said.

Genet took a bite of the cake and looked up, startled at its delicate balance of sour and sweet.

"Is he a friend of liberté?"

"Indeed," James answered in French. "He is sure he invented it."

Genet's smile grew wider. He turned his head and shouted across the loft. "Did you hear that, Mr. Denmark? Mr. Jefferson will use his influence over the president. You must use your influence over your captain. Don't you want the revolution to succeed?"

From the base of the ramp came a deep, ringing sound. It was a sound so rich James could taste it—a heavy lubricious boudin noir, but carried along a tone that rang clear as beef consommé. It took a beat for James to register that the euphony was an assembly of words.

"More than you know."

James looked over. The source of the astounding voice had a beautiful mouth and a heavy brow split by two furrows. A plain linen shirt stretched across the man's broad shoulders. As he approached them, his gaze passed quickly from Genet to James, where it remained. For what seemed. A very. Long. Time.

James stopped breathing. His hearing failed, and the loft fell silent. He felt in his gut a coup de foudre, a strike of lightning. Years ago in Monticello he'd fallen out of a tree, landing in a way that knocked the breath out of him. This was the same feeling. It was not pleasant.

When sound returned, Denmark was mid-sentence.

"...the Declaration of the Rights of Man.

"Saint-Domingue cannot be lost to the English."

"You will side with the Africans?" Denmark said. He did not take his eyes off James even as he queried Genet.

Genet hesitated, then rushed ahead. "Of course. If they are loyal to France, we welcome them as we welcomed the gens de colueur into the Republic."

"Reluctantly."

Denmark's voice—or his unblinking stare—reached into James's chest and squeezed away what little air was left in his lungs.

"Non!" Genet cried out, insistent. "We welcome them— you—as brothers. With enthusiasm! As citiyons of the new French Republic."

Denmark shifted his eyes back to Genet. "If you side with the Africans in Saint-Domingue, you lose any chance of President Washington's support."

Genet chewed on his lower lip as he considered this problematic insight. "President Washington owns slaves, yes," he conceded. His eyes narrowed then brightened as he found his escape. "Secretary Jefferson will be our champion! He helped Lafayette write our Declaration of Rights; he will surely defend it. That is why he has sent his man to invite me to dinner tonight!"

Genet turned to James for confirmation.

James drew in a breath and cleared his throat to get his voice working again. He meant to tell Genet that Jefferson enslaved twice as many people as the president but discovered his jaw was paralyzed. Instead all he was able to manage was, "Dinner is at seven."

Denmark took another long look at James.

"Jefferson—he is your master? Does he have a dinner invitation for me too?"

James found his jaw could, at last, move again and that he could even manage a small smile. "You don't need an invitation from him. I can invite you to my kitchen."

Denmark raised an eyebrow. "Your kitchen."

"I am Jefferson's cook."

"Employed or enslaved?"

James's smile disappeared. "It is not so simple."

Denmark's eyebrow tugged somehow higher.

"Can you sail away to New York if you wished, find a new employer there?"

James coughed into his fist.

"You are enslaved, then."

"I come and go as I wish."

"Then why don't you go?" Denmark waited for a response. Hearing none, he offered his own. "I see."

James grimaced, then did what he could to recover his poise. "My apologies, but there is dinner tonight. I'm needed in the kitchen."

James turned to leave and thought he heard Denmark snort. What did this sailor know? The workers looked up from their sewing to watch him hurry down the ramp.

"Vive la révolution!" Genet shouted down to James.

He was nearly out the door when he felt Denmark's hand on his shoulder and was brought around with a sharp yank to face him. "There is dinner tonight, and there will be dinner every night thereafter," Denmark said.

He moved his hand to the back of James's neck and grabbed it, and now there was nothing in James's vision but the two deep furrows between Denmark's brow.

"Join us. You were not born to be a slave."

It was all too much. James's innards twisted, his liver tangled among his kidneys. He felt as if a church bell was ringing inside his skull, painfully loud.

Denmark held tight James's neck and leaned in close. James felt Denmark's breath hot against his ear. "We need a cook. Come join our ship. We sail tomorrow."

Suddenly released from Denmark's grip, James took hold of a large bolt of cotton cloth to steady himself. A wind blew into the loft, strong enough to lift the scraps from the floor and rustle the sails hoisted along the posts. The workers had stopped cutting and sewing. All eyes on James, they seemed to be waiting for his response.

James took a last look at the man before him. "Bon voyage then, sailor." He tried to flash his winning smile. It died on the vine.

Away from the loft and back out into the morning air, the sun still gleamed off the surface of the river. On the far shore was the forest, a familiar jumble of birch and cedars. The dogwoods, James knew, were ready to bloom. Dock workers struggled against their carts. James took a deep breath. Something in that loft had grabbed ahold of his senses; back out in the open air, he was free of the bewitching. But Denmark's voice echoed, faint but audible still.

You were not born to be a slave.

James woke with blood roaring in his ears. How much had he drunk the night before? He remembered the bottle of Bordeaux, gone by the time dinner was served. He remembered starting the Madeira. Surely he did not finish it. He tried to sit up and managed a few inches. The bed, unfamiliar, seemed to rock as he lowered himself back down. Perhaps he did finish it.

James searched his memory, gingerly. Ambassador Genet had greeted him by name. The poisson à la meunière was overcooked, but Genet had barely looked up when James served it—the ambassador was pressing Jefferson about trembling before a just God. James left the kitchen after serving the coffee and headed to his favorite tavern. Someone caught him as he nearly tumbled off the gangplank boarding the ship.

The ship?

James's eyes flew open and he sat up. His forehead met the plank with a thud. He sank back down and realized the swaying he felt was only partly internal. This really was a ship. James pressed his palms against the ridge of his brow. So he had gotten drunk. Drunk enough to get on this ship. Because a rough-looking sailor named Denmark had asked him to sail away. James groaned.

He had to get back, of course. Jefferson was surely upset at the lack of breakfast, and growing angrier by the minute.

James forced himself out of the bunk, then up the ladder. Everything on deck was far too bright. The sun ricocheted off the water and cut daggers into his eyes. James squinted and searched along the horizon, hoping for a glimpse of land.

"Don't remember how you got here, do you?"

A knowing smile played on the questioner's cracked lips as he offered his hand and introduced himself as the coxswain. The man had a build and color that reminded James of the first time he'd made pork chops. The fire too hot, the thick cuts came out of the oven both tough and undercooked.

"Wondering how to get back to shore." James noted the man's shoes were torn along the seams. "There's cash for my return."

The coxswain laughed. "We're not turning back. We're on our way to Saint-Domingue." The coxswain touched his finger to his forehead in pantomime of doffing a hat. "Welcome to the *Golden Dragon*. I'll let the captain know you've joined us."

The coxswain ambled off, pausing to talk to a sailor resting his back against a small cannon. The sailor slurped from a bowl, not quite ignoring the coxswain but also not paying much attention. James leaned forward to see what the sailor was eating. The gruel that dripped from the man's spoon had bits of gristle suspended in the oozing slime. A small panic rose in James's throat.

It was clear even to James's inexperienced eye that the *Golden Dragon*, gleaming black with red trim, was built for speed. Her sails were tightly fit. Her bow sliced through the water without a figurehead. There was, in fact, no ornamentation of any kind. The ship's sleek line was interrupted only by a longboat, strapped tight starboard. James wondered whether he might be able to lower the boat to the water and make an escape. This was certainly not the first instance he'd found himself in unexpected surroundings after a few too many glasses of wine. There was the time he woke up in the grand-duché's carriage ten miles from Chantilly, requiring him to make an embarrased request to disembark for the long hike back.

This was a decidedly different circumstance. In every direction as far as he could see, there was nothing but water. A sudden clap of fear cleared away the stuffing in his head. He was trapped aboard a ship sailing at a fantastic clip away from Philadelphia. Away from the breakfast he did not prepare and place in front of Jefferson this morning. How will he react when he discovers James gone? Might Jefferson sell Critta or another of his siblings as punishment or a warning?

James pressed the palms of his hands against his eyes and muttered a mix of curses and prayers. He was interrupted by a familiar voice.

"I had to come see for myself." Denmark tried to suppress his smile but failed. A sailor at the foremast called for Denmark's attention. "Make yourself at home. We've never had a real cook aboard."

As James watched Denmark stride off, all seemed hopeless. He dropped his head back into his hands and resumed his muttering. What to do? There were fewer prayers and more curses, at the completion of which he resolved to do what he usually did in hopeless situations. He would make a cake.

The sailor, still slurping from his bowl of gruel, pointed James below deck, back towards the stern. There, dimly lit by a pair of portholes, a galley stove hulked against the back wall of the hold. It was an entire kitchen compressed into an iron rectangle six feet by seven. There was an open fire at the front of the range, two large boilers, and an oven that could be opened on either side. A roasting spit spanned the range.

The clever arrangement cheered James for a bit, but when his search for cooking utensils turned up only a cracked spatula, despair returned. There was a large pot, two pans, and a single dull knife. As for ingredients, there was beer, flour, salted pork, butter, cheese, and oatmeal. A small cask of pickled oysters sat open among the barrels of salt cod. James found two eggs hidden among the dozen chickens huddled inside a tiny cage, the poor creatures too depressed to cluck. That was all. There was no sugar for his cake.

"You didn't say you're our new cook."

James spun around, an egg in each hand.

"Denmark said to show you the kitchen." The coxswain stepped into a patch of light. "Seems you found your own way."

"These are all the provisions?"

"Something missing?"

"Sugar."

The coxswain shook his head. Denmark found sugar as offensive as slavery, he explained; the former was only made possible by the latter. Nothing made of sugarcane was allowed aboard the ship.

The coxswain looked James up and down, considering whether he could be trusted. The coxswain's talent was in making judgments, but this fellow clutching a pair of eggs was an odd one. His stomach growled, encouraging him to take the chance.

"I might 'ave a bit I keep for myself, tho. I'll give you some for half of whatever you're making."

The cake turned out crumbly and dry, but the coxswain grinned with his teeth—enormous, yellow and cracked teeth—as he divided it. He savored his portion crumb by crumb. "So you'll stay on as our cook, then."

James, miserable, pushed the final piece to the coxswain. "What choice do I have?"

"Not much, true." The coxswain wet his forefinger and gathered up the last bits of cake. "How'd you learn to make a cake like this?"

James's cake had its genesis in a hognose snake that flared its hood and spooked a horse. The horse threw its rider, an ill-tempered slave dealer named John Wayles, who was James Hemings's owner. And father. A rock angled just so killed Wayles, and ownership of the boy James passed from dead man Wayles to his son-in-law, Thomas Jefferson. The rest of the Hemings family as well: James's mother Elizabeth, his older siblings Mary, Martin, Betty, Nancy, and Robert, his younger siblings Thenia, Critta, Peter, and the infant Sally.

Elizabeth Hemings understood the danger in the move to Monticello: James, barely eight but tall for his age and as yet without skills, was the most likely of her children to be selected for sale. And so she quickly negotiated a place for him in the kitchen under the tutelage of Ursula, the short, stout woman who ruled over the kitchen and pretended not to hear the tinge of sarcasm when others addressed her as Queen.

Within a year, James made himself indispensable in Queen Ursula's kitchen. Young James learned how to tilt the paring knife to spare the flesh of the fruit. He learned smoking, pickling, and salting. Ursula taught James how to count money and calculate sums for the week's shopping, then to write out the lists in a beautiful script.

When Ursula taught him plum cake, James thought he could do better. He snuck into the kitchen after dinner and gave the cake another try. Better. James tried another. Then another. The kitchen came alive. Hiding in every bin were sweetnesses and savories, each waiting to be fired into being. James felt about these tastes the way other boys felt about salamanders: quicksilver wonders he needed to capture before they slipped away.

When Ursula discovered the reason for the sudden decline in flour and kindling, she hid her delight at her student's cleverness and sent James out to slop the pigs. Still he was permitted to continue his experiments, though they did not all succeed. Failures he offered to his younger siblings. Thenia and Critta refused after the first unctuous bite of shepherd's pie made with too many onions. Peter accepted only the fallen breads. It was Sally, possessing an iron-lined stomach, who happily ate whatever James handed her. At three, she polished off an entire apple tansy. At four, she downed a pot of peanut soup thickened nearly to paste. At five, Sally valiantly ate bowl after bowl as James tried different herbs to brighten the porridge.

Sally became James's favorite, his shadow in the kitchen. Whenever James sat to peel a bowl of potatoes, Sally squatted across from him and piled the slivers into little pyramids. When it was time to stoke the fire, she helped by making blowing noises. The other Hemings treated her like a pretty little doll. James never did that. He had her fetch the firewood. He asked her opinion. Sally adored her brother completely.

The first time James prepared a full dinner on his own, Jefferson called Ursula into the dining room to complement her on the tenderness of the roast. James was then eleven years old.

Jefferson wrapped the remainder and took it with him

to Philadelphia, where the Continental Congress was meeting. *All men are created equal,* Jefferson wrote. *They are endowed with unalienable rights.* He took a bite of the succulent meat and enumerated *Life* and *Liberty.* Pepper, rosemary, and a trace of red wine filled his mouth. He added, *and the pursuit of Happiness.*

When Jefferson was invited to represent the United States in France seven years later, Elizabeth was the one, as always, to see the opening. She made her case one evening after dinner, as James carried away the plates. She stood tall and rested a hand lightly on the table. Was that not an excellent veal sausage and potatoes? Jefferson turned his head and regarded her with a wary eye. Elizabeth pressed ahead. Veal sausage was good, but in France, a man as talented as James could be trained to cook a more sophisticated cuisine. Imagine, Elizabeth said, setting a table for your guests as fine as any in Paris.

Jefferson looked at his plate. Yes, this was a good idea. Fey, pretty-faced James. Jefferson made a calculation. James was clearly not the sort to increase the estate's net worth by siring offspring. But having James trained in la cuisine moderne. That would increase not only Jefferson's net worth but his reputation as well. What a splendid idea. Jefferson nodded to congratulate himself. How lovely it was to have such good ideas.

The night before his departure, Elizabeth sat with James in the kitchen as he selected pots and pans for the trip. Her beautiful and tender-hearted son. She wished she had the power to give him his freedom. She did not.

All she could do was make plain to James what she had done to get him closer to freedom, so he could do it for himself. Accept reality, she told him, however dire. And then make the next best move, however small, to improve your position. She could see he was terrified, and for a moment she regretted having arranged for him to be away so far from home, alone with Jefferson in a treacherous sea of whites. But she could not call him back, not now. This was his next best move. This was the most she could do.

In France, Jefferson sent James away to learn at Château de Chantilly, a castle that made Monticello seem a backwoods cabin. The kitchen struck James mute the first time he entered it. Heat flowed from the ovens, an entire wall of them, tended by a boy holding a little rake to scrape at the coals. From the roasting pit the smell of meat—lamb chops stuffed with artichokes and raisins—thickened the air.

Mademoiselle Madeleine welcomed James and said a dozen things to him in rapid French. The words flew over him like a flock of sparrows. She enumerated items six seven eight nine on her fingers, and James was utterly lost, cut loose from every binding of family, home, and language. His tutor only stopped when the boy raking the ovens yelped from touching a hot coal. It was a sharp animal sound of pain, and James felt an overwhelming desire to run away. He would have run if he had not been at that moment wearing such fashionable but too small shoes.

James learned in that kitchen how to turn leftover roast game into a perfect salmi. With the geese whose livers were to become pâté de foie gras, how to coax one more fig down their throats. James learned how to lay delicate filets of sole atop a sheen of butter. Salt cod was crushed into balls, smothered in cream, dunked into a bouillabaisse. In that Chantilly kitchen, James learned how to squeeze his way through the palisades guarding the hearts of men. Butter, patiently incorporated. A shake of powdered vanilla. A dollop of crème fouettée dite. It was the art of the irresistible, practiced with sauces and knives.

James would have been delighted to remain in Chantilly

longer, but in 1787 Jefferson called him back to Paris to resume work as his cook. Not long after, Jefferson's daughter Patsy arrived. She was chaperoned, much to both James and Jefferson's surprise, by Sally.

As her coach rolled into Paris, Sally looked down the long boulevard and knew immediately: this was where God had meant for her to be born. Hats! Crowds! Her brother was a real chef! She could barely sit still long enough to give James the family updates. Yes, their brother Robert's baby Elizabeth was still healthy. No, there was no improvement in Peter's leg. Yes, Critta had kept her word and named her firstborn after James. It was an ugly baby, though.

James, for his part, could barely believe this was his baby sister. They had been separated only three years, but in that time Sally had grown into a young woman nearly as beautiful as him. Jefferson installed her as the femmes de chamber. It was an expense adding to his already significant debt, but Jefferson justified it as… It was unclear how he justified it.

James studied Jefferson's face as the older man announced his decision. James was ecstatic to have his sister with him, but there was something off about the way Jefferson looked at young Sally. It was subtle, the way a wagon wheel wobbled, ever so slightly, when a hub rivet came loose.

A dozen other servants made for light cleaning work for Sally, so at every opportunity the Hemings siblings stepped out of their front door onto the Champs-Elysées. In Paris, where the Freedom Principle declared that there were no slaves in France, James and Sally were free to come and go in a way they never could have back in Virginia, and James was paid a wage equal to any white chef. James helped Sally with her verb conjugations as they strolled the Tuileries Gardens and bought chocolates at the newly opened Palais Royal shopping mall. They drank café au laits and eavesdropped, the gossip now almost totally replaced by arguments over politics. The whole city was abuzz—Louis XVI was losing control.

As spring passed into summer, Sally tossed off her bonnet and hired a coiffeur to raise her wavy black hair into a tower atop her head. Then from one season of masked balls to the next, she grew three inches and an ample bosom. She radiated health. James credited the good butter.

Sally loved Wolfgang Amadeus Mozart's operas, but it was the dashing gens de couleur Joseph Bologne who left on James the deepest mark. Bologne, a champion fencer, was a maestro of the violin and rumored to be a lover of Queen Marie-Antoinette. When he appeared on stage at the opera house for a demonstration of his fencing prowess, James was in the third row. The young chef watched as Bologne thrust and parried with his sliver of a blade, gliding as if on oiled feet. At the final touché, the audience rose in a collective roar, and James felt a flood of desire swell inside him. James wished to be a gens de couleur as famous as this, to have his talents recognized by a standing ovation. He wished this with every hair on his handsome head. He wanted nothing less. What Bologne did with his épée, James would do with his spatula. He wanted nothing more.

One evening, James took Sally to visit Pierre Givenchy, a friend from the Chantilly kitchen. Moved by the revolutionary spirit, Givenchy was bringing his high training to the common people by selling restorative bouillons out of a store he called a restaurant. Barbers sipped their soups next to financiers; wig makers sat elbow to elbow with lawyers.

"Don't be fooled by the calm," Givenchy warned as he ladled out soup. He said that France was spiraling into chaos, and the Jacobins filling the streets were braying ever louder, pressing the king to declare the end of absolute monarchy.

Givenchy shook his ladle at the bustle around him. People crowded into his restaurant for the soup, yes, but mostly to hear and pass along bits of news. He needed help. Would James consider joining him in the kitchen here?

James peered through the steam that rose above the pot

of bouillon. He saw his friend was serious. Pierre was certain that the Société des Amis des Noirs would take James in, would hold him up as an example of what was possible after the abolition of slavery. You and Sally must stay in France, Pierre insisted.

James laughed and bid his adieu, pulling his sister away from the men whose stares leeched onto her neck and wrists. Can you imagine, he said to Sally, us as Frenchmen? He said it as a joke, and laughed as he called out Bonjour, mon frère! to every passerby.

But Pierre's words burrowed their way into James's consciousness. Was such a thing possible? Although the Freedom Principle meant there were no slaves on French soil, a foreigner who wished to bring his "property" ashore was permitted to do so, so long as he registered such "property" with the admiralty court. But James knew that Jefferson had neglected to register. That made his own status unclear. He had a salary. He could come and go as he pleased. James felt himself, while not exactly free, remarkably libré.

Here there was a revolution brewing, one where he was included in the fraternité demanding liberté and egalité. Here he had a reputation for both his well-formed face and his fabulous desserts. No one could pile a tower of profiteroles as high as he (his secret: a thin glue made of spun sugar). Nowhere in Paris was there a lighter mousse. As for his version of cherry clafoutis, why *not* add candied lemons and top it all with rosewater-infused crème fraise?

When a mob hungry for bread stormed the Bastille, James found Sally in her bedchamber and pulled the door closed behind him. What if they really did remain in Paris? With the right introduction to the right nobleman's kitchen, he could command a wage sufficient for both of them. She could find work as a seamstress.

Sally folded her arms and laughed with a dense little conker shell of a laugh. James had expected her to hesitate.

He had not expected her to dismiss him outright. Her love of Paris was as strong as ever—just last week she had insisted on extra lessons from their French tutor, to improve her pronunciation. So why this rejection?

It's a chance for us.

A chance for what?

A revolution—

Like the one in Virginia?

This is different.

It is not different for us.

Our mother would want us to—

Our mother would understand my situation better than anyone.

Silence filled the room as Sally's words took on their full meaning.

"You're his daughter's age," James could barely speak, choking back the bile that rose in his throat.

His sister clenched her jaw and looked hard at him.

"My children will be free. This is my best chance."

Sally's face softened as she saw the tears welling in her brother's eyes. She took his hand and pressed his palm to her cheek. "What's yours?"

That night, sleepless, James turned the question over and over again in his mind, worrying it, searching for a crack along its edges. Was his best chance to risk escape? It felt impossible to leave Sally behind. He was her brother. Yet— the thought cut through him, sharper than the sharpest of his knives—a brother powerless to protect her. He could hear his mother's voice. *Improve your position.* He wished she were here to tell him how to make such an impossible choice.

His second morning on the *Golden Dragon*, James made oatmeal for the crew and considered his options as he scraped out the pots. They would soon be anchoring in the port of Savannah. James could go ashore and try to make it back to Philadelphia. But he would have to travel on roads full of slave patrols. In all likelihood, he would be captured and sold within the week.

In his pocket he carried, as always, his best chance. Or at least the best chance he had been able to negotiate after his bitter return from Paris, over the course of many years. A promise, written in a cramped and resentful script:

> *I do hereby promise and declare, that if the said James shall teach such person as I shall place under him to be a good cook, he shall be thereupon made free. Given under my hand and seal in Philadelphia Pennsylvania this 15th day of September 1793.*
> *Th: Jefferson*

If he were snatched up by a patrolman, he could pull out this agreement, point to the signature, and… He could hear the white men laughing as they crumpled the paper and threw it to the ground.

James looked down at the reflection of his face at the bottom of the pot and realized his best chance was not worth much. At least not in Georgia. It had taken him four years after returning from Paris to negotiate that promise. James told himself not to cry. Accept reality, however dire. And then make the next best move, however small, to improve your position.

He set down the pot and went looking for Denmark. If he was going to stay aboard and cook in that miserable kitchen, he would need provisions.

James made a list and set the paper atop the cod when he delivered Denmark's dinner plate. Denmark glanced at the paper and offered only a brisk thank you before continuing his conversation with Captain Mai.

James cleared his throat and interrupted. "I need these ingredients," James declared. "It will raise the morale of your crew."

"You think their morale is low?" Denmark laughed and glanced at Captain Mai. She was from the east, China or Malay maybe. A thick queue of black hair flowed from the top of her head down to her waist, and a scar cut a dark line from her earlobe up to the bridge of her nose. When she looked up, James saw her left eye was made of glass.

Unnerved, James gave a shallow nod and backed out of the room.

The coxswain was waiting for him on deck. "No luck with your grocery list?"

"What do you know about Denmark?"

"Denmark is just the first mate. It's Captain Mai you should be asking about."

"What do you know about Mai, then?"

"The woman is rich." The coxswain examined a coil of rope. "That porcelain in the hold is worth ten times its weight in indigo. She bought Denmark off another captain. Him and the ship, a two-for-one deal. Captain Mai loves a deal."

"She is still his master?"

The coxswain shook his head as he finished one rope and moved on to the next. "Bought himself out after the last run."

"But he is still onboard."

"The first mate believes people are ready to join the Saint-Domingue uprising and raise the flag of liberty."

"Who?"

"Africans everywhere. Cuba, Jamaica, the Carolinas. Denmark intends to spread the fires of revolution." The coxswain found a fray in the rope and marked it with a ribbon. "Our little ship will bring the word." He lowered his voice into an imitation of Denmark's baritone. "Liberty and equality. The Rights of Man."

"That seems…" James searched. "Ambitious."

"He recruited you, didn't he? Right out of Philadelphia, even."

James wanted to ask more, but at that moment Denmark appeared on deck. The coxswain saluted and stood up straight to get his orders, but it was James whom Denmark addressed.

"Your list of provisions is not cheap."

"Without them, what I can cook will be inedible," James said. He hesitated a moment, then added, "Sir."

Denmark called over a sailor. "Have you complaints about your meals?"

"None, sir."

Denmark turned to the coxswain. "And you?"

The coxswain looked off over the helm as if remembering an old love. James thought he was remembering the contraband cake. It was only later, when he understood the coxswain's role as the crew's representative, that he realized the coxswain's long pause was to weigh whether each crewman would be willing to give up a few pesos of pay in exchange for tastier meals.

"Some variety wouldn't hurt," the coxswain finally said.

Denmark looked skeptical.

"No one has complained to me," Denmark said. "Or to Captain Mai. Have they complained to you?"

The coxswain shifted from foot to foot but held his ground. "No crew's ever mutinied when the food's good."

"You realize every peso we spend on spices is that much less to be divided at the end," Denmark said, his question directed at James.

James had not realized—he had no experience with the practice of equal shares. He assured Denmark the ingredients were worth the cost.

"Basil? Rosemary? Thyme?" Denmark seemed insulted by the very mention of herbs. "We're a merchant ship, not a botany expedition. These are sailors."

"Sailors deserve fine meals," James said. "As *citoyens* of the sea. A delicious dinner is a fair reward for a day's work."

This seemed to find a crack in Denmark's guard.

"Good coffee and an omelet in the morning changes the sound of the first bell from a dreadful tone into a beloved one."

Denmark frowned in an encouraging way.

James continued in a rush. "It's in the spirit of the revolution to bring the richness of royalty to your crew."

"Our revolution is for equality, not the excesses of nobility," Denmark said sharply. He motioned the coxswain to follow him and gave James a curt nod good night.

A few steps on, Denmark turned back.

"You are persistent."

James grinned. "But are you persuaded?"

"Perhaps." Denmark turned back to join the coxswain. "Let's see if I surprise myself."

Chapter 2

At Savannah, Mai and Denmark disembarked with a single set of porcelain, the plates and soup bowls carefully packed in moss. They returned the next day with forty chickens and five drays towering with provisions. Denmark himself carried the herb plants in their pots to the bow of the ship and built an elegant little wood trap to secure them.

James turned the fresh tomatoes and the day's catch into a bouillabaisse. It was delicious. As for the bread, when James opened the stove to turn it he upended a bowl of seawater used to cool the stovetop. A cloud of steam billowed inside the oven. When the long loaves came out with an unusually thin, crisp crust, James wondered whether the salty steam was the reason. It was a miracle of a loaf of bread. The sailors clamored for more. Before James could accommodate them, a ship's boy came into the kitchen to let James know his presence was requested.

The captain's quarters were built into the stern with space enough for a mahogany table surrounded by a dozen chairs. Lanterns and skylights lit the space, showing off a bookcase filled with books in various languages. Set deepest into the stern was Captain Mai's bedchamber, which remained closed.

"Join us," said Denmark, and returned to his conversation with Mai. The four others at the table glanced up from their bowls but did not stop eating.

Captain Mai continued poking at the map with chopsticks, ignoring James. She said without looking up, "You are wrong—more commerce, more capital, more slavery. Capital builds capital, more more more, always more."

"The cook is here," said Denmark.

Mai glanced up at James. "Good bread," she said. "What do you cost?"

James looked at Mai blankly.

"Your price, on land," Mai demanded.

Denmark saw James's discomfort. "It's no insult," Denmark said. "We're arguing about the future of trade."

Denmark picked at his bread. The crust really was splendid.

"No matter," said Mai. "Increasing production is very easy. Now with cotton gin, it's even more easy. Every bank wants to give credit to make farms for cotton. Twelve cents a pound, one slave makes 1,000 pounds equals $120. But with new cotton gin, one slave makes 2,000 pounds. With more whipping, one slave makes 4,000 pounds, equals $480. You need credit to buy slave? So easy! When one slave equals $480 in one year, easy to pay 10 percent interest on credit. Every bank gives credit. More credit, more slaves, more profit."

Denmark explained. "We had dinner in Savannah with a tutor. A tutor and a tinkerer, named…" Denmark looked to Mai.

"Eli Whitney," she said.

"Yes, young clever Eli. The contraption got Captain Mai here very excited. She believes it will prove Adam Smith wrong."

James nodded as if he knew this Adam Smith.

Denmark was not fooled by James's nod. "Adam Smith," Denmark said, "thinks only of buying and selling. As does Captain Mai. Mr. Smith believes slavery will end on its own. He believes the work done by free men is cheaper than the work done by slaves, which has to be squeezed out by violence."

Mai jumped in. "Adam Smith is right about everything

else. Here he wrong. Violence is free. More violence equals more cotton, zero additional cost."

"She is trying to make me a good *capitaliste*," said Denmark to James. Then to Mai, Denmark said, "You know I'll never touch the trade, no matter how profitable."

Mai stood and reached across the table. With the heel of her palm, she gave Denmark a hard rap on his forehead. "You stupid man! I talk cotton gin for your protection. Not for your profit. Capital is most powerful. If indigo down, capital go to sugar. If sugar down, capital go to cotton. No sugar in Santo Domingo? Yes in Cuba. Man is not free, capital is free."

Denmark rubbed his forehead. To James, he said, "She thinks I've been unduly influenced by the French notions of *liberté*."

"French *liberté* is no match for Spanish *libertad*," said Mai. "*Liberté* is idea only. *Libertad* is real, is free trade in Blacks. *Libertad* brings silver pieces." She snatched the last piece of bread from Denmark's plate and stuffed it in her mouth. She chewed ferociously. "*Libertad* forever stronger than *liberté*."

"We should have brought more flour on board," said Denmark. "So what can I do about this monster *libertad*, other than fight for *liberté*?"

Mai pressed her lips together. James thought she looked sorrowful, though it was hard to tell on such an unflinching face.

"Stay at sea," she said. "You safe at sea."

The *Golden Dragon* continued southward, threading a line between the Florida Keys and its reef. Inspired by James's cooking, the sailors became enthusiastic fishermen. One evening, it took three of the crew to wrestle onto the deck a goliath grouper. James steamed it and served it with pickled berries.

The chickens felt the change in atmosphere. They fluffed their feathers and produced eggs with aplomb.

Denmark asked for his dinners on deck after the crew's meal, eating as the sun touched the horizon. As they sailed past the final Florida island, James presented a bowl of bouillabaisse. He flourished it with a wave of his hand.

"The last of the tomatoes." Dark water stretched before them. "It feels like we're sailing to the edge of the earth."

"Not the edge, the opposite." Denmark examined the green bits in his bowl. Herbs. "We're sailing to the center of the new world."

"It has some competition then—Philadelphia has the same ambition."

Denmark glanced at James. "Your former master believes that. He's wrong. Philadelphia will not be the center of the world." Denmark accepted the piece of crusty bread James offered. "It will be Saint-Domingue."

"The coxswain says we're going because Captain Mai knows how to make profit out of chaos."

Denmark laughed. "She certainly does. It didn't take much to convince her to take this route."

"Why Saint-Domingue?"

"There is someone needing rescue."

"Like me."

"No." Denmark cocked his head. "Maybe a little like you." Denmark bit into the bread. "There is no more butter?" He sopped what remained of his bouillabaisse with the bread.

Across the deck, a flap of sail caught Denmark's attention. "Thank you for dinner. Good for my morale." Denmark handed his empty bowl to James and walked away before the cook could ask another question.

The days aboard a ship, James discovered, were all the same.

There was breakfast, a midday break for beer and biscuits, then supper. In between, the crew swabbed the deck, mended the ropes, kept watch, prepared the oakum, and did the dozens of other tasks necessary to keep the ship tidy and afloat. The routine had a soothing effect on James, and after a while he felt almost accustomed to his new life and stopped calculating whether he might be able to swim to shore. His nights, though, reamined littered with dreams of Critta or another of his siblings being sold away to recoup the cost of his running away.

Favorable winds carried them quickly to Saint-Domingue, where they dropped anchor in Le Cap's harbor. As the anchor pulled taut, James was at the galley stove making breakfast. Shouts from the deck suggested trouble.

Yelling was common but not at such an early hour. Some of the voices sounded angry. Others were lined with a sharp edge of excitement. James kept his eyes on the ladder as he sautéed shrimp in cayenne pepper and poured the remainder of the stock into the grits. He did not want to leave his post— corn grits were tricky business. Pulled off the fire an instant too late, they would harden into a stone. Also, if the ship were under attack, what use would he be, shaking a wooden spoon?

The noise from the shouting increased. The usual group that pushed to the front of the breakfast line each morning was nowhere to be seen. James sighed and put a cover on the pot.

His hand was on the top rung of the ladder when the first musket shot popped off. James ducked below and considered returning to the safety of his stove. His curiosity nudged him up the ladder onto the deck.

The sailors were pressed together in a jumble, straining to get a better look at something happening off the ship's port side. A few men balanced on the yards and hooted at the action below, yelling and pointing.

James saw it was Captain Mai they were watching. The Chinawoman stood at the edge of her ship, feet planted wide and hands gripping the railing. She leaned over the side of the ship and shouted at something below her in the water.

The harbor was a frenzy of boats, the water barely visible in the most crowded areas. There were twenty or so two- and three-mast ships at anchor, a typical number for a port of this size. What crowded the water were more than a hundred dinghies and skiffs, each of the small boats overstuffed with passengers. A yawl intended for half a dozen passengers sat low in the water with twice that number. A longboat with seats for twenty had every seat filled while, quite incredibly, another dozen people in the water clung to its sides. The small crafts moved to and fro with frenzied desperation.

Captain Mai's yelling was unintelligible. She was trying, James suddenly realized, to yell in French. Mai did not speak French. Acting against his better judgment, James elbowed his way to the front of the scrum.

He waited for Mai to pause for a breath. "Can I help? I speak French."

Mai pointed down at the water. Seven or eight boats were crammed in a chaotic huddle. "They don't understand me!" she yelled. She was agitated, insulted by their stupidity.

The men and women and children on the water looked up pleadingly at Captain Mai. Denmark was not around to give James an explanation. James noticed that the ship's own longboat was gone. Was Denmark out there in the harbor among this chaos of boats?

"Tell them we—" Mai paused to search for the word. "—auction each berth, one at a time. One hundred berths total."

James tried to ask Mai who these poor people were.

"We auction now one by one! Silver full value. All else half. No credit! No exceptions!"

James repeated her declaration in French, and then as she laid out the rules of the auction, James translated those as well. Some words he made up. Five years in Paris and

Chantilly learning French cooking made him fluent in every shape of spatula but less so in terms of commerce.

A man with jowls that hung below his chin reached into his blue velvet coat and pulled out a purse. Golden wisps of hair blew back in a thin plume as he lunged to the front of the dinghy. With the bag held aloft he opened the bidding. James asked him to repeat the amount, certain he had heard incorrectly. Another man raised the bid. James glimpsed across the water a woman trying to climb up another ship's anchor chain. Before he could see whether she made it to the deck, the shouting from the dinghy below reclaimed his attention. The noise increased, and James did his best to match his translations to the shouts.

The bids grew more desperate with each berth gone. The crescendo reached a screaming frenzy when the hundredth and final berth came up for bid. James could not keep up with the shouts and was relieved when the *Golden Dragon*'s own longboat pulled up, forcing a pause. James saw Denmark at the small boat's bow. With him were five of the crew and someone James did not recognize. Covered in a mean-looking shirt, she did not seem like someone who could offer a winning bid for a berth.

The woman's eyes, dark as coals, scanned along the gunwale and came dead stop on James. Her stare went through James like a lance, and he had a sudden impulse to reach over the edge and pull her up.

As Denmark caught the ladder thrown down to him, the woman pulled from her rags a long, deadly looking sword. Its blade was tarnished, but dozens of jewels set into its hilt caught the light and flung it about in every color and direction. It was a spectacular weapon. She held it aloft and pointed the tip to James. Without thinking, James turned to Captain Mai and told her the woman in Denmark's boat was making an offer for the final berth. Mai glanced between Denmark and the woman and accepted the payment with a curt nod.

As those left in the boats wailed in protest, the coxswain appeared and pointed a pistol at the remaining refugees to insist on their departure. James was utterly exhausted. He considered the new passengers lined up on deck, the men and women clutching one another as they received their berth assignments. They were all white, save this last, most curious one. He had no time to wonder about the woman with the jewel-hilted sword. Now cooking for twice the number of people, he had dinner to make. And not nearly enough ingredients.

The next morning the sun came up grey and timid. The crew crowded on deck, all eyes on the line of warehouses along the waterfront being eaten by a roaring, orange fire. Black smoke billowed from further inland. The volume of smoke suggested the entire city of Le Cap was burning. When James was passed the spyglass, he watched a white man run into a building where the flames had nearly died down. The man was still inside when the fire flared up again. James had to pass the spyglass along before the man reemerged.

The crew argued about what was happening ashore.

"The man who took my berth said the French sailors are to blame. They came ashore and attacked without provocation."

"Impossible! French sailors don't attack without provocation. Too lazy."

"They've been lounging for months," the coxswain said. "Boredom makes you do things."

"The woman who tried to bring her dog aboard says the gens de colueur have been ruined by Commissioner Sonthonax. They're picking fights with the sailors."

"Hardly a reason to burn the city. And you shouldn't have thrown her dog overboard."

The man growled and yipped like a little dog.

"It was the slaves who set the fires, I'm sure of it," said the coxswain. "But they've not managed to fire the armory, or we would have heard the explosions."

"Perhaps the slaves have control of the armory."

The men considered the possibility. The spyglass came back to James. He raised it to his left eye. "I heard the commissioner declared any slave freed who joined the army to defend the city."

"Absurd. The governor would never do that. It would be suicide."

"Henry says the French sailors are in control of the armory. He would know—he was ashore with Denmark."

"Sailors don't want an armory. They just want to go home."

The black smoke was now so thick James could see nothing through the spyglass. He handed it off once again. "Maybe they think a different commissioner will let them sail home." He was glad to be on a ship and not ashore.

A new voice behind the group said, in French, "There are two thousand people dead. At least, perhaps three."

The crew turned from the fires ashore to the stranger behind them. It was the mysterious passenger Denmark had brought onboard the day before. Dressed in the tattered strips of calico that had once been a shirt or a dress, she offered up the name Romaine.

The coxswain looked up and sneezed. Soot from the city was drifting into the harbor. "Romaine the Prophetess?" The coxswain sneezed again. "Romaine the Prophetess is not real. That's a ghost story."

"Not real?" said Romaine. She laughed, a quick fluttering breath. "It was a ghost who captured Léogâne and held it for a year?" She grabbed the coxswain's arm. He flinched away but was neither fast nor strong enough to escape her grasp. "Does this feel like a ghost to you?"

The coxswain yelped to be let go. "The Prophetess was captured and executed," he said, voice trembling.

"They captured me, but they did not have the courage to kill me," said Romaine. She released the coxswain and pulled her hand back to pat down her spectacular halo of hair. The coxswain backed away, rubbing the red marks left by Romaine's fingers.

Denmark's voice rang over the group, ordering the men to pull up the anchor and unfurl the sails. With relief, the men leapt away to do their duty, leaving James alone with Romaine.

"You do not follow orders?" Romaine said.

"You are the person Denmark came to rescue," James said.

Romaine smiled, thin lines leaping up around her eyes. "Am I? His name is Denmark, then."

"He came looking for you." James meant to remain silent, but the words came out of his mouth as if scooped by a net. "He said you didn't know he was coming."

"True," Romaine said, her lips closing over her smile. "Mary said I would soon be released, but did not say how."

"Your jailer was a woman?"

Romaine cocked her head to the side. "You have not heard of me?"

James admitted he had never heard of anyone by the name of Romaine the Prophetess.

"It's just as well," Romaine said. "You are not afraid of me then. Mary is not my jailer. Mary is the Blessed Virgin Mary. She is my godmother. How far to our destination?"

"Nuevo Orleans," James said. "Denmark says two or three weeks to the mouth of the Mississippi if the winds are good but then double that to get to port."

"Your French is very good. You will help me be understood, and I will help you cook," said Romaine. "I know a thing or two about stretching provisions."

James was not enthusiastic about being joined in his kitchen by someone who communed with the Virgin Mary. Romaine lifted her chin up, and James led the way to the galley. As he descended into the hold, he realized he had not said anything about being the ship's cook.

Captain Mai sent the coxswain to the hold for a bolt of painted Indian chintz, scissors, needle, and thread. The next morning, Romaine appeared on deck in a voluptuous gown that flowed from her shoulders to the ship's deck. Her hair was piled into a turban adding another foot to her already impressive height.

Denmark scowled as the crew paused to watch the Prophetess stride the deck. He let them stare for a while before yelling at them to get on with their work. They returned to the ropes and sails but kept their eyes on the Prophetess. The gossip was that Romaine's recruits had, two years earlier, captured first the port of Léogâne, then the town of Jacmel. Then she was betrayed and imprisoned. The sailors gave her wide berth whenever she paced the deck.

Denmark called James for help translating, so he could ask the Prophetess about the movement of troops, about weaponry and ammunition, about food supplies, about alliances and betrayals. The Prophetess talked at length, and Denmark stood with his thick forearms crossed in front of him, listening intently to all of it.

The paying passengers regarded Romaine with fear bordering on panic. Ten days after escaping Le Cap, a group of them gathered up their courage and requested an audience with Captain Mai. This Romaine, they complained, was a menace. Captain Mai listened patiently as James translated their descriptions of the havoc wrought by Romaine and their fears for their safety on Mai's ship. When they finished their litany, Mai pointed over the side of her ship and told them they were welcome to leave.

"You must restrain her, at least," the leader of the group pressed. Blood rose up in the man's cheeks as he spoke, bringing a blush of pink to skin that was usually the color of cheese curds. His fellow refugees muttered agreement.

"She pay same as you pay," said Captain Mai. Her face showed no emotion, but the impatience in her voice was sharper than usual.

The pink cheese-curd-colored man turned to Denmark. Perhaps a man would better understand the dangers. "We hear she has access to knives, even, from the cook." He gestured to James.

"There are a hundred of you and one of her," said Denmark.

"You do not understand the risk, she has *powers*. You will wake up tomorrow morning, and the crew will have taken up arms against you."

Denmark turned to Captain Mai. "He believes the crew will mutiny." They both laughed.

"Why are there no mutinies on pirate ships?" Denmark said loudly, to no one in particular.

The group of white refugees looked at one another in confusion.

"Yet there is constant threat of mutinies on merchant ships," Denmark continued. The passengers fell quiet, mesmerized by his voice. "I will tell you. On a merchant ship, the seaman's pay is one coin to the captain's fifty. On a pirate ship, the seaman is paid one coin for every two taken by the captain. Captain Mai here has made a study of this—the more lopsided the ratio of captain's pay to the ordinary seaman's, the more likely a mutiny."

"No mutiny here," Captain Mai said. "We pay like pirates."

"Mutiny or no, Romaine with a knife can pick any of us and slit our throats," the white man said. "For no reason."

"She would have a reason," said Denmark.

"You have taken all our money. You owe us some measure of safety from this beast you have taken aboard."

Denmark's smile disappeared. "We owe you nothing." The words came out as a low growl.

The skin on the white man's face flushed a deeper shade of pink. Nostrils flared, he stepped up to Denmark. A space no wider than the blade of James's paring knife separated the two men's noses.

The white man spoke first. "The situation in Le Cap is temporary. Be assured that the natural order will eventually be restored. In the meantime, we're giving you the chance to extend a courtesy. Don't be a fool. What you do now, we'll remember later. You should…"

Before he could finish, Denmark hoisted the white man up by his shirt and pressed him backwards towards where James stood. The crowd parted as Denmark plowed through, slamming the man up against the mast with such force James was sure he felt the ship tilt. To the passengers, it appeared Denmark held his opposite up against the mast for a moment before dropping him. Only James was close enough to hear Denmark's response.

"So will we. Remember."

That night, James handed Denmark a plate of saltfish accras. "Eat it while it's hot. You left your rice porridge to cool this morning—it's no good cold."

Denmark gave James the smallest of smiles. "You're giving me orders?"

"Never," said James. "Merely a suggestion."

"There was sugar in my porridge this morning," said Denmark. "Where are you getting sugar?"

"That was honey," James said. "You brought it onboard in Savannah."

Denmark's mouth receded into its familiar frown. "That was very expensive, a small jar of it. There can't possibly be any left." He looked hard at James. "Not if everyone is getting their porridge sweetened."

"The crew's porridge is plain," said James."

Denmark's left eyebrow shot up. "You can't favor me. This ship only runs if we keep equal shares. You sweetening your own porridge?"

"I don't eat porridge," said James. "Your accras are getting cold. They must be eaten hot. I had to refire the oven to fry you a fresh batch."

"Not necessary," said Denmark.

James dipped one of the accra into a green sauce and held the fried saltfish ball at Denmark's mouth. "Try it."

Denmark kept his eyes on James and opened his mouth. The spicy cilantro sauce glistened atop a perfectly crisped fritter. James pushed the accra into Denmark's mouth and let his finger and thumb linger a moment as Denmark bit down. James had an urge to push his fingers deeper into Denmark's mouth, but willed himself to withdraw them.

"You will admit it's better hot," said James.

"You're a good cook," said Denmark.

"But you don't eat the dinners I cook you."

Denmark smiled. "I have a ship to sail, you know."

"And you must eat," said James. "You never missed dinner before Romaine."

The smile disappeared and the grooves between Denmark's eyes deepened. "I took a risk taking her on."

"Romaine?"

"Yes," said Denmark. "If they discover Romaine onboard, the Spanish will sink this ship." He looked at James. "And you will be sent back to Philadelphia as a gift to the Americans."

"What do the Spanish care about this ship?" said James.

"They don't, so long as Captain Mai's business in Nuevo

Orleans is to sell her porcelain. But now we have a shipload of Frenchmen to explain."

Denmark put the last fritter in his mouth and turned to leave. "My rice porridge tomorrow—will there be honey in it?"

"Not if you're going to let it sit until second watch before eating it," said James.

"Then I'll eat it hot," said Denmark.

James watched him go, the twilight sky striated with clouds soaked in brilliant shades of red. Back in Philadelphia, Denmark's certainty had filled the sailmaker's loft. He was the most solid person James had ever met. The way Denmark seemed unsure of himself when talking about Romaine was the smallest of cracks in that solidity.

It was, James thought, a lovely little fissure. He closed his eyes and felt the wind pushing a mist of saltwater against the skin on his arms. His wrists were tired, as they were every night, from whisking and chopping, and hefting pots. His fingers tingled at the tips, where they had touched the inside of Denmark's mouth.

At the mouth of the Mississippi River, a dinghy from Fort San Felipe de Placamines rowed out to meet them. Captain Laveau, young and well-built, braids swinging from his uniform's epaulettes, puffed out his chest and sniffed the air. White cords dangled from buttons. Chevrons covered two sashes crossed under his jacket, and a third sash over his jacket was studded with metal badges. Laveau demanded to know how much the French were paying them to sneak into New Orleans to attack the Spanish colony.

"I no French," Captain Mai said. She jammed her toes against Captain Laveau's. She tilted her head and shouted, "I serve King Charles of Spain! You too!"

Captain Mai waved a stack of papers in Captain Laveau's face. He took them from her hand, glanced at the first page, then at Captain Mai, then back at the page. He squinted and looked hard at the paper.

"This is in French," he finally said.

Captain Mai snatched the papers back from him. "Of course it is! These words too complicated for you because you are Spanish! Come with me—I show you something Spanish easy to understand."

Denmark held the door to the captain's quarters open, then followed the two inside. As soon as Denmark closed the door, the crew started making guesses about the size of the bribe Captain Mai would have to turn over.

"Fifty pieces of eight, no less."

"Ha! *Captain* Laveau indeed—the whole pardo militia is fake. He'll be happy with a ribbon if it's colorful enough."

"But if we are a ship full of Frenchmen come to attack the city, he'll be hung. His own neck is worth a few picayunes, at least."

"He knows there's no chance of that. What Frenchman in his right mind would want that swamp of a city back?"

"What Frenchman *is* in his right mind?"

"I'll give even odds for no more than twenty pieces of eight," said the coxswain. The crew drew in close around him and put down their bets.

Those who bet short won: it was twelve silver coins Captain Laveau jingled when he saluted Captain Mai and sent them on their way. The crew leapt into action, but the near-gale wind that had hurried them to the mouth of the Mississippi faded to a whisper. No matter how quickly they tacked, the turns of the river appeared even more quickly. No matter how vehemently Denmark cursed, the wind did not pick up. The ship barely budged. Some days, there was no wind at all, and the *Golden Dragon* had to drop anchor to keep from being pushed back downriver by the current.

They fought the hot, thick air for three weeks, finally dragging it all the way into the port of Nuevo Orleans. Even before the gangplank could be secured to the wharf, the refugees rushed off the ship, pushing past one another along the narrow boards. They were greeted by the corpse of a dog, three days old at least. The once wealthy planters gagged at the smell and assured themselves they were safe now, far from the savagery of Africans in uprise. It was only a matter of time, they muttered, before their island returned to order. Until then, this would do.

The crew folded their hammocks and returned to their berths. They were accustomed to the layovers, where Captain Mai disappeared into town with pieces of porcelain and came back with bags bulging with silver. She sometimes finished her business in days, but other times it took months. It was a matter of selling the delicate blue trimmed porcelain from Canton and making a deal for a lucrative next destination.

Selling the porcelain would be quick. Everyone on the Mainland with some bit of fortune was mad for porcelain. Cups and saucers, plates, and bowls. Pickle tureens, cider jugs, mustard boats, flagons, footbaths, and lidded dragon jars. It was a full-blown mania. But the second half of the equation would take time. Captain Mai wanted to return to Canton with something to sell, but the Canton market had little interest in tobacco or corn. What the Canton factory owners wanted was silver. The stone faced Hongs had their pick of customers—the hulking, high-sided oak ships of the Dutch East Indian Company floated next to ships from France, Denmark, Portugal, and England. But whatever flag they flew, all were stymied by the unsmiling Hong, who wanted only silver.

Captain Mai understood this and asked no favors in her dealings with her countrymen. Rather, she took to the task of amassing silver with meticulous energy. Her singular focus on silver—specifically, specie from the mines of New Spain—had moved her from being an orphan girl running amok among the Canton warehouses to assistant to the supercargo on a Danish East Indian, to supercargo for a London merchant, to Charleston, South Carolina, where she became the owner of a fine and fast schooner. She bought the schooner off a drunkard named Joseph Vesey, deep in debt. The schooner came with the young sailor Denmark, a boon that Mai immediately recognized as the most fortuitous turn of her most fortuitous life.

Denmark commanded the respect of everyone on the ship, whites included. It was the timbre of his voice, certainly. But it was also how he carried out every task with utter efficiency. If there was ever a man destined to captain a ship, it was Denmark. Captain Mai saw it in a flash. Her great talent was to recognize the true value of things. She struck a business deal with young Denmark: the benefit of his talents in exchange for a full share of profit and, if they both survived eight years, the sale at fair market value of a deed of manumission securing his freedom.

It was, like all of Mai's business deals, a well-constructed bargain. It gave Denmark an interest in keeping Mai alive for the next eight years while she took unseemly risks to maximize profits. With Denmark as first mate and Mai as captain, the *Golden Dragon* raced between the East Indies and the newly formed United States of America. Mai's talent for sniffing out sources of silver specie was matched by Denmark's skill at keeping the ship on time and on course.

A few months earlier, Mai had decided it was worth the risk to hold back her shipment of porcelain from the grasping hands of the Philadelphia elite. She would try instead to sell it in Nuevo Orleans, a Spanish colonial town awash in silver. Denmark convinced her to take a detour to Saint-Domingue, where the uprisings were producing refugees in search of safe passage. There would be a good profit to be made from their desperation, he'd argued, and he'd been right.

Now, with more silver than she'd dreamed of locked in a secret hold behind her bookcase, Mai needed only one more great deal to guarantee her retirement. Even as they dropped anchor, she was calculating profits, and the profits that would in turn flow from those profits. They would remain anchored, she decided, until she had a deal worthy of her final sail.

Chapter 3

The ship now docked in a town full of enticements, Captain Mai needed to do what she could to keep her crew intact. She offered James an unusually generous salary to remain onboard as the *Golden Dragon*'s cook. To her surprise, he refused.

Finally anchored at a real city—one that was not being burned to the ground—James despearately wanted to get ashore and feel the solid earth beneath his feet. He wanted to walk farther than eighty feet before having to turn around. Also, he could not bear the smell aboard the ship. They were anchored among twenty other ships, and the two closest were both slavers. They emanated a stench that pushed through the handkerchief James held to his nose.

Denmark paused his pacing.

"How do you stand it?" James asked, waving his handkerchief towards the starboard slaver.

"You've seen this before," Denmark said. "There was an auction house outside the sail loft where you and I met."

On the ship next to them, a line of women blinked at the sun's glare as they climbed out of the hold. A trio of men worked their way down the line. One oiled the women's arms the way a carpenter might varnish a chair. Another picked through their hair. The third man ordered each woman to squat and pull apart their buttocks. James and Denmark watched in silence until a woman refused and the man pulled a thin board from his belt.

"I didn't stop to gawk," James said.

"I don't pretend," Denmark said.

James turned away from the sight of the man raising his arm. "Pretend?"

"That this does not exist." The woman's sharp cries cut into the velvet of Denmark's voice.

"Captain Mai asked me to stay aboard but I'm afraid that is impossible," James said.

"We won't eat so well then," Denmark said.

Was that disappointment in his voice? James could not tell for sure. From the corner of his eye, he saw the woman squat. Her curses flew over the ship's masts, settling in among the line of pelicans that flew along the river.

Captain Mai emerged from her captain's quarters, cradling her money pouch with both hands. Mai studied the cook with her one good eye. She grabbed his hand and squeezed as if to crush it.

"You refuse my offer!"

James gulped and started to explain how he wanted a chance to maybe try… Mai made a sharp noise to cut him off.

"What they offer to pay you to cook, double it," she said. "You are a very good cook! If they say no, you come back here." Mai raised herself up on her tiptoes and said with great urgency, "Understand?" James was not certain he did, but the woman's glare was terrifying. He nodded.

James felt the rough cloth of the satchel in his right hand. It contained all he owned, but he was not afraid. He knew what it was to start in a new place. Twenty-eight years old, he had already made three new starts: in Monticello, in Paris, and in Philadelphia. He did not know what would become of him here, but he knew he needed to find the markets and a kitchen to cook in. Once he found the markets, he would be able to plan a proper meal. Something with oysters or turtle. A good chicken liver pate, even, if he could afford the butter. Once he cooked it, Nuevo Orleans would become home.

"Nuevo Orleans," James said as he stepped onto the wharf. Romaine followed close behind. James needed a sous chef if he was to cater anything larger than a family dinner, and Romaine had quickly accepted his invitation to come ashore with him. As well, James knew he had a better chance of luring Denmark off his ship if Romaine was with him.

James and Romaine walked away from the river, through the town square. To one side stood the prison and the guardhouse, on another the cathedral half rebuilt. The whole town had been burned to the ground a few years earlier, and the new buildings smelled of fresh cut cypress.

Everything else smelled of rot. In theory, the streets ran in a downslope from the river at the front of town to the marshes in back. The path of drainage, on paper at least, appeared rational and clear. French designs, alas, were better in theory than practice. The city's drainage lacked momentum, and left the streets covered in two inches of muck. Desperate for a good bottle of wine, James was forced to purchase instead a pair of sturdy boots.

The cobbler looked back and forth between James and Romaine as he shook his head no, there were no rooms to rent, nothing they could afford anyway. They could, he suggested, ask Henri D'Arcantal, treasurer of the Spanish royal household. He knew every residence in town—all that paid taxes, at least.

James and Romaine found D'Arcantal at the tavern suggested by the cobbler. He was exactly as the cobbler described: a cabbage atop a winter squash, eating.

"Monsieur D'Arcantal?"

The man nodded, chewing.

"You seem a man worthy of a finer meal than this rat stew."

The eyes of the tavern turned and narrowed at the Black stranger speaking a familiar French to the most powerful of the town's government officials.

"And you are?"

"Trained in Paris," said James.

D'Arcantal dabbed his mouth with a stained napkin and asked James's business. Heads turned back to their mugs of ale as the two men spoke. James offered first a bit of flattery, about D'Arcantal's obvious nobility. How difficult it must be, James offered, for a man of refined upbringing to live in such rough surroundings. Did he miss Paris? D'Arcantal admitted he did. The theater, especially. James discussed the theater, then various streets and celebrities. Ah, Paris. Pushing away his empty bowl, D'Arcantal offered to rent James a stall in his stables.

"You have employment?"

James pretended to cough to give himself a moment to think. He could lie and say he did, or he could tell the truth and ask for a job. James wished he knew more—or anything at all—about the customs of this town. Surely, wealthy people like D'Arcantal had chefs in their employ. But why then would he be eating this tavern's slop? Maybe there were not enough good chefs in Nuevo Orleans. Maybe there were no trained French chefs at all. The possibility that he might be in great demand gave James a shot of courage.

"You need a chef," James said. "Are you willing to pay for the best?"

"And give up this stew?"

"A gentleman from Paris should not suffer so."

D'Arcantal laughed. He liked the man's pluck, even if it bordered on impertinence. He suggested a trial, and the two agreed to a rehearsal dinner in ten days' time, a chance for James to show off his worth as a cook.

"You are both at liberty?" D'Arcantal said, his eyes sliding to Romaine.

"No one is more free than Romaine," James said. He put a hand on Romaine's lower back and steered her towards the door. The Prophetess ducked for her headwrap to clear the doorframe, and then they were outside. James was elated. In town for less than a day and already he was on his way.

D'Arcantal's stables were at the back of town, next door to a tippling house. To his delight, James discovered that the tavern's proprietor poured cups of wine nearly free of charge. The tavern's profits came from dice games, billiards tables, and a dizzying array of roulette wheels. On his first night in Nuevo Orleans, James fell asleep in the horse stall with his satchel as a pillow, pleasantly drunk on an enormous quantity of Malbec.

The next morning, James returned to the riverfront in search of provisions. In the stall market near the levee at St. Ann Street, the butcher's pavilion abutted a set of stalls where fish sellers offered up croakers and crabs. Further in, peddlers had mounds of beets, artichokes, radishes, and potatoes. Rough-looking Kaintucks squatted behind piles of brick they had floated down the river in flatboats, nicking at their toenails with pocketknives. The women selling coffee and chocolates flirted with James, handing him samples to sniff and taste.

From the peddlers, James learned half of the people in Nuevo Orleans were white, a third enslaved, and the remainder free people of color. There was another, much smaller, group as well—the maroons who lived in the cypress swamps behind the stables. Any runaway who managed to survive there longer than a year was considered a maroon and left largely alone. Those who were hunted down before the year mark, however, were made to suffer. The slavers under French rule, he was told, had been free to punish runaways in whatever manner they pleased.

"Is this not the case now?"

The white man behind the pyramid of bread looked carefully at James. He seemed to be assessing the color of his skin.

"The Spanish king is a fool," the bread seller said carefully, in French. "They deluge us with Africans, then meddle in how to keep them under control. Try this bread. It is better than the others—I don't mix my wheat with rice flour."

It was suppertime when James returned to the stables, carrying cheese and a loaf of bread. He'd eaten the meats and drunk up the ale some hours ago, but he hoped he could make a dinner for Romaine with what remained. A cook who did not eat well did not cook well. This basic gastronomic principle applied especially to sous chefs in training.

Expecting to find Romaine in their stall, James was startled to find instead a horse. In the adjourning stalls, empty that morning, were more horses, seven or eight at least. They smelled hot and exhausted. When his eyes adjusted to the dim light, James saw the horse in his stall had a spotted coat, its mane braided with beads and feathers in spectacular fashion. A young man in a loose, deep red shirt hummed as he brushed the animal's flank. For an instant, James wondered whether he had returned to the wrong stables, but no—this was the right place. James waited to be noticed. The groomer did not look up as he moved his attention from one haunch to the next, happily humming the same few notes over and over again.

James looked around for Romaine. Seeing no sign of his friend, he loudly cleared his throat.

"Bonjour!" the young man said, looking up. He gave James a once over, raising an arm in greeting while continuing to brush the horse. "Hola! Hello!"

"That is my stall," said James, first in French, then in English.

The groom stopped grooming and stepped out from behind his horse. He rested his forearms along the stall gate and looked behind James, a smile playing at the edges of his mouth. "But where is your horse?"

At the closer distance, James saw the man was younger

than he had seemed at first glance, no older than perhaps twenty, and clearly not a Spaniard despite his flashy red shirt. He was an Indian of some sort, the sharp angles of his face softened by dark brown almond shaped eyes. His hair was pulled back into a heavy braid.

"My name is James Hemings, and this is my stall." He and Romaine had put some effort into cleaning and setting down the thick layer of straw bedding that was now being enjoyed by a horse bedazzled in beads.

The young man cocked his head to one side. "My apology," he said, settling into English. "I will help you and your mother prepare another one for your horse."

James was confused for a moment. "That is not my mother," he said after a beat. "And we don't have a horse."

Now it was the horseman who looked confused. "She is not your mother? The woman who offered this stall to me."

"Where is she? And what do I call you?"

The young man stuck out his hand. "I am Red Eagle. Red Eagle of the Wind Clan from the talwa of Octiapofa, where the Coosa River and Tallapoosa River meet. Sehoy is my mother, Sehoy is my mother's mother, and Sehoy is my grandmother's mother. Whites call me William Wetherford, after my father Charles Wetherford, an Englishman no longer welcome in the confederacy. My mother's sister is Sophia, whose children are…"

"And where is Romaine, the woman who offered you the stall?"

Red Eagle did not seem to mind the interruption. He opened the stall door and gestured upwards to the loft. "She went to keep Mary company."

Now James was more confused than ever. Mary? Was Romaine keeping company with the Virgin Mary, as she had in Saint-Domingue?

"Mary is…" Red Eagle paused to find a word. He muttered a few in languages James did not understand before finding the right words. "Very dry. Easy to break. We should let them be alone for now."

"I'm not a danger," James said. He held up the bread and cheese, wishing he had not gobbled down the sausages earlier. "I have food."

Red Eagle looked up to study James's face, looking for clues. The brown-skinned man spoke with the accent of a wealthy white man. But he wore a rough shirt and was connected in some way to the woman Romaine, whom Red Eagle had immediately trusted. He decided he would trust this man. Red Eagle stepped out of the stall and led the way up the ladder to the loft.

Romaine sat on a low stool, waving smoke from a bundle of sticks. A body lay at Romaine's feet, hands clenched into fists and their body twisted as if suddenly frozen in the middle of a fight.

James wondered if by "very dry" Red Eagle meant "dead?" James leaned down for a look. The woman was young, similar in age to his sister. But where Sally seemed to stand still even when she was walking, this young woman gave the opposite impression. She seemed to be thrashing and clawing at the air as she lay still, no movement other than her barely perceptible, jagged breathing. James felt the girl might spring up at any moment and attack him.

"What happened to her?"

Red Eagle knelt beside the young woman and sat back on his heels. "This is Mary. She is a jockey. Fearless. Faster than anyone. So I wanted to race her. I like to race the best."

"And you did?"

"In Natchez the Saturday before last. Virginians, Choctaws, Americans, Catholics, everyone brought their fastest horses. Larger than the derby in Virginia. For eight races, Mary won. Then she lost."

Red Eagle glanced sorrowfully at Mary.

"You beat her."

"Yes. I did not know about her master."

James waited. After a while, Red Eagle continued.

"Mary's owner loves to win at horses. Mary has a sister, and her master told her he would not sell her sister, as long as she wins for him."

There was a long silence in the loft. Romaine ate a bit of cheese and waited. James shifted from foot to foot. After so many years tending to Jefferson, James expected men to speak in one long constant stream. He found silences unsettling. Finally Red Eagle started again.

"I did not know about his threat. Mary told me after the race. Her master sold her sister, right at the racetrack. I was very sorry. So I helped her run away. To here."

A mosquito buzzed around the girl's face and Romaine waved it away.

James switched to French. "Is she asleep? Did you put a spell on her, Romaine?"

Romaine kept waving at the air. "A small spell. Rum, mostly. Some time away from this world will do her good."

"Did you understand your new friend here?"

Romaine nodded. "He told me what happened. His Spanish is good."

"How long will she be … away?" James asked.

"A week. We all know French."

"And then?" James asked in French.

"She might be calmer by then," Romaine said. "Mary was a handful when she came in this morning. She was ready to ride back out and tear her owner's throat out."

"She will try to escape and find her sister," said Red Eagle.

James looked suspiciously at Red Eagle. "Did you help her run away, or did you kidnap her?"

"If she goes back to find her sister it is…" Red Eagle searched for the right word. "Hopeless. She will be recaptured immediately. She is famous everywhere, and valuable. Her owner will offer a large reward."

"I can't keep her under for longer than a week," said Romaine.

"I will go find her sister," said Red Eagle. "When Mary wakes, tell her I will return with her sister."

"That will take longer than a week," Romaine said, eyeing Red Eagle.

"I am the best horseman, the fastest. No one knows this land better than me." Red Eagle said. He did not sound boastful, just stating a fact. "Yes, it will take longer than a week. But if she knows I am looking, she will not rush away. You tell her—"

James interrupted, suddenly worried for the stranger. "Who is this woman's master who sold her sister? It is his fault, not yours."

"It is his fault, yes, but the debt is mine," said Red Eagle. He started down the ladder. "I caused her great harm. These debts must always be repaired."

James did not understand. "You didn't know what would happen—how can it be your debt?" Red Eagle ignored the question, forcing James to call after him. "It's the master who has the debt. What's his name?"

Red Eagle was already halfway down. He climbed back until his head reappeared. "His name is Andrew Jackson." Nodding at Mary, he said, "Tell her when she wakes up I have gone to find her sister."

Red Eagle gone, James turned his attention back on the dinner for D'Arcantal. He had only a few days to prepare. James headed back into town to do research. To create a meal that surprised but did not startle, he had to understand the tastes of D'Arcantal's guests.

James noticed the markets were well stocked, but the excellent ingredients seemed wasted. Space too was in good supply and wasted in the same casual way. When he went to examine D'Arcantal's kitchen, James saw the entire bottom floor sat empty. It was as if the town was waiting for someone to come make something good of the ingredients and fill the empty spaces.

The day before the rehearsal dinner, James was sleeping off another late night at the tippling house when someone knocked on the stall door. It was Denmark, a crawfish stuck to his shoe.

"This is foolish," Denmark said, peering over the gate.

James had to admit he was, indeed, bunking down in a horse stall. "How did you find me?"

"I asked for the Black cook."

"This town is full of Black cooks." James did not know whether to ask Denmark in. It seemed rude to leave him at the door, but there was nothing to sit on in the stall save a shoeing stool.

"So I learned. But you've made an impression."

"My first dinner is not until tomorrow," said James, surprised.

"Not the food—your looks. The tall pretty one, they call you."

James blushed. This was unusual. Ever since he was a boy his good looks had received compliments, all of which he received without embarrassment. But having Denmark say he was pretty made the blood rise in his cheeks. James corrected himself: Denmark had said nothing of the sort. Denmark had merely said other people had said he was pretty. That he had blushed at Denmark not saying he was pretty made James blush even harder. He turned and swept his hand from wall to wall. "There's not much for me to invite you into," he said.

"That's too bad," said Denmark. "I was hoping for a good meal."

"You miss my cooking!" James said brightly. "Admit it."

Denmark smiled but shook his head. James was suddenly afraid he might leave and never be seen again.

"I am cooking tomorrow for the town's treasurer." James stopped himself before he added, "a rich white man." It was not the sort of detail that impressed Denmark. "Come with me to the market."

The two walked down St. Phillip towards the river. Two girls ran between them, laughing and chasing a ball. The smaller one outpaced her companion and reached the ball first, kicking it at an angle that sent it flying into an open doorway. The two girls stopped as if yanked back by a string and stared first into the doorway, then wide-eyed at each other for a long second before spinning around and sprinting back past James and Denmark.

Denmark turned his head to watch the girls turn the corner. "You prefer a horse stall to a berth on my ship."

They passed the doorway. Back in the shadows, an old woman sat on a cane chair, the rattan weave spread like a peacock tail behind her. The accordion folds of her brown skin suggested she was not merely old but ancient. For an instant James wondered if perhaps she was already dead, a carefully preserved mummy, but as he and Denmark walked past, her eyes followed them. James felt the hair on the back of his neck come alive.

Denmark glanced towards the doorway and seemed unaffected by the woman. "One of the sorcerers from the islands," he said. "This town is full of them." He turned his attention back to James. "You left the ship because you hate seeing the trade. But closing your eyes does nothing to end it."

"Your opposition to the slave trade kept me from making sweets for your crew," James said lightly.

Denmark's brow tightened into its familiar furrow. "Stewed prunes are a fine way to complete a meal."

James laughed. "Stewed prunes are a menace in such tight quarters."

Denmark's face softened, and he allowed himself a grin. "It's no laughing matter. If we're going to end slavery, there are things we need to give up. Indigo, Carolina rice, rum. Sugar is just the worst of it."

"We are going to end slavery?" James said. He immediately regretted his teasing tone. Denmark's furrows deepened.

"Yes, people like us." There was no levity in Denmark's voice.

James had no idea what Denmark meant by it, but he liked the sound of it. He liked it so much he repeated it. "People like us."

"Who have seen enough of the world to know there is revolution rising everywhere."

"You mean in France and on Domingo," said James carefully.

"Yes," said Denmark. The street opened before them into the parade ground. "It will take people like us to spread the revolution."

"People like us," James said again. If he said it enough times, perhaps Denmark would make clear his meaning.

"Who see what is possible and are tired of waiting for it to happen."

What a high opinion Denmark had of him! "You will someday be a captain," said James, "but I will never be more than a cook. A great cook, to be sure, but I don't recall a battalion ever rallying behind a chef's spatula."

"Your owner was rich, paid you a wage for your work. Yet you decided you would rather live free in rags than remain enslaved in finery. For that, men will follow you. It was an act of courage for you to steal yourself away on Mai's ship."

James nearly blurted out, "I only did so to follow you!" but said instead, "I have no intention of living in rags." They arrived at the edge of the market. "I hope the bakers still have bread."

Inside the market, they were greeted by peddlers shouting the superiority of their hazelnuts and bison meat. At the first stall, small clay pots were arranged in tidy rows, one row tiered atop another, each pot filled with a different spice. A string of ducks were hung farther down the lane, the carcasses tied up tightly to show off their brilliant teal. To their right, a stack of crates soared towards the ceiling, leaning with a precarious tilt. A girl leaned far too far over from atop the tower and sang out, smile bright, "Oranges from Florida six pesos a crate, oranges from Florida!" Something caught James's attention, and the cook stopped. It was an unfamiliar smell, teetering between sour and sweet.

"Do you smell that?" James asked, sniffing the air.

"I smell horse manure," said Denmark. On the ship, there was not a sliver of oakum that escaped his attention. But here on land there were too many new details to know what was important and what was not. It made him feel off balance.

James located the source of the smell at a fruit stand. Atop a box of dried brown pods, the fruit seller had placed a bowl containing a thick, brownish red mash. James leaned in to examine the paste. The pungent sour was shot through with sweetness.

"Tamarind," said Denmark, standing very close behind James.

"How is it used?" James said, picking up one of the brown pods. It was dry, shaped like peanut shells but twice as large.

"My mother turned it into a mash and pounded it into goat meat, to make it tender. And a drink too, with the sugar slop that did not crystallize." said Denmark. He added after a pause, "When I was a boy on Saint Croix."

Of course Denmark had once been a boy with a mother. Still, to hear him say so surprised James. It seemed more likely Denmark had sprung a full grown man from the hull of a ship.

"You were born on Saint Croix?" James offered Denmark the pod of tamarind.

Denmark opened his hand and accepted the pod. "You could say that," he said.

James waited for Denmark to continue. Instead, the first mate frowned as he rubbed the lumps of the tamarind pod with his thumb. "But you could say something else as well?" James prodded.

Denmark felt himself lifted up and forward, the way a ship rises up slightly when its sails catch a good wind. Something about James made Denmark feel up ahead of himself, talking despite himself. Denmark did not like it. He looked up to a point over James's shoulder. "My mother's village was raided when she was a girl. She became pregnant while in the factory hold, and then she was sold to a Danish ship. They sailed, and, the day they sighted land, I was born. I was not listed on the manifold, so the register noted an ekstra, the property of Christian VII, King of Denmark."

The din of the market continued around them, but a bell jar descended around the two men, quieting the noises. "Did you have a name?" James asked gently.

Denmark shook his head. "My mother said she would not give them any other thing they could take away." There was a long silence too heavy for James to lift. Denmark finally said, "She became pregnant six more times that I remember. What she could not kill in the womb she drowned when it was born."

James did not know what to say, but he knew he did not want Denmark to stop talking about his mother. "She made a marinade out of tamarind to tenderize the goat," said James.

Denmark unhitched his gaze from the spot over James's shoulder and looked at James. "A marinade," Denmark said. "Yes, a marinade."

They stepped out of the market into the muted light of dusk. A line of wooden steps trudged up the levee to their right. "It's curfew." There was a slight quaver in Denmark's voice.

"We are in Nuevo Orleans. There is no curfew here."

Denmark looked around, shaking his head as if waking from a nap. "I need to get back to the ship," he said.

"You have not eaten yet," James said. He was sorry the conversation had taken such a dark turn.

"There will be something," Denmark said, the low, steady bass back in his voice.

"Gruel," said James.

"Is fine," said Denmark.

James could see Denmark had already decided. "Listen, there was a string of quail in there, for my commission to-morrow night. Come at four and the first plate is yours. A well-roasted quail is very good. Tender, layers of flavor."

"You're very enthusiastic about dinner."

James flashed his dazzling smile. "What you can do with a ship, I can do with dinner." He told Denmark how to find D'Arcantal's house. "I'll put a plate aside for you."

The quails emerged from the oven with skins so perfectly crisped they glowed. James could hear the guests arriving as he settled each little bird on its plate. With all ten done, James rang the brass dinner bell, and two young women appeared. They balanced the plates up their arms and carried them out. An eleventh plate James put back into the oven.

He waited.

The sounds of the dinner party took their usual course. There was chattering at the table, then the clatter of knives against plates, then silence. "This!" someone exclaimed. The chattering resumed at a higher volume, peppered with com-pliments to D'Arcantal and demands to know the name of his caterer. James kept his eye on the back door, waiting for Denmark. The quail warming in the oven was by now too dry, but the sauce might still save the dish. James waited for the first guests to depart before he gave up waiting and ate the last quail.

James was draining the grease from the drip pan into a canister when D'Arcantal came into the kitchen. The white man paused at the doorway, as if unsure whether the space belonged to him or to James. Behind D'Arcantal, the last of the dinner guests peered over his shoulder.

"Ah, there he is," the guest exclaimed. Addressing James, the man continued. "Whatever this stingy old Frenchman is paying you, I'll double it!"

D'Arcantal frowned and turned to usher the guest away. D'Arcantal hoped James did not take the guest's outburst seriously, lest he understand he was now able to command a much higher catering rate.

As the guest protested his ouster, James in a flash saw the possibilities. If he wished to become wealthy and famous—and he wished to become wealthy and famous!—here was his chance. D'Arcantal's bottom floor was empty. What he'd done tonight with dinner, he could do every night. James cleared the bowls and knives off the table and waited for D'Arcantal to return.

In French, with as calm a tone as he could muster, James made his argument to D'Arcantal. Eating establishments called *restaurants* were becoming popular in Paris and Philadelphia. They were like taverns but with better food and fewer fights. Might a savvy businessman like D'Arcantal be interested in investing in such a venture? The bottom floor of his house, now sitting empty, would serve as the dining room. The space was filled with light. They would serve fine wine rather than cheap ale. There would be no spitting on the floor.

The accountant looked skeptical. James's experience with figures hurried forth to serve him. Pulling a sheet of brown paper from the trash and smoothing it out on the butcher block, James used a piece of charcoal to fill the page with figures. The numbers crowded the page, showing the income such a venture would generate, half of which would inure to D'Arcantal for doing nothing at all. A better set of stoves, more pots and knives, and a set of sturdy tables and chairs were all the investment he had to make. With a flourish, James circled the number at the bottom of the page. An impressive sum. One that would go to another willing investor should D'Arcantal demur.

D'Arcantal reviewed the figures and found no lie. "And I eat for free," he said.

James countered, "The servant's room behind the ovens— it would be convenient for me to lodge there."

D'Arcantal hesitated, then thrust his hand forward. "You have a good instinct for business, Monsieur James."

The two clasped hands, each one grinning at his good fortune.

Back at the stables, Romaine listened to James's recounting of the deal and immediately appreciated the genius of the setup. "Knives and gossip," she said. Here was a place where a large stock of knives would cause no alarm. A place where people could come and go at all hours without raising suspicion. A place for sailors, merchants, and nuns to drink wine and discuss their days, ready to be overheard by someone with an ear for rumors. In such uncertain times, what better place than this so-called *restaurant* to keep abreast of news and opportunities for revolt?

Romaine's delight was interrupted by a shattering scream. It came from above, a girl's furious yell.

"I'll kill him!"

As if snatched up by the hand of God, Romaine flew across the stables and up the ladder to the loft. The horses snorted and pawed at the walls of their stalls.

"I'll kill him! Sarah! I'll kill him! Sarah! Sarah!" The

name turned from anger to bewilderment. "Sarah. Sarah. Sarah." From bewilderment to grief. "Sarah. Sarah…" Until it faded into a sobbing cry.

James followed to the top of the ladder and paused, where the orange glow of an oil lamp spread across the straw. He saw Mary, crouched and trembling in the far corner, and she saw him, emerging from the place below. For one breath they stared at each other in silence. Then with a screeching cry Mary leapt towards James with hands outstretched in murderous rage. James flinched as he watched Romaine throw herself to catch Mary by the waist, bringing them both crashing down. James's brother Martin once brought into the house a bobcat, its legs crushed by a trap, eyes wild with pain and rage. Mary's eyes drilling into James's had the same look. He hoped Romaine's grip on the girl was solid.

James forced himself to climb into the loft. She was half his size, after all, and restrained. He held a blanket out before him as an offering. Or as a shield. He heard Romaine assuring the woman that James had nothing to do with her sister's sale. James repeated the assurance, in English, adding, "I am James, I will not harm you."

"Tell her she has been asleep for a long time."

James did as requested. Mary's questions sounded like she was choking. "How long? Where is my sister? Who are you?" Romaine loosened her hold on Mary as the younger woman's eyes cleared and the tension in her body uncoiled. She collapsed to her knees. James knelt beside her and answered her the best he could.

In this way, Mary learned her memory was a true one, she had lost a race to a Muskogee, and as punishment her twin sister had been sold away. The Muskogee Red Eagle, who bested her on the track, snuck her out with the train of horses he was taking down the river to sell at Nuevo Orleans. "I should not have gone," Mary said to the floor. "I should have stayed and killed him."

"You tried to go back," James said, translating for Romaine. "We made you—we let you sleep. Red Eagle has gone out to find your sister."

Mary was up on her feet. She moved with alarming speed. "Why should I believe that? He has no reason to do so."

Mary's thick eyebrows and nearly black eyes sent James backing away to stand a bit behind Romaine. "He believes he does."

Romaine stretched her arm out to Mary. "Tell her she must promise to remain here with me."

Mary did not respond to James's translation. Outside, a wolf howled.

"Tell her Red Eagle knows this land. If anyone can find her sister it will be him."

Mary sat heavily on a hay bale and covered her face with her hands. "She needs me, I can feel it. She is afraid."

Romaine sat beside her and drew her close. James held his breath, expecting Mary to swing a fist into Romaine's face. Instead, she collapsed into the Prophetess and sobbed. It was the saddest sound James had ever heard.

"I once had a daughter your age," said Romaine, speaking to the air above Mary's head. "Her name was Louise-Marie."

James did not believe in spirits, but it seemed to him the air in the loft was heavy with spirits. It made it difficult to breathe. The bullfrogs went suddenly silent. Below, the horses shuffled back to sleep. James sat on the other side of Mary and put a hand on her back. It was as much to comfort himself as it was to comfort her, but the touch did not soothe. To prepare a soup, the chefs in Chantilly taught James how to tie together a bundle of herbs, a bouquet garni. It was a simple threesome: a stick of thyme, a bay leaf, and a strand of parsley, wrapped together with string. He felt the three of them were being bound together as such.

Ready to be lowered into a pot of boiling stock.

Chapter 4

The invitation was carried to the *Golden Dragon* by one of the dockworkers, a compact man with arms as big around as most men's legs. "The good cook James," the man called up from the dinghy, "wants you to come in for dinner tonight. Says you know the place."

Denmark thanked the messenger and continued his climb up the mainmast. It was a morning ritual, unnecessary in these layovers, where the view each day was the same as the day before. Ships cluttered the river bend; Nuevo Orleans sprawled out beyond the levy. Denmark shouted down to the man in the dinghy to send back to James a polite excuse, but the dockworker was already out of earshot.

Denmark swung his leg into the crow's nest and pulled himself into the bucket. There was no reason to accept James's invitation, yet perhaps he should. Denmark rubbed his temples to dislodge this unfamiliar feeling of indecisiveness.

Something had prompted him to goad James into abandoning his master in Philadelphia. And that same instinct had prompted Denmark to go ashore a few days ago to look for him. On the rare occasions Denmark went ashore, he liked to remain within sight of the ships. This time, he had surprised himself by venturing deep into the city, nearly to the back gate. Then, even more surprising, he had gone with James into the city market, a chaotic place where Denmark exerted no control. It had been disconcerting. But, Denmark had to admit, not entirely unpleasant.

He'd not returned the next night for the quail dinner James had promised him. For that, Denmark felt a touch of regret, knowing he'd missed out on something delicious. Perhaps he should accept this invitation after all. He could go ashore, eat dinner, and be back aboard the *Golden Dragon* before nightfall. There was that crusty bread that held its crunch even after being dipped into a crab and fish stew. James had served that stew just before they entered the mouth of the Mississippi. The memory made Denmark's mouth water. A quick dinner. What harm could come of dinner?

Under James's knife, an onion became a pile of tiny dice. He looked up to see the pot boiling over. The oven gave uneven heat. "If you can give that pot a stir, Denmark." James asked for news of Mai's search for the right trade deal.

"Not much business here," said Denmark. "Captain Mai will find the right people, but it'll take time. Where's Romaine?"

"Back at the stable, keeping watch over someone." At Denmark's quizzical look, James continued, "A runaway, a young woman. Romaine is afraid she will run back."

"Runaways don't tend to run back," Denmark said.

"Her twin sister was sold away. She wants to find her sister." James spread walnuts onto the table and crushed them with the flat of his knife. "Have you ever met someone and thought you knew them already?"

Denmark said he had not. He thought a moment, then added, "Though perhaps a bit, with you."

"Yes," said James, careful not to smile too obviously. He tore a loaf of bread into the bowl, poured a slick of oil into the bowl, then thrust his hands in to mix everything together. "Like in some other life we have already spent a good deal of time together, as brothers."

"Or brothers in arms."

"Or lovers."

James waited until Denmark gave the barest of nods before continuing. "Having a twin must be like that but more so. I can imagine why this woman feels she has to go find her sister."

"This woman has a name?"

"Mary. She is a jockey; one of the best, it seems. You must be parched. The wine is there behind that door."

Denmark returned with a bottle, and James tossed him a corkscrew.

"These new devices," Denmark muttered as he examined it. When James looked up from his skewers, the bottle was clenched between Denmark's knees as the first mate struggled to open it. The corkscrew, James saw, was twisted into the cork at an unlikely angle.

"You have never used a corkscrew," James said, laughing.

Denmark made a face of mock despair.

"It's endearing," James said. "You're masterful at everything. I'm glad to see there are some things you've not perfected."

Denmark sat back from his efforts and smiled. "I know ships. The kitchen..."

"We choose our realms," said James. He wiped his hands on his apron as he walked to Denmark. "Yours is sailing. Mine is cooking." He pulled the bottle from between Denmark's knees and twisted out the corkscrew, then reset the tip back into the center of the cork. With a quick twist of his wrist and an authoritative tug, the cork popped free. "And drinking." He poured two cups. "Santé!"

Denmark held up the cup to James's toast but set it back down without taking a swallow.

"No slaves touched the production on this bottle. The French peasants who plucked the grapes were destitute but not enslaved." James touched the rim of his cup to Denmark's. "Come now, join me—you drank on board the ship, I know."

"It's dangerous to drink ashore."

"I have been drinking ashore for years now, to no ill effect," James said.

"You might reconsider, now that you're a fugitive from justice."

"A fugitive?" James knelt before the oven to assemble the rabbit fillets onto a turning rack. "Let's not make me sound like a pirate. I'm hardly the sort."

"Anyone who wants a quick dollar can snatch you up and drag you back to Philadelphia. The same as Mary."

"That seems a lot of trouble," said James. The turning rack was not well made, and forcing the last of the fillets onto the contraption threatened to topple it.

"Sure," said Denmark, "but you're tempting. The man who owned you will pay for your return, won't he?"

"This is not Charleston," said James. "This is not even the United States. Those laws have no force here." With a final shove, the string of rabbits were skewered on the rack.

"You should make yourself papers," Denmark said evenly. On the high stool, he shifted his weight and rested his hands on his upper thighs. Even seated, he seemed to be standing at attention.

James set the skewer of rabbits onto the roaster and poured himself another cup. "If freedom papers allow me to drink without fear of the slave catcher, then I'll forge a deed of manumission for you as well. Would that allow you to take a drink?"

Denmark held his cup, still full, against his chest. "Papers might persuade someone to move on to easier prey."

"Then ease up and enjoy the wine," said James. "Are you always such a careful man, Denmark?"

Denmark kept his eyes on James as he took a small sip from his cup. "I do like to be in control of my surroundings."

"Which will make you a great captain someday but a terrible dinner guest," said James. "Every once in a while, you must want to get away from this..." James swept his hand in the air dismissively. "From all this."

Denmark took another sip. "No."

The sailor's dark eyes, James realized, were not looking at him but through him. James nearly said, "You should try letting down your guard," but he held his tongue, suddenly unsure of what to do next. It was clear Denmark was bound for some destination past this kitchen, far beyond this town. He was terribly beautiful, a storm cloud that appeared without warning, blackening half the sky. The air surrounding Denmark was filled with an intensity that scared James. He turned back to the roaster and gave the rack a quarter turn.

"Tell me, what is the best meal you have ever eaten?"

"Meals are simple on a ship."

"A simple meal is sometimes the best." James did not turn around. He would calm himself by keeping his attention on the meal.

"The fritters you made were good."

James brushed the meat with drippings from the pan. "You will be brave and try things you've not tried before?"

"I'm not afraid of rabbits."

"It's not whether you're afraid of it," James said, dipping a ladle into the pot of bouillon, "but whether you appreciate it." He stepped up to Denmark and brought the ladle up to the first mate's lips. "Taste this."

Denmark allowed James to tip a sip of the broth into his mouth. He did not close his eyes. He made a sound at the back of his throat, between a grunt and a question.

"It's perfect as it is, no?" James brought the ladle up to his own mouth and tilted his head back, downing the remainder in one swallow. "And from a great bouillon come great soups."

"The rabbit is burning."

"It's the drippings. The rabbits are fine." James smiled down at Denmark. "Do you want me to go check them to make sure?"

For a while, the only sound in the kitchen was the sizzle from the roaster and the two men breathing.

"Show me something else."

James leaned in, reaching over Denmark's right shoulder to break a piece off the almond cake.

"This is sweet," he warned, feeding the cake to Denmark. "As is this." James leaned in again, this time reaching over Denmark's left shoulder to scoop up two fingers worth of crème fraîche. James offered up the crème, expecting some tentativeness. Instead, he felt Denmark's hand clamp down around his wrist as the first mate took the length of James's fingers into his mouth. Denmark's tongue, thick and rough, split James's fingers for the crème, his free hand grabbing the back of James's head. James felt himself pulled close with forceful efficiency and thought, a moment after the fact, *He's going to kiss me.*

And he did. Denmark took James's face in his hands and kissed him with the sureness of a king tide. In the time it took them to navigate around the chopping blocks and stoves—limbs twining, hands searching for skin, a pan sent clattering—and into James's room behind the kitchen, the smoke from the roaster turned succulent with char. The rabbit was burning. James pulled away to see whether there was anything to be saved. Denmark laughed and said "too late now," and removed James's shirt. The small room was overly warm. James let himself be guided onto the bed and was surprised, then gratified, then delighted at how Denmark took his time, unhurried, sailing a ship in familiar waters, attentive and responsive to any change in the atmosphere.

After, as James felt under his head the rise and fall of Denmark's chest, he wondered how long it has been since Denmark had spent a night on land. James knew Denmark had slept every night on the ship while docked in Philadelphia. Had it been over a year, then? Five? Was it possible that Denmark had, since leaving Charleston on Captain Mai's schooner nearly a decade ago, always returned to the ship at night, able to sleep only where the rocking of the water let the sailor know he was safe to rest? A mourning dove hooted not far above the house. James vowed to ask Denmark in the morning. And then, whatever the answer, to do what he could to keep the good man ashore.

Sure enough, as Denmark predicted, the slave catcher came looking. But it was not James he came looking for. It was Mary.

He was a lanky white man, limp hair spilling onto thin shoulders, a small downturned mouth, eyes squeezed in a hard squint. James knew immediately the stranger in the doorway of D'Arcantal's stables was trouble. The horses smelled it too and whinnied, stamping at the ground. James looked back behind him to the loft. The white man's squint followed, shifting upwards to the loft.

Denmark was gone, back at the ship for the day, and Romaine was out in search of the church. James realized there was no one else in the stables to stand between the slave catcher and Mary. The slave catcher legged into the stables and pushed past him. In a dozen long, fast strides the man was at the bottom of the ladder that led up to the loft. Only then did James move, yelling out a warning as he sprinted to catch the man now halfway up the ladder.

"Mary! Mary!" James felt a stabbing regret. If this slave catcher had come looking for Mary, James should not be screaming confirmation of her name. From the bottom rung, James leapt upwards to grab at the white man's leg. For an instant, his hand closed around shoe leather, but then it slipped away quick as a fish. James scrambled up the ladder as the man's ankle disappeared into the loft.

The loft was tall enough for James to stand but barely so. In the grey light, the bales of hay formed a staggered wall.

Two pallets. A trunk. A single chair on the floor, knocked to its side. The man whirled around to face James. He had a coil of rope in one hand and a pistol in the other. He used his foot to poke at the blankets on the closer pallet.

"Where is she?"

James willed himself not to look down into the stalls. If Mary had managed to drop herself down from the other edge of the loft, she could use a minute to find a horse to ride out on.

The white man kicked at the other pallet, his eyes never leaving James. He raised his pistol and closed the distance between them. James felt the cool of the barrel against his forehead. He backed up two inches, until he felt the edge of the floor under his heels.

"I come a long way to collect her. Where is she?"

The man's breath stank of rotting cabbage. He was not tall and he had to lift himself up on his toes to keep the pistol pressed against James's forehead. James leaned back into the open air, no floor left for him to retreat onto. Fear locked his joints tight.

"There is no one here," James said. Behind the white man, a flash of movement. James closed his eyes to keep from looking. The odor from the man's mouth grew twice as strong.

"Ya lie. Ya said Mary, I heard ya. Where is she?"

James felt the wisp of cool air an instant before he heard the crack of breaking wood. The gun pressed against his forehead flew away, and half a curse hung in the air as the slave catcher fell. Mary lifted what was left of the chair over her head and with a sharp grunt of effort brought it down hard towards the white man's face.

But the man was quick. He rolled to one side and took the blow on his shoulder. With cat speed, he drew himself up on his knees and lunged after Mary. James startled himself as he flung himself onto the white man's back, arms in a clinch around his chest.

The slave catcher writhed to pull himself from James's grasp, eyes on the pistol that had pinwheeled across the floor and now lay under the table. He pulled one arm out and brought his elbow back hard. James heard the crack of his nose breaking and felt blood flood his face. James's hands flew up, and, suddenly free, the white man pounced for the pistol.

"You are Mary, run away from Andrew Jackson," the white man said, eyes darting from Mary to James. He settled the gun and his attention on James. "If ya move I'll put a bullet between your eyes."

The three stood and watched one another, their breathing and the horses' breathing the only sound. James felt the blood flowing out of his nose but was too dizzy to lift his hand to staunch it. In a daze, he watched Mary smooth her dress.

"I'll get my things then," she said. She said it as casually as if she was commenting on the weather. She went to the chest and opened it, pulling out a bundle of cloth. The colors of the calico swam before James's eyes, and he knew he was close to fainting. He went down on one knee.

Mary placed the bundle of cloth on the table and opened it. A sparkle of light bounced off the jewels in the handle of Romaine's sword. With astounding speed, Mary grabbed the handle of the weapon in both hands and ran at the slave catcher. The barrel of the pistol started towards Mary. James screamed. The pistol swung back to James and fired. The bullet cut through the air at James's right ear, taking an impossibly long while to whistle past. Mary brought the sword around her body in a wide arc, and the slave catcher folded in half.

Eyes wide, the white man dropped the pistol and then himself onto the floor. His hands went to his stomach. A pool of red formed around him.

James tried to stand, but a wave of nausea forced him back down. He and the slave catcher eyed each other from their low positions. James pulled his shirt up and pressed it gingerly against his nose to stop the blood. The slave catcher looked down to see intestines spilling out. His hands grabbed at the slippery mess and tried to press things back into place.

Mary lowered the sword. Satisfied there would be no more shooting or slashing, James's eyes rolled back into his head, and he finished fainting.

James woke to the noxious smell of a slaughterhouse.

"Hold still." Romaine's face, upside down, hovered above him. His head was being held immobile between the knees of the Prophetess, who pressed a finger against the side of James's nose and pressed hard. The pain was sharp and excruciating. She released him. "Now it will heal straight."

Romaine stood up, and James turned his head to look for Mary. He came eye to eye instead with the white man and his intestines, the source of the putrid odor. James turned his head back, closed his eyes, and moaned. His face throbbed, and it was hard to breathe. He pushed himself up on his elbows and then made his way into sitting. The air was damp and warm. "Where is Mary?"

"Selecting the horses," Romaine said. "Can you ride?"

"I'd rather not," James said. He touched his cheeks lightly, testing for pain. It was everywhere.

"We can use your help," Romaine said. "If only to translate. What happened here?"

James explained the best he could, forcing himself to stand and make his way to the body as he did so. He wanted to search the man's pockets, but James found it difficult to bend back down without getting dizzy.

"You are looking for this." Romaine handed a folded piece of paper to James. "He was not carrying much else. Coins. A compass."

James unfolded the paper and saw it was a runaway advertisement. He translated into French as he read.

"*Fifty dollars reward. Eloped on the 5th of January last, Mary, a mulatto girl slave, about sixteen years old. Will pass for a free woman. The above reward will be given any person that will take her, and deliver her to me, or secure her in jail, so I can get her. If taken out of state, the above reward and all reasonable expenses paid*—" James stopped reading and looked up as Mary climbed back into the loft. He reread the paper for Mary in the original English. "*And ten dollars extra, for every hundred lashes any person will give her, to the amount of three hundred.*"

James handed the paper back to Romaine. The Prophetess folded it back and offered it to Mary. She refused. Her dress, James noticed, was covered in blood. She seemed quite calm for having just sliced open a white man.

"Ten dollars extra for every hundred lashes," she said. "I will kill him."

"You already have," James said. He moved his foot to avoid an approaching rivulet of blood.

Mary glanced at the body. "Andrew Jackson, I mean. This man is nothing. Jackson is the one who needs killing."

Romaine shook her head. "Tell her the Spirit has a higher use for her. She is the one."

"The one what?" James asked, confused.

"It is prophecy. Where this sword draws blood, the revolution will come to pass. Mary will rise and lead us into liberation. Tell her."

James translated the gibberish the best he could, expecting Mary to protest or at least have questions. Instead, she and Romaine looked at one another for a long while, having what seemed to James to be some kind of conversation without words. James felt the air spatter with energy, the way water jumps off a hot oiled pan.

"Ask her where we are going, then," Mary said.

Before James could translate, Romaine said, "To get rid of this body. Tell her she will have her chance later. I promise."

James cut his eyes between the two women. His face hurt less when he kept it still. There was some kind of sorcery happening here. It did not frighten him, but he preferred it to be over. The bloody rivulet crept closer. He preferred this all to be over.

The sound of the stable door opening sent all three of them scrambling to the back of the loft.

"James, you here?"

Denmark's baritone boomed through the stables. James's heart leapt with joy and relief. The first mate would know what to do. James opened his mouth to call down, but the pain from taking a breath kept him from yelling. It was Romaine who went down to confer with Denmark, and, in the end, it was Romaine's plan that they all agreed was the best.

The cicadas, loud at the edge of town, screeched louder still as they entered the swamp. There were four of them, five counting the dead man, but no one was counting the dead man. Or five counting Red Eagle, since these were his horses they were riding. They were fine animals, strong and light, bred to make their way through this kind of terrain. At the edge of town, their hoofs disappeared into the muck. A hundred feet on, they were up to mid-cannon, slowed to a high-kneed prance by the sucking mud. Romaine led the way. At the rear, Mary rode next to the horse carrying the dead man. Bullfrogs bellowed. Mosquitos swarmed. James cursed under his breath.

James wondered why he had agreed to come along. Mary was needed to handle the horses should they become skittish. Romaine was present because she was the one who made the plan. Denmark was the muscle they needed to carry it out.

But James? With a broken nose and weak from blood loss, what help could he offer in the task of finding a congregation of alligators to eat the body of a slave catcher? Yet Romaine had insisted he come.

"The prophecy," she had said. "And to translate."

James pointed out that Denmark had enough French and English to translate. As for the prophecy, he had already seen three revolutions—the American, while enslaved at Monticello; the French, as a servant in Paris; and the one in Saint-Domingue, from the deck of a ship. Three were plenty enough. Yet an hour later he found himself on a white-faced bay, trudging through the swamp with the rest of them.

The moon streamed in mustard yellow through the cypress. At any moment James expected the shimmering black ground to come to life, a mass of alligators emerging from the muck. An arrow of fear shot through James every time a dark lump rose up out of the ground—in the dark, the gnarled cypress knees looked like knobby snouts. He wanted to find the alligators quickly, so they could be done with their task. But he was not ready to find them quite yet. If he could slip away and ride quietly back to town without being missed, he would certainly do so.

"Here!" They were on firmer ground, out of the muck. Romaine dismounted and crouched for a closer look. From her horse she untied a chicken carcass with one hand and ran her other hand along the length of a makeshift scabbard hanging from the saddle. She pulled free her long sword and turned towards a cluster of dwarf palmettos to their right. She moved slowly forward, swinging the chicken by the legs like a thurible and using her sword to prod the ground before her. The swamp grew suddenly quiet.

A feeling of dread poured through James. He looked at Denmark and Mary, but if they felt the same desire to bolt, they hid it well. Mary sat calmly on her horse, watching Romaine's slow progress through the dark water. Denmark talked in a soothing tone to his horse, which seemed as nervous as James, ears swiveling back and forth and eyes darting from side to side.

"Let's just drop him here and go, don't you think?" James hoped they could not hear the tremor in his voice. "No one is going to come looking for him."

"I'm scared too," Mary said. She did not seem the least bit frightened.

"The gators will find him on their own," James said. "They really will. Let's *go*."

"Romaine's the captain here," Denmark said.

"She's going to get us all eaten alive," James said miserably. His heart pounded in panic.

Denmark put a hand on James's shoulder. "Perhaps."

In the distance, a barn owl screeched. For a moment, James thought the eerie shriek was what made Romaine leap backwards. Then he saw her toss the chicken in a tall, gentle arc. The long jaws of an alligator rose up and followed the flight of the lifeless bird. The primordial beast whipped itself around and the flash of white feathers disappeared into its maw.

Now the ground *was* moving. Romaine did not retreat as the water around her started to simmer. Incredibly, she turned and motioned for the trio to come join her. More incredibly still, Mary did as requested, using all her skills to urge her horse and the horse carrying the body towards the mass of predators emerging from the water.

The barn owl screeched a second time, closer now, and the quiet sound of individual alligators coming out of their holes merged together gurgle by gurgle into a terrible murmur. Romaine stood in the midst of it with the composure of a priest preparing to deliver a well-rehearsed sermon. Halfway to the convocation, the horse carrying the slave catcher's body stiffened its forelegs and refused to go any farther. Its eyes rolled and rolled, wild with fear. Mary made noises meant to comfort but got in response a terrified whinny.

The whinny was too much for Denmark's horse. The animal wheeled around twice and bolted back the way they had come. James saw Denmark's experience with ships was useless on horses. The first mate had no control over the galloping horse and soon disappeared into the darkness.

"James!" Romaine called his name with her back still turned. How did she know it was James who remained?

Years of riding and tending to horses gave James good command over his mount. He could turn and ride after Denmark. Or he could walk his horse forward to join Mary and Romaine.

Where this sword draws blood, the revolution will come to pass. Mary will rise and lead us into liberation.

Pain and fear combined in James's skull into a raging fire. It blurred his vision, and for an instant he saw a dozen or more people in a semicircle around Romaine. There was his mother and Sally beside her. There were his brothers Robert and Peter. There was Thenia, and Critta. Was that Ursula and her children? They shimmered in the dark, grey against black. James suddenly understood that he would never see them again. Whatever it was Romaine was doing here was more than disposing of a body. Whatever revolution was meant by her prophecy, there was no place in it for him to return to his family in Monticello. Grief fanned the flames in his skull. The seconds felt like hours, the fire intensifying until there was nothing left to burn. Then there was only char, and before him there remained only Romaine and Mary.

"James." This time Romaine did turn around, impatient.

Without intending to, James dug his heels into his horse and urged it forward. He kept his eyes on Romaine to keep from seeing what he was riding into. As he dismounted, he felt the alligators all shift their tails to move a bit closer. Mary calmed the horse as Romaine and James wrestled down the sack containing the body. James gagged at the smell of human offal. They opened the sack, and James did as instructed, kneeling to hold an arm or leg this way and that. He turned his face away as Romaine swung her sword to separate each limb from the torso. He did not understand the words she intoned as she threw each piece of the slave catcher into the swamp. It seemed each piece was an offering. It seemed the constellation of scaled, knotted eye sockets that hovered above the waterline receded a bit with each hand, foot, calf, thigh.

The moon disappeared behind a cloud, and for a moment all was blackness. James felt Romaine's hand on the back of his neck. It was as if the Prophetess was reaching inside him and placing something in the charred cavern of his skull. James could not turn his eyes inward to see; he could only feel that it was small and dense.

"The revolution will pass through here," Romaine said.

James closed his eyes, completely exhausted. "The revolution." His face hurt. He was unsure his legs could stand. "When does it start? I will be sure to be unavailable."

Romaine laughed. "It has already started. And by your own telling, you've been at the start of three. You have a talent for being available."

Dozens of eyes stared unblinking from the murk, but James was suddenly too tired to be afraid. The alligators and Romaine seemed to have come to some kind of understanding. They were creatures of the water, satisfied by what she had brought them from beyond the swamp.

Mary swung her leg onto her horse and turned it around. She tugged at the rope to encourage the now unburdened horse behind them to follow along. Romaine cleaned her sword and wiped it dry with a clump of Spanish moss. In the distance, a figure on horseback came trotting to meet them. The good sailor, James thought, was the sort of man who returns. The relief he felt was smothered by a blanket of exhaustion. James gathered the last of his strength to climb atop his bay and went to meet him.

Chapter 5

They emptied the horses' trough twice to scrub the loft clean of blood and evidence. As the water faded from red to pink to clear, so too did Romaine's prophecy fade from James's thoughts. From experience James respected the power of revolutions. If one was brewing—or if, as Romaine claimed, there was one already afoot—he should prepare for the fervor. A secluded place to wait it out, perhaps, or a way to take part. The possibility of taking part was so novel to James he laughed as he wondered where the thought came from. Was it how Denmark referred to the two of them as "men like us?" Or how easily Mary grabbed and used Romaine's sword? Perhaps it was how it felt to feed the slave catcher to the alligators. *Satisfying.* He might be able to cook. He was good on a horse. He knew how to sharpen knives He knew how to *use* knives. It was almost pleasant to consider the future possibilities.

But for the present moment, they had to make some pesos. Romaine, even more than James, insisted they all work together to make the restaurant a success. For James, the restaurant was the necessary first step to fame and fortune. For Romaine, it was a way to attract information. Most important of all, the venture kept Mary busy, distracting her from her desire to ride off in search of her twin sister. Day after day, sometimes twice or three times in one day, James translated the same conversation between Mary and Romaine:

"I am leaving to find her."

"If anyone can find her, it is Red Eagle."

"I know my sister. She is in trouble, I can feel it."

"Red Eagle knows every river and town from here to Savannah. He speaks twelve languages."

"He is taking too long."

"You must stay alive. If you go you will be captured within two hours."

"He has no reason to look for her."

"He is bound by his moral duty to find her."

Through this recurring exchange Mary learned some French while Romaine learned some English. By the beginning of Lent, the two were able to carry on their argument in either language while helping James serve bowls of restorative soup. It was a Catholic soup composed of soft shell river turtles, with a shot of sherry to liven the pot.

Word spread that the soups being ladled out of James's pot were far tastier than the swill served at the taverns, and soon ministers and colonels were jostling in line with coopers and draysmen. The ground floor of D'Arcantal's residence at the corner of St. Louis and Chartres became known as James's Café. Denmark came nearly every evening, bringing Mai's crew for supper. Some nights he returned to the ship to sleep. Some he remained behind.

James discovered his best chance for having Denmark stay the night was by setting a final table as the last customers departed, opening a bottle of Malbec and starting an argument. One night, handing a glass of wine to Romaine and pulling back a chair for Denmark, James asked with casual interest, "What is the one element most necessary for the success of a revolution, I wonder?"

"Ships, no question," Denmark said. "There is no revolution without a navy. How else will the revolution spread?"

"Guns, of course," Mary countered. "What is there to spread if you can't win the first battle?"

"Faith, obviously," Romaine said. "Unless they know they can win, you won't have anyone to carry that gun."

"Butter," James suggested, pulling a hot loaf of bread out of the oven.

By the time the four agreed ships, guns, faith, and butter were all necessary, it was well past midnight, and the cozy little room behind the kitchen James now called home was, to Denmark, preferable to making his way through dark streets back to Mai's ship.

Another night, James opened an expensive bottle of Burgundy and innocently asked, "If Denmark had a navy, which port city should be its base?"

"Havana," Romaine said. "The hands in Cuba are ready to be in revolt. Even a few ships in Havana will light the fuse."

"No, no—it's Charleston we want," Denmark said. "There is rice in the Carolinas. You will not win even Saint-Domingue if you have no source of food."

"Why not Nuevo Orleans?" James offered. "It is close to Cuba. And I am here to keep everyone well fed and satisfied."

Mary shook her head. "Denmark should take his navy to Port-au-Prince, where there is already an army fighting."

They discussed another dozen port cities along the coasts of the mainland and among the islands of the West Indies. As James had hoped, by the time they conceded there was no one clear answer, it was too late for Denmark to return to the ship. But alas, Denmark wasted the night in James's bed muttering to himself about Cartagena and Havana.

The next morning a long-limbed white boy was squatting by the café door when Mary went to open up. He had a message from Red Eagle: following a trustworthy source at the racetrack, Red Eagle had a good lead on the location of Mary's sister. He was on his way now. Mary took ahold of the boy's shoulders and tried to squeeze more information out of him, but that was all he knew.

As Lent ended and the Catholics resumed eating meats, James's Café started serving roasts. The faithful hurried out of the cathedral Sunday mornings and raced one another up two squares for a seat at the table. Señora Ribeau came the day she bought her daughter's freedom with pesos made from sewing dresses. Setting her remaining coin on the table, the mother ordered a bowl of bouillon, laughing at the novelty of having someone else serve her a meal.

There was soon another message from Red Eagle, this time from a trick rider who was in town performing for Sir Astley's Fabulous Circus. He tried to make Mary prove her identity by racing him but wisely changed his mind when Mary pressed the tip of her paring knife against his crotch. Her twin sister, the trick rider told her, was on a farm in the Cumberlands. Red Eagle was on his way there. No, he did not have any other information, could the young lady please move her knife?

One day in June the governor himself came to James's Café and asked the chef to prepare a feast for the pardo militia. The men were returned from fighting on the Florida border. The Spanish king owed the men a raise in pay, but the white militia would not stand for it. The governor hoped a fancy meal and a new slew of ribbons might serve to convey sufficient gratitude. Would James prepare something to show honor to the pardos?

"Of course," James said.

"Tonight?" The governor asked. A line of perspiration sprung up above his lip. He smiled in a pleading way.

James laughed. Dinner for fifty on four hours' notice? Impossible.

The governor's smile disappeared. Teeth bared, he looked around the room. "There are regulations, you know, for taverns of this sort."

James accepted the governor's coins and glanced at his watch. The governor left with his retinue of deputies, and James flew into action. He sent Mary to the market and hurried downstairs to make a bouillon. Romaine shucked oysters. Mary returned with eggs, two chickens, a dozen crabs, and apologies for the scanty haul. In his despair, James remembered the instructions from his Chantilly instructor Mademoiselle Madeleine: when in doubt, first make a roux.

When the lard and flour turned the color of a hickory nut, James added chopped onion and the oysters' liquor. Into the pot went the crabs, eggs, and oysters. There was no time to make bread, so he made rice instead.

James dipped a ladle into the soup and retrieved something far too thick. Using both shell and roux had been too much. What it produced was a dark brown slush that resembled the muck clogging the street gutters after a hard rain. A feculent mess. James meant to set the ladle down in disgust, but momentum carried it onward to his mouth.

With some reluctance, he opened his mouth to receive it. His eyes flew open. He took three quick breaths through his nose. He could not swallow. It was that good. This was not soup at all. It was something else entirely. It was the sea and the swamp and the earth struggling one against the other for dominance. It was not merely the succulent meat of the oysters and crabs that bonded into some other thing, but their marine souls as well, briny and dark. It was a trickery of grief and joy. It was the taste of worlds long gone and oceans yet to come.

It was too rich and too thick, fraught with too many flavors. How to serve this dark pot of magic? James had been instructed in Chantilly to strive for clarity in all soups. But this was not a soup. And the French king was dead. There was nothing to stop a cook, trained in France but forced to improvise in Nuevo Orleans, from pouring this unctuous new creation over rice. And so James did.

Between slurps, the pardo captain made clear to the governor they still expected full and fair monetary compensation for their service. For now, though, they could be satisfied with another bowl of this strange stew.

The governor returned the next evening with a retinue of lieutenants and captains, asking for another bowl of the same.

The pardos returned, clamouring for more. Within a week, half the town was at D'Arcantal's door, hoping for a taste of this dark wonder.

It was Denmark who named it. "Ngombo," he said, *magician*. He meant James.

Word spread that James was willing to take payment in trade. Guests began to arrive with ingredients instead of coins to exchange for a meal. Thomas brought a wealth of chicken giblets, secreted out of his master's kitchen. The Senegambian Constantine brought a pot of ground cayenne made from peppers grown in a square of land he worked after a day of cutting indigo. An Isleño shrimper with arms thick as a cypress trunk brought shrimp. An unnamed Manilaman brought a considerable amount of alligator meat and blue crabs. From one of the German Coast plantations came andouille sausage.

Most important of all were San Maló's maroons, who brought rice. The rice from their bend of the swamp was good, long-grained with a nutty taste. But what they really brought to James's was business. Nothing drew more customers than their presence. What food was so good that the maroons came in from the swamp to eat at a table not fifty feet from Maspero's slave traders? Their leader Juan Maló had been condemned by the Cabildo and, in front of the church of St. Louis, hung by the neck ten years ago. Yet his people, the maroons, persisted and came to eat, bright red handkerchiefs tied tight around their necks as a tribute and a dare.

Here was the kind of égalité James could understand: everyone who came into his restaurant ate like a king. What place in all the world was more democratic in spirit and in fact?

Spring turned to summer when another message came from Red Eagle. The emissary this time was a fellow Muskogee, in Nuevo Orleans with a mule load of deerskin. Mary's sister had been sold, he told her, to a dealer who specialized in subterfuge. The buyer was known for changing names and identifying information to turn runaways into more valuable stock. He assured Mary that Red Eagle would nevertheless find the dealer—having caused such harm, he was obligated to do all he could to bring things back into balance. Mary frowned, still not believing Red Eagle owed her a debt, but glad he believed he did.

To James's barely suppressed delight, there was no sign of a deal for Captain Mai. Once or twice a week she came to the café after an afternoon across the street at the tables of Pierre Maspero's trading house. The deals the traders made at Maspero's were for sugar and humans. They listened closely to Mai's explanations of wealthy Americans' love for porcelain and tea, and the Chinese love for silver and otter pelts. They examined her samples of silk, muslin and nankeen. They studied her profit sheets, hefted her bags of silver coins, and agreed with her appraisal that the French wars threw open the doors of opportunity for a merchant willing to take the risk. But each negotiation ended the same. The men dipped their dry biscuits into the last drops of their coffee and explained to Captain Mai they prefered the certainty of the slave trade to the risks of the China trade. After each failed negotiation, Mai stomped into James's restaurant and pulled out her whiskey, her face as hard as her glass eye. James rejoiced at the flash of Mai's silver flask. So long as the captain remained without a commission, she would keep her ship—and thus Denmark—in Nuevo Orleans.

In the bedroom behind the kitchen, James felt the little room fill with a wild happiness that he did not know existed in the world. Denmark was as contained as ever in the restaurant among his crew, but in James's bed, the first mate uncoiled and his edges softened. What was hard turned tender, his carefulness turned to care. His splendid body, so stimulating in action, was comforting in repose. Inside those tough calloused hands, James learned, was a startling gentleness.

After a while, Denmark relaxed some of his guard. He allowed himself to be the first to fall asleep, his muscular back as quiet and vast as the sea. James draped his long legs over Denmark and hoped for a slow arrival of the rising sun.

It was late summer, the long tables at James's Café glowing in the morning light. Denmark waited until they were alone to tell James his news.

"Captain Mai has made a deal."

James, walking to the kitchen, froze mid-stride. The tureen he carried slipped from his hands. It hit the ground with a sharp crack, exploding into a splash of ceramic shards.

"When?" James did not turn around.

"Yesterday."

James bent and reached for the largest pieces of what had been the best of the restaurant's soup bowls. He saw there would be no repairing it. One side was only cracked, but the other side had shattered into pieces too small for any glue or gum to hold. "No. When will she sail?"

"As soon as we can gather the crew." After a pause, Denmark added. "It may take a while to complete the crew."

James knelt to gather the fragments into a pile. He felt as if he had been kicked in the gut with a hobnail boot. He placed one ceramic bit after another into the upturn of the half bowl and stood to face Denmark but did not trust himself to speak.

"A week at least, perhaps two." Denmark said.

"You can stay," James said. He did not believe it even as he said it.

"You can come," Denmark countered. "A good cook is important when you're at sea this long."

James set the remains of the tureen down on a table and looked around the room. Fourteen tables of four chairs each, all well squared and sturdily built. The wood floor was marked by scratches and stains. The oil lamp's hazy light reflected off windows that needed another wash. The space from front door to back wall was not large—a quarter the length of Captain Mai's ship. But just yesterday, half the Cabildo had come through for a bowl of ngombo. One suggested, only half in jest, they take up their official meetings here while they waited for city hall to be rebuilt.

"My place is here," James said.

Denmark nodded. The silence hung heavy between the two men.

"You will be famous by the time I return," Denmark said. He tried to smile but the attempt failed.

"You plan to return?"

Denmark swallowed hard before answering. "This deal is a good one. I may have enough to buy the ship."

"Mai will sell you the *Dragon*?"

"That I can't predict."

"But if yes, would you return here?"

Denmark opened his palms to the sky. "I can't say. I will go wherever the revolution spreads. Perhaps here."

James clenched his jaw to keep from crying. He hated this about himself, how forcefully his emotions leapt to the surface, demanding his attention. "Stay with me," he wanted to say, but to speak would be to lose the small measure of control he had over his tears. Instead, he picked up the tureen with both hands, careful not to let any bits fall back to the floor, and turned back to the kitchen. Mary was probably already there. Mary always arrived early to start the dough.

"I was happy here with you, James Hemings."

James pulled the remnants of the bowl to his chest, not wanting to drop it a second time. Careful as a funeral cortege he made his way across the dining room and into the kitchen. Mary waited for him at the bottom, her hands outstretched to take the broken tureen from James.

"I heard," she said.

James smiled, grateful for the help of this young woman whose temperament was so much older than her age in years. "Captain Mai will be off soon," James said as lightly as he could.

"I will miss her," Mary said. "Denmark too."

"It was nothing unexpected," James said. He had known, of course, from the first night they spent together that Denmark would leave and that no wish or hope would keep him ashore once it was time to sail. The miracle was that it had taken so long for Captain Mai to make her deal. It was enough time to create this restaurant. It was enough time to grow fond of a person.

"Being expected doesn't make it any easier," Mary said.

James nodded. This seemed true enough.

"You can go with him," Mary said.

"Cooking swill for sailors."

"Sailing the world."

James cocked his head at the twinge of jealousy in Mary's voice. "You go then," he said. "You've learned enough cooking here to make a good cook for any ship."

"I have my sister." Mary laid the pieces of the tureen down on the chopping block and tried fitting the larger pieces back together.

"If Red Eagle rode in here tomorrow with your sister, would you join Mai's ship?"

"Of course," Mary said, without hesitation. "Here I'll always be looking over my shoulder."

"Your master will give up looking for you at some point," James said. He did not know whether this was true for Mary. It was what he believed for himself—that Thomas Jefferson might be looking for him still, but he would soon give up his search. Jefferson's reputation as the champion of liberty could tolerate ownership of slaves but not sending out slave catchers.

"Andrew Jackson will never give up. Me walking around

free is an insult to him." Mary shook her head, searching for the right word. "A danger. An injury. He won't stop until I'm back riding for him. Or dead." She closed her hand around the clay fragment she held, breaking it in half. "This is too broken to repair."

Denmark appeared at the kitchen's doorway. James looked up expectedly, but Denmark looked past him.

"Mary. Red Eagle is here."

Mary dropped the broken tureen and pushed past James. He started to follow, but reconsidered and turned back around. James lit a candle instead to take into the wine pantry. Good news or bad, either could use a bottle of good wine.

When he acquired his first casks of wine, James had lined the back of the pantry with stones to try to keep the alcohol from turning to vinegar. James was proud of the wines he had on the shelves. There were not only jugs of Madeira and port but also a respectable collection of Burgundy and Bordeaux. It was not as large a collection as he had helped Jefferson amass after their return from Paris, but, passing the candle over the labels, James imagined that his wine collection was possibly of better quality. What would Jefferson think of him now, making an independent living?

James's reverie was interrupted by a furious scream, followed by a loud bang of something heavy hitting the floor, then the sound of shattering glass. James's hands found the two heftiest bottles of Burgundy and, against his natural instincts to remain hidden in the pantry, he forced his legs to carry him to the source of the commotion.

In the dining room, Red Eagle stood close to the door, next to a window apparently broken by the chair that lay beneath it in a glimmer of glass. Across the room, Romaine had her arms wrapped around Mary, who was struggling to free herself.

The struggle continued in silence until Mary's thrashing slowed, moving from frenzy to exhaustion. Red Eagle stepped gingerly around the glass and went to Mary and Romaine. As he approached, Mary made a sudden movement towards him that Romaine smothered. Romaine shooed Red Eagle away with a jerk of her head.

"You did not find her," James said. It sounded like an accusation, though he did not intend it as such.

Red Eagle glanced at James without expression. "I found her, but we were discovered. She was punished for trying to run away."

"Whipped?"

"Sold."

Mary shook herself loose from Romaine. She strode across the room to Red Eagle, eyes hard and angry. She thrust an accusatory finger towards his face. "Did you forget to show her my ring?"

"I showed her," said Red Eagle. He took a half step back away from Mary. "She thought I'd stolen it and refused to come."

"I told you she would be afraid," Mary said. "You should have forced her."

"I persuaded her. She was ready to come."

"So why is she not here?" Mary yelled.

"She must have told someone, the wrong person. When I returned the next morning with a horse, she was already gone. Sold."

"There is something you're not telling me," Mary said, squinting hard at Red Eagle.

Red Eagle blinked rapidly, but his eyes did not leave Mary. "She is pregnant."

Mary staggered and caught herself on the edge of the table. "Pregnant," she repeated under her breath.

Romaine put a hand on Mary's arm to steady her. "The last dealer, what do you know of him?"

"He resold her to a trader who does business along the coast."

"Can you find him?" James asked.

At the same time, Mary said, "You will find her."

"I will find them," Red Eagle said. "I know all the taverns and ferrymen along the Lower Path. I will find her."

Mary was unconvinced. "It took you eight months to find my sister, and then you immediately lost her." The Muskogee's confidence in his own abilities aggravated her.

"I know the coast well. I am sure I will find her."

"You can't promise that," Mary shot back. "You've already failed once."

"I did find her, as I said I would," Red Eagle said carefully. "I will find her again."

Chapter 6

Red Eagle rode off the next morning. Not a week later, Captain Mai pulled anchor and sailed the *Golden Dragon* around the bend in the river, carrying Denmark out to sea. For both departures, James hid in the warmth of his bedroom, protected by a generous jug of brandy.

Romaine the Prophetess knew it was part of the divine plan for Denmark to be gone—to build his navy, God willing—but she was sad to see her friend go. There was so much more to discuss with him.

The dissemination of gombos, for instance.

Since its creation months earlier, James mysterious little soup had taken on a life of its own. Denmark on first tasting the smoky brown liquid had called James a sorcerer, an *ngombo*, but when it became apparent that anyone could produce the same magic, the dish lost its *n* and simply became known as *gombo*, a pot of sorcery that made the leap from James's Café into pots all around town.

The Spaniards used filé powder, it being less work, while the French made roux of every shade. Cooks from West Africa used okra. Acadians, shellfish. But in this common alchemic quest, cooks quickly set aside group loyalty and freely borrowed from their neighbors.

The speed of the spread of gombo seemed to Romaine to have something to teach about the spread of rebellions. Gombo spread quickly because there were few rules: there must be a thickener, and there must be rice. In rebellions too, there had to be some thickener to gather the forces. Beyond that, no particular set of ingredients was prescribed. People used what was available, and into their pots went chaurice and shrimp, crab and andouille pork sausage, chicken gizzards and alligator, turkey and unmentionable parts of the pig. People experimented with gusto. Some chickens were wasted, but the possibility of success was worth the sacrifice. This confirmed Romaine's belief that people everywhere were willing to take part in something as uncertain as an uprising so long as the result—liberty, equality, and the end of slavery—was worthy the risk of death.

Romaine pulled the meat cleaver against the whetstone and watched the dinner guests slurp their gombo. If uprisings spread in the islands and around the Main as quickly as gombo was spreading throughout Nuevo Orleans, the question of liberty would soon be settled. Romaine tested the edge of the cleaver, and, satisfied, moved on to the carving knife. The *sssshwt, sssshwt, sssshwt* of the blade sliding across the stone punctuated the hubbub of diners as they emptied their bowls. If uprisings spread as quickly as gombo, the revolution in Saint-Domingue would soon come complete. Slavery would be ended everywhere.

Romaine stopped her sharpening. She set down the carving knife and made her way to a table of dockworkers.

The Prophetess slapped down a loaf of bread in greeting. "I have a proposition for you gentlemen," she said. The burly men nodded to let her know they were listening. They continued to slurp down their bowls as Romaine laid out her terms.

Before nightfall, every worker on and around the merchant ships crowding the riverfront knew of Romaine's offer: fresh and reliable news—whether through word of mouth or in the form of recent newspapers from the port cities—would be rewarded at James's Café with a hot bowl of gombo. The Prophetess promised an additional half loaf of crusty bread when the news was of her homeland.

The very next day, three draysmen raced one another to James's Café, each determined to be the first to tell Romaine about the discontent brewing among those enslaved in plantations in Pointe Coupee, a hundred miles upriver. Food portions, the tallest of the three told Romaine, were being cut in half. The second of the draysmen shouldered his way to the front and reported secret meetings were being held in the arbor at the back of Jacques Vignes's plantation. Among the trees, they were studying copies of the Declaration of the Rights of Man.

"Can you get word upriver?"

The three nodded in unison, their bowls held at the ready.

"Let the leaders know the Decree of the National Convention has ended slavery in all of France's colonies," Romaine said. She ladled out their prize.

"But Pointe Coupee is Spanish," the tallest said. He picked a shrimp out of the gombo and popped it in his mouth.

"No matter. The conspirators will believe the Spanish Crown has done the same. How many total?"

The third draysman spoke up. "Seven thousand enslaved in Pointe Coupee."

"And whites?"

"Two thousand at the most. The Mississippi Legion Militia is weak."

Romaine nodded, calculating in her head. "If they come through the German Coast, there might be enough to take Nuevo Orleans. Tell them the Prophetess will be waiting for them here."

If Denmark was off to build his navy, she had better get started building her army.

Romaine was not always the Prophetess. Romaine was in fact not always Romaine. Forty years before she became the

Prophetess, Romaine was Roman, born in Spanish Santo Domingo. As a young man, Roman, in an act of religious devotion, followed a Catholic priest across the border into French Saint-Domingue. There on a plot of land in Trou Coffy, he learned to grow coffee and fell in love with Marie-Rose, oval faced and serious. On Sundays, Roman rode into the bustle of Léogâne to attend Catholic Mass and visit his beloved.

Roman was free, but Marie-Rose was enslaved and so the three children she bore with him were also enslaved. It took thirteen harvests for Roman to accumulate the 6,000 livres he needed to buy Marie-Rose. In 1785, at the Church of St. Rose de Lima in Léogâne, Roman married Marie-Rose, and the priest declared as *libre* their children Louise-Marie (age eleven), Pierre-Marie (age nine), and Marie-Jeanne (age seven).

Roman did not mean to have a favorite, but his oldest daughter was his pride and joy. Louise-Marie, as serious and unsmiling as her mother, calculated in her head the plantation's yield in pounds raw, pounds roasted, livres gross, and livres profit, first as absolutes and then as percentages. She walked around the farm with a palm-sized notebook and pencil stub, taking notes on the plantings, prunings, and harvests. One day Louise-Marie invited her father to walk with her along the northern edge of his property. Here, she pointed, you can add a crop of cocoa. And our Sundays, she continued, can be more profitably spent gathering the indigo that grow without cultivation in the crags of the mountainside.

Roman smiled and declined. His devotion to the Virgin Mary was profound. Did he not name his children as he did in order to be able to call her name dozens of times a day? He turned his oldest child by her shoulders to face him. Here was a lesson he wanted to be certain she heard and understood: remaining faithful to your namesake the Blessed Virgin Mary, he told Louise-Marie, is the only way to ensure lasting prosperity. To forsake Sunday's worship for the sake of profit was greed, a deadly sin.

"They are all sinners, then," Louise-Marie said, waving her delicate hand towards the horizon.

Roman agreed that perhaps they all were. There was no place on earth that produced such wealth as this colony. Coffee, cocoa, and indigo grew with hardly any care. There was a large-leafed tobacco native to the land, and cotton too. But, most of all, there was sugar. It was shipped out raw and in cakes, as molasses and as rum. It made the white colonists extraordinarily wealthy and covetous for more. The owners of the cane plantations cast a jealous eye on their neighbors to the north. If the American colonists with their long winters and poor soil managed to increase their profits after shaking off Great Britain, imagine what was possible if the planters of Saint-Domingue broke free of France? The white owners doubled the lashes to make up the profits they imagined were theirs *if only*. Those enslaved suffered under the whip and plotted an end to their suffering. The entire island glistened with riches and rage.

A few years after Louise-Marie gave her advice, the fever of revolution spread through the colony. In the north, the fearsome Boukman and the priestess Cécile Faitman led mass incantations in the mountains that loomed over Le Cap. Men and women from two thousand plantations set fire to their misery. For three weeks, the black smoke of burning cane turned day to night, and, in the darkness, the rapes and tortures endured for a hundred years by those enslaved were returned, with brutal efficiency.

In the south, a miracle struck Roman's coffee farm like a flash of lightening. The Blessed Virgin Mary, eager to push forward the revolution, used the channels of voudon to do her will. She chose as her vessel Roman, whose devotion, gentle and fierce, was so like her son's.

One evening, Roman knelt in prayer, and the Virgin took possession.

When Roman opened his eyes, he was on a dusty road among a flock of believers, following Jesus at Calvary, the

Messiah's back bent in half under the weight of a wooden cross. Roman rushed forward to help when Jesus fainted but was pushed back by soldiers. Roman tried to yell out to Jesus to fight but discovered he could make no sound.

Roman searched the crowd for Mary but could not find her. At midday, the sun disappeared, and the world went from bright daylight to the darkest night. The soldiers went stiff with fear. In the blackness, Roman placed his hands on his own body to be certain he had one still.

He touched his face. It was unfamiliar. His fingers slid along soft and beardless cheeks, wet with tears, Roman realized he was not merely one of the faithful. He was not Roman. He was Mary of Nazareth, daughter of Saint Anne, mother of Jesus.

Then the sun reappeared, and the crowd started screaming as lightning came down from the skies. When Jesus finally died, the soldiers wrapped his body and set him into a cave. How does a mother who has just watched her child be killed then endure his burial? Roman—Mary—followed the soldiers to the mouth of the cave, and, as they rolled the stone to seal the tomb, she fainted into a deep sleep.

On Sunday morning, it was not Jesus who rose from the dead. It was his mother who awakened. Mary had collapsed in grief on Friday, but then on Easter morning she rose. She rose in fury.

When the possession lifted, Roman woke and flew into a frenzy of action. He turned Trou Coffy's stable into a chapel, replete with relics, adorned with orchids, lit by a thousand candles. A dull old sword, given to him as a boy by the Catholic priest, lost its coat of rust and found its edge. Jewels gleamed from the handle. Roman placed his head on the tabernacle to receive further word from the Holy Virgin. She whispered in his ear, her words dragged across the boundary to the spirit world, a rasp pulled against a rough block of wood.

Raise me an army, the Holy Virgin said.

Roman gathered his neighbors and told them about what happened at Calvary, how Jesus was nailed to the cross and killed, the lightning, all of it. When he got to the part about sleeping outside his tomb, someone yelled out, "And then Jesus is risen!" *No*, Roman said, *No, Jesus did not rise. They were not forgiven.*

Roman laid his ear against the tabernacle, and the Virgin Mary said to Roman, *Again.* Ten, fifteen, twenty times he told the story. *They were not forgiven.*

Each time Roman told Mary's story the crowd got bigger.

Warriors and soldiers, men and women of destiny. Jesus did not rise, and their sin was not forgiven. The sin of slavery cannot be forgiven, it can only be redeemed. I am Mary of Nazareth, the mother of Jesus Christ our Lord, and I have risen. There is freedom at hand for those who seize it. Who will follow me to the Redemption?

Roman preached in this way, sword in one hand and an inverted cross in the other. Each time he incanted he felt a part of himself fall away and something new rush into the space. His confusion at the swirl of change turned to wonder, then wonder turned to gratitude. When gratitude turned to resolve, the transformation was complete. Trou Coffy became a rebel camp. Roman the coffee farmer became Romaine the Prophetess.

The Prophetess had two gifts. The first was to attract followers. They came and trained and marched across the south. One plantation after another fell—some abandoned, others after vicious fighting. Each victory brought more recruits. The Prophetess's second gift gave her followers courage—she had the power to heal. A gunshot wound was no longer fatal. Her army believed themselves under the protection of divinity.

The whites were frightened but dismissive. Only imbeciles will follow this hermaphroditic tigress, the mayor of Léogâne sniffed. At year's end, the mayor was on his knees, trembling before the spears and cannons of Romaine's ten thousand troops. The mayor ceded the city to save his own skin, and the colony's largest port city on the southern coast was in the hands of the rebellion.

It did not last.

It was the free gens de couleur who betrayed the Prophetess. Roman the coffee farmer had been one of them, free and prosperous, seeking equality with the whites. Romaine the Prophetess was another matter entirely. Her followers had been enslaved and sought freedom and vengeance. Even as she led the troops into Jacmel, capturing for the rebellion the entire southern coast, the gens de couleur abandoned her.

The end of Romaine's reign came as quickly as it started. Her soldiers, outgunned and weakened by the desertion of its gens de couleur, retreated to the safety of Trou Coffy. A final betrayal by a white Catholic priest brought in a military assault that destroyed the camp.

Romaine's son Pierre-Marie was killed defending the tabernacle. Her youngest, Marie-Jeanne, was shot through the back. When the Prophetess could not be found, the French commander stopped the execution of Romaine's wife and most favored daughter Louise-Marie, calculating the two could be used as bait to lure Romaine back.

A finger a day, the French commander announced. He let loose two of the rebel lieutenants and bade them to let the Prophetess know: once twenty fingers were gone, the next cut would be to the throat. Romaine received the first finger, disbelieving. She received the second, furious. She received the third, defeated. On the fourth day Romaine walked back in to Trou Coffy, her tall turban topped with a riot of black crow feathers. "I am here," the Prophetess said. "Bring me my wife and daughter."

"We made no agreements," the Commander replied. A dozen soldiers rushed in to grab the Prophetess, who made no move to resist.

Romaine could do nothing but pray in the black hole of her prison cell. She made a scratch in the dirt each time a circle of light appeared above her and her guards dropped down a half loaf of bread. When the guards came to tell her Rose-Marie was dead, Romaine felt something at the base of her throat come undone When they threw down the news that Louise-Marie was killed, Romaine fell to her knees and knocked her forehead against the ground, and her faith drained out of her body in a violent rush.

She continued to pray, but now it was for deliverance. By death, if nothing else was available. A hundred days her prayers went unanswered. Then the daily bread stopped, there was a fluttering of black soot, and the air turned acrid. A sailor calling himself Denmark appeared and hauled her out of the hold.

The Prophetess grabbed the jeweled sword her jailers had dangled from the grate to mock her. She and the sailor rushed through the burning streets of Le Cap and onto a ship that sailed her to Nuevo Orleans.

Where once the Holy Virgin spoke to Romaine in clear directives, now her signs were muddled and hard to understand. Was it the Virgin Mary's will that placed Romaine in James's kitchen, surrounded by knives? Was it the Virgin Mary who brought to Romain the girl Mary, the same age as Louise-Mary, needing help to find her twin sister? Romaine asked in every way she knew how. *Is it you? Is this you? Please, this?*

There was no answer.

When James peered into the gombo pot and learned the reason for the dwindling of his soup, his eyes grew wide. He replaced the lid and looked Romaine up and down, the way a butcher assesses the carcass of an unfamiliar animal.

"You will have us killed," James said.

Romaine did not deny this was a possibility. But the risk was worth the reward, wouldn't he agree?

James frowned at the question. With Denmark gone, he had hoped Romaine would let go of her wild ideas about revolution and settle into her place as his sous chef. The restaurant was doing very well, far beyond what he had hoped. Just last week, they had added four tables and extended the hours, nearly doubling the already impressive weekly income. As important as the profit was the fame. Everywhere James went in Nuevo Orleans, the townspeople—white, Black, free, and enslaved—acknowledged him with a respectful nod. The nod sometimes even turned into a small bow. The last thing he needed was one of Governor Carondelet's lackeys investigating his restaurant on suspicion of inciting a slave revolt.

"There will soon be uprisings everywhere," Romaine said. She said it as if such a prediction would soothe James. "I can't be blamed for them all."

Over the next months, rebellions did indeed flare. A dockworker came to the restaurant to report the maroons in Jamaica were rising in revolt. A sailor from a ship turned back from Grenada reported the free mulatto French-speakers, siding with the revolutionaries, had seized control of the island. Less than a week later, the coxswain of a merchant ship carrying sugar from Cuba found Romaine to report that a conspiracy had been discovered among the enslaved and put down. He insisted on the loaf of crusty bread, for including the detail that the men and women in Cuba were inspired by their counterparts in Saint-Domingue. As Romaine waited for word from Pointe Coupee, more news rushed in. There was an uprising in Saint Vincent Island, a revolt in Curaçao, an insurrection in Venezuala, a rebellion in Guyana.

For every message received, Romaine sent back out a carefully crafted piece of encouragement. Let the cane cutters in Saint Vincent know Grenada is nearly won. Tell those who escaped in Cuba they will live to fight another day, as the maroons in Jamaica are doing. Send word to Curaçao that Guyana has joined them in revolt. In the mornings, she drank her coffee at the restaurant's front table and read the newspapers. The rebellion in Saint-Domingue was spreading fast as gombo.

And then there was word, finally, from Pointe Coupee. The same three draysmen came with hats in hand to give Romaine the news, eyes downcast.

The plan to burn the plantations and kill all the white men, then march down the river to Nuevo Orleans, had been discovered. The betrayal came from two Tunica women who feared they would be among those killed. Within two days of discovery, the Pointe Coupee commandants arrested and conducted trials of sixty-three people, ending in the execution of twenty rebels and banishment of the rest. The draysmen concluded their report with a description of the twenty severed heads set on high stakes along the river road.

The draysmen did not ask for payment. Romaine gave them each a bowl of gombo anyway. They were putting their hats on to leave when James emerged from the kitchen, glaring at Romaine.

"You have some responsibility for those deaths," James said when the draysmen were out the door.

"I do," Romaine said. A wave of nausea rolled through her as she tried to quell the bile rising from her stomach. Not only these deaths, but hundreds more, in Saint-Domingue.

"And what if they named you in their confession," James said. "Or me."

Romaine knew that people like James, who wavered in moments of trouble, needed strong assurances. "There's no possibility of that," she said with as much confidence as she could muster. "We'd already be strung up if we'd been named."

James touched his throat. "Or they were too busy chopping off heads to get to us yet."

Romaine forced a light laugh. "It takes no time at all to put a head on a stake. We were not named, I assure you." She did not know her hands were shaking until she set a bowl down on the table and it gave the barest clatter.

James kept one eye on the front door, a tingle at his throat each time a group of white men walked in. He was certain each time they were a posse come to take him or Romaine away to be hanged. But the Pointe Coupee commandants did not come to the restaurant with nooses in hand. Not that week or the next. What came instead was a letter, delivered by the captain of a two-mast brig sailing out of Charleston. The captain had been *very* well compensated to make the delivery by hand and, upon handing over the oilskin packet containing the letter, did nothing to disguise his surprise that the recipient was a Black man.

"We are the Jockey Club of Charleston," the flowing script read, "and most desirous of making your acquaintance in person."

James wiped his hands on his apron and shook open the rest of the letter. The paper was whiter than any James's had ever seen, with such a fine grain it was almost creamy to the touch. This was an expensive letter, sent by someone of significant wealth. Mary put down her stack of plates and slipped her arm through James's, prodding his side until he read out loud.

"The city of Charleston has completed construction of a new Horse Track that we are certain will soon become the United States' preeminent horse racing facility. The Jockey Club will be hosting an inaugural banquet at the Horse Track's opening and require the talents of a great chef. An admirer of your cooking has recommended you." The letter specified that the banquet should be "of French technique and presentation, as we have been assured you are expert." At the bottom of the letter was an offer of payment so generous that James paused his reading to recount the zeros. This was no fiddler's pay. Quite the opposite. This was a king's ransom.

"An admirer," Mary said. "How mysterious." She took the oilskin packet and peered inside. It was empty of further clues. "Will you go?"

James was flattered by the recognition and even more so by the fee. How could he not go? It was exactly what he needed: a chance to have his fame spread far beyond this single Spanish town of Nuevo Orleans. The wealthiest, most powerful men of Charleston would all be present. And with the gentlemen of the Jockey Club wanting renown for the new horse track, they were sure to extend invitations throughout the Carolinas and beyond. With a single elaborate banquet, James's fame could spread among the moneyed plantation owners as fast as mushrooms after a rain.

Yet he knew he had to decline the offer. Charleston was the center of the American slave trade, and the scions of the Rice Coast made no secret of their intent to keep the United States a slave nation forever. What if the members of the Jockey Club were bringing him to Charleston to cook a feast, but instead of making good on their payment they intended to snatch him up afterwards and offer him up at the slave market? What if it was Thomas Jefferson himself who, having discovered James's whereabouts, was enticing him to Charleston? It was precisely the kind of deceit Jefferson would fashion, setting out as a lure a spectacular promise that he had no intentions to fulfill.

James refolded the letter and slid it back into the oilskin. It was maddening, to be able to see the fame and fortune he so desired just across the river, and then to see the river was impossible to cross.

"I'll have to think on it," he said to Mary. There had to be a way across.

Chapter 7

As James pondered, Red Eagle was riding back towards Nuevo Orleans at a gallop, the blues and browns of the pine barrens streaming past. It took four days of fast riding to put him inside the sagging wooden gate that separated Nuevo Orleans from the swamp.

"Tell me you've found her," Mary said when Red Eagle stepped into James's Café. It was past midnight. A group of white women—well-to-do by the fashionable cuts of their dresses—crowded around a front table cluttered with empty wine bottles, but the place was otherwise empty.

"Your sister is in Charleston," Red Eagle said. "I can take you."

"Charleston," Mary said. Her face shifted into a hard, determined smile. "You will take me."

"Yes," Red Eagle agreed. He searched for something else to say, to try to coax a bit of warmth or welcome from Mary. Finding nothing, he scratched behind his ear. His fluency in so many languages did not make him a better conversationalist in any one.

For months, Red Eagle had regretted his failure to bring Mary's sister back with him after he'd found her on a settler's farm built—illegally, as all of the farms were—on Cherokee land. Here was a chance now to finally settle his debt to Mary. He did not intend to fail again. At home, there were too many tasks needing his time and attention. To the east, white Georgians were streaming through the line separating Georgia from Muskogee land. To the north, Dragging Canoe was dead, and the Cherokees were threatening to revert back to their longstanding status as rivals to the Muskogees. To the west, whites were pushing in from the Mississippi River, shoving their rifles under the chins of Choctaw chiefs while handing them packets of gifts to force them into friendship. If the Cherokees and Choctaws took the side of the Americans, the Muskogees would be surrounded. Red Eagle's mother, Sehoy, had other children, but Red Eagle was the one everyone knew would one day take her place as the head of town. For that, his days racing and selling horses up and down the coast, and along each river from the Ogeechee to the Coosa to the Alabama to the Mississippi were, alas, certain to end. And soon.

Mary beckoned Red Eagle follow her into the kitchen. "Let's tell the others."

Romaine was bent over the chopping block, slicing a pork shoulder into thin rounds.

"Romaine," Red Eagle said, nodding his hello. "It is a pleasure seeing you again." Red Eagle chose Spanish and modulated his tone carefully. He was reminded by the way the air thickened around Romaine that the warrior woman from the islands was not one to be taken lightly.

"We need to go to Charleston with James," Mary said. She tried to keep her voice low, but James's head snapped up at the mention of his name.

The redheaded Scotsman helping Romaine prepare the meats set down his mallet to pick at the scab that crusted over the side of his nose. Head tilted to one side, he asked James, "When you going to Charleston?"

"I'm not going to Charleston," James snapped. "You're done for the night. Don't be late again tomorrow." When the Scotsman disappeared out the door, James joined them around the butcher block.

"Tell us what you know," Mary commanded.

"Mary's sister was sold to the coast. The man's name is Charles Pinckney. Very wealthy."

"Pinckney," Romaine said. "I know the name." It took her a moment to place it. Pinckney was the governor of South Carolina, mentioned in a news story about the influx of refugees from Saint-Domingue into the port of Charleston.

"Why would we want to provoke Pinckney?" James asked. He examined the rounds of pork shoulder.

Mary felt a twinge of aggravation at having to explain. James was always asking for explanations for things that were plain as day. Red Eagle had finally located her sister. This Pinckney man who bought her was somewhere near Charleston. She was going to Charleston to find her sister. What further explanation was needed?

"You'll get snatched up before you're even halfway to Charleston," James said.

"You don't know that." Mary scowled. But how James refused to look up from the rounds of meat told her the chef knew *something*. "What do you know about Pinckney?"

"Nothing," James said.

"You're a terrible liar, James." It was why Mary found him trustworthy. She took a hold of his chin and turned his head to force him to look at her. Mary waited.

James shook his face free of Mary's grasp and returned to his close inspection of the slices of meat. "Really, nothing. Pinckney's just one of the Jockey Club. There are dozens of other members."

Mary understood immediately what James's denial was meant to conceal. "The banquet they want you to cook!" Mary smacked the back of James's head. He yelped but did not look up. Mary persisted, "Pinckney is the host, isn't he?"

James's silence was all the affirmation Mary needed. "James! You must take the commission. And you must take me with you."

"I, by myself, am merely tempting to the slave catchers," James said. He picked up a slice of pork and shook it at Mary. "You, on the other hand, are irresistible. If I take you, they'll just snatch me up alongside you and double their profit."

Mary squeezed her hands into fists and clenched her jaw. "I will go with Red Eagle, then," she said, turning to Red Eagle. "Why are you looking at them? Look at me. I'm the only one you have to take with you."

"James has a point," Romaine said. She slid her eyes to Mary, and Mary felt the familial closeness to the Prophetess that she felt with no one else but her twin sister. Perhaps it was because the people of Nuevo Orleans assumed Romaine was her mother and Romaine did nothing to dissuade this belief. Mary's own mother she could barely remember. It shamed her to see only a smudge of grey when she tried to recall her mother's face. "It is dangerous."

"Dangerous," Mary muttered. A rush of blood reddened her ears. Romaine was only trying to protect her, but what had that achieved? If she had gone with Red Eagle to search for her sister, she and Sarah would be together now, safe and well, in Nuevo Orleans. Sarah would be right there, ten feet away, crouched by the ovens coaxing a fire out of the coals. Mary tried to tamp down her emotions, but her displeasure seeped through. "You just want me to stay here and wait some more. I'm done waiting."

"How about you chop some onions while you wait?" James said. He tossed two yellow onions into the air between them.

It seemed Mary was going to let them drop, but at the last moment her arm whipped out, and she caught both onions in one hand.

"I will say she belongs to me," Red Eagle said. "And she can be hidden. She only needs to show her face to her sister."

"And then?"

"I take them to Muskogee country. They will be safe there."

Romaine's eyes shuttled back and forth in their sockets. "Muskogee country," she murmured.

"Runaways are welcome in my town," Red Eagle said. "My mother believes they make us stronger."

Romaine looked bewildered, then, a long blink later, delighted. "You have runaways in your town." Mary felt something in Romaine shift. It felt nearly exactly the same as those many times during an argument when her sister switched from disagreeing to agreeing—or, at least, acquiescing.

"Close by," Red Eagle said. "They are in the old fields on the other side of the river."

"How many?"

"Fifteen, sixteen," Red Eagle guessed.

"How long?"

"They arrived after the British lost the war," Red Eagle said.

"Ten years. They are maroons." Romaine turned to Mary. "You ready to be a maroon in Muskogee country, my dear girl?"

"What are you—" James started, startled.

Mary clapped her hands. "Yes, absolutely. And you will come with us."

James looked wildly between the three of them. "Where are you—"

Romaine cut him off, "We're all going to Charleston. You should join us, James. It will be hard to run the restaurant here without me and Mary."

"There's nothing but trouble in Charleston," James sputtered.

"There's Mary's sister," Romaine said. "And for you, opportunity."

Red Eagle watched Romaine with wonder. She was, Red Eagle felt, spinning something into the air, casting a spell. He pressed his lips tightly shut to keep from interrupting whatever was being cast.

"You want me to take the Jockey Club's commission." James sounded a bit drunk.

"*You* want to take the commission," Romaine said smoothly. "But you are afraid of being kidnapped and sold off. That will not happen. You are a guest of the governor himself. He has a reputation to protect. He's a rice planter, not a kidnapper. You want to do this, James—it's a chance that might never come again."

Like a shrimp net descending into dark waters, a feeling of inevitability settled over the group. Red Eagle rolled his shoulders forward to try to shrug it off before realizing there was nothing covering him. It was just air, Romaine's voice. Romaine's spell.

"They will write about your banquet all the way up the coast. *James Hemings, formerly of Thomas Jefferson, now a free Black*. Once the newspapers write it like that, the matter is settled. Better than any manumission paper. *The greatest chef this side of the Atlantic Ocean*. You will be famous, James. Rich and famous."

The reflection of a candle flame flickered in James's pretty brown eyes. He swayed a bit before steadying himself on the edge of the stove. After a moment, James's face softened and he nodded to confirm yes, he would take the commission. Whatever spirits were being summoned, they'd come and done their work.

"Tomorrow morning, then," Red Eagle said.

"Yes!" Mary said in triumph, slapping Red Eagle's shoulder with enough force to send him staggering. Mary clapped her hands together, squeezing hard to keep them from flying off in celebration. Red Eagle studied her as she struggled to contain her delight. Her physical features were identical to her twin sister's, but it seemed that in their mother's womb the life energy meant for each had all pooled in one. Life radiated from Mary with vivid excess. It was something Red Eagle often saw in his travels, in the bend of a river, or a particularly bright break of day, but never before in a person. It fascinated him. She fascinated him. He wondered whether Hickory Ground was ready for someone like her. He wondered if he was.

Mary could not sleep and spent the night loading up the catering wagon. From the outside, the wagon was not much to look at. The driver's seat was well worn, and, behind it, the sail canvas that arced over the high-sided bed had more patches than original cloth. The four horses were harnessed in straps thick and plain, made for pulling heavy loads.

Inside, the wagon had been modified months earlier into a catering dray, to James's fastidious specifications. There was a place for each pot and utensil, and a stack of butcher boards contained slots sized for each knife. There was a collapsible roaster, a vat of cooking oil secured so as not to slosh, and rows of spices. A series of drawers held rolls of twine, jars of vinegar, and cakes of salt. The cabinets were raised and arranged to keep clear space enough for two to sleep. As Mary packed the wagon, she grew skeptical that this cabinet of curiosities, built to produce delicious meals, was sturdy enough to withstand the journey up to Charleston. Unlike the messenger flying east on a light, sturdy horse to accept the Jockey Club's commission, this meticulously wrought wagon was both heavy and fragile.

Shortly after sunrise the next morning, they rode out of Nuevo Orleans. With James at the reins and Romaine in her white turban sitting ramrod straight beside him, the lead horses pulled the wagon foward. Red Eagle and Mary rode ahead. The wagon's back left wheel, slightly misshapen, added a loping lurch to the already rough ride. When Red Eagle turned them eastward along the Lower Trading Path, the road narrowed and got rougher still. Two days in, the loping wheel went askew, stopping all forward progress.

Mary unhitched the horses and took them to water while Red Eagle and Romaine worked to fashion a lever out of a tree limb. The river was fresh and fast, and the horses quickly had their fill. When they returned, the back of the wagon was lifted half a foot off the ground as Red Eagle pounded at the axle skein to force it back into position. James hovered above, exhorting him to please take more care.

"It's my only one," James said. "There are no paillards without that mallet."

Red Eagle examined his handiwork and, unsatisfied, resumed pounding. Romaine leaned against the wheel to steady it. "Are we still on Choctaw land or is this Muskogee country?"

"This is Choctaw still," Red Eagle said.

"You are allies?"

Red Eagle paused in his work and frowned. "This is a complicated question," he said. "The Choctaws are part of the Southern Confederacy, but there is no agreement about what that means."

Mary saw Romaine squint the way she did whenever dockworkers ran into the restaurant with news of the uprisings sweeping through the islands.

"I've not heard of this Southern Confederacy," Romaine said.

"Muskogees, Chickasaws and Cherokees. The Chickamauga too remain welcome and Shawnees in Muskogee country."

"All these nations are united?" Romaine asked.

Red Eagle resumed his hammering. "In a way." He seemed finished with his explanation.

Romaine glanced at Mary, silently asking her to help keep Red Eagle talking.

"Tell me more," Mary prompted. "If we're about to join you in Muskogee country, we should know something about the Choctaws and the Chickasaws, don't you think? What is the Southern Confederacy?"

"It's the doing of my uncle, Alexander McGillivray," Red Eagle said. "The brother of my mother, Sehoy. When the British retreated after their war, my mother and uncle agreed it was time to call together the nations."

"In order to…?"

"To band together and push the Americans back to the sea. They are a covetous people."

"Covetous indeed," Romaine agreed. The possibility of an alliance among the Indians quickened her blood. "You were ready to fight?" she asked.

"We did fight. We went to war against Georgia."

"When? Together as a confederacy?" Romaine abruptly stood up. Red Eagle motioned for her to lean her weight back against the wheel. Red Eagle swung the mallet hard against the axle skein, forcing the cylinder into place. He stood and counted with his fingers.

"Eight years ago. They all came to Little Tallassee. Not only the southern nations. Hurons, Mohawks, Oneidas, and Shawnees too, for the Northern Confederacy." Red Eagle was satisfied with the wheel and tossed the mallet to James. He was surprised by the intensity of Romaine's interest. "We joined together as a Grand Confederacy of North and South. We made an agreement to attack the Americans in every place they passed over their limits, to never grant them lands, and to no longer allow surveyors to roam about the country."

"I am ignorant of this Grand Confederacy," Romaine said.

"It no longer exists." Red Eagle went to help Mary re-hitch the horses. "My uncle helped build it, but then he destroyed it. It was not his intention—still, he is responsible for the mistake that ended it."

"I am always interested in the mistakes," Romaine said. "I made plenty myself.

Red Eagle secured the breast collars on the wheel horses and ducked under the shaft. He liked very much how easily

Romaine admitted to making mistakes. It was so unlike his uncle. "The president Washington called my uncle to New York, to make a deal to stop our war with the Georgians. They agreed on a boundary line between Georgia and Muskogee country."

"He ceded too much land, then?"

"No, that was not the mistake. They offered my uncle a bribe: a yearly payment for life, three plantations and sixty Africans as property. They wanted, in return, a promise to send back all current and future runaways. My uncle accepted. That was his mistake."

"The confederacy broke apart because its leader was not trustworthy."

Red Eagle considered this. His uncle McGillivray had tried to keep the payments a secret. Once discovered, McGillivray lost status. But that was not what destroyed the confederacy. "It broke apart because we are split about slavery. Some of the Muskogees are willing to send runaways back to the Americans. But, for others, the runaways have married into our clans. It was not for my uncle to say someone's kin must be sent back to be a slave in Savannah. The Seminoles, especially. They were the first to leave the confederacy."

"It's easier to form an alliance than it is to keep it together," Romaine said sympathetically.

"He thought it was a small thing, to include this in the New York treaty. It was not a small thing."

Mary handed the reins up to James in the driver's seat. "You said your mother welcomes runaways," she said to Red Eagle.

"She does. After my uncle took the bribe, he and my mother parted ways. It was when they took different paths that the entire Confederacy split."

"Can they be brought back together?" Romaine asked.

Red Eagle swung his leg over his horse and smiled down

at Romaine. "You should ask my uncle. It will be good for him to have to answer these questions from you."

Late in the afternoon of the next day, the lead horses stepped over an invisible boundary and everything changed all at once. Gone was the chaos of bushes and trees climbing over one another, branches intertwined and wrapped in vines. The only trees in this orderly forest were longleaf pines, aloof of the earth and one another.

"The Open Pines," said Red Eagle. He swept his arm left to right to indicate he was naming not the trees but the terrain.

As they continued east, they started to encounter travelers heading west. Those on foot or traveling alone on horseback, Red Eagle greeted in a friendly way. His demeanor changed, however, with those travelling by wagon. Americans hauling all their possessions in horse-drawn wagons intended to stay.

Past the Flint River, there was one day when they encountered a wagon near dusk. A woman with milk-white skin and a washbasin jaw rode shotgun. She reached under the seat and came up with two pistols, one in each hand. The man who held the reins spat over the side of the wagon and lifted a long gun from under the bench, placing it across his knees. The woman lifted a pistol and pointed it at Red Eagle's head. Mary stopped breathing, trying to be as still as him. Behind them, Mary heard James curse and pull the wagon over to make way. As they passed, the heads of three children peered out from the back of the wagon. They made guns out of their fingers and mouthed *pow pow pow* as Mary and Red Eagle rode by.

From James's warnings, Mary imagined Charleston to be a place where slave catchers ran through the streets chasing after their prey and in the town square runaways writhed in a flaming pyre. Such a town must be guarded by packs of snarling dogs, hordes of men on horseback, whips snapping overhead. What she saw when they rode past the guardhouse at the western wall was a single white man tipped back in a chair, asleep with his hat pulled over his eyes. She felt a touch of disappointment.

Beyond the guardhouse, the town more ably met its reputation for wealth. Once the crown jewel of the British empire, then the center of the slave trade, Charleston was now home to families of unfathomable fortunes. The street was lined with handsome buildings, residences above and stores below, a church steeple visible in the distance. On every block or two a mansion rose, its marble columns and steps hinting at the treasures contained within. They seemed to Mary designed to emphasize the chasm between their own colossal prosperity and their neighbor's more modest fortunes. From the recessed doorway of one such mansion, two women emerged, a mother and daughter hand in hand. Their satin petticoat dresses overflowed with tulle and lace, their shoes were trimmed with jewels. They stared as Mary rode by, their lips pursed at the procession.

The sky was bright and blue, not a cloud in sight. On the right, the grand courthouse soared upwards, a mountain of sandstone that blocked out the sun. It was so recently built the soil around it was still upturned. A crowd of men milled around the front, shouting at the auctioneer who stood atop a platform, clutching a stack of papers. An unusually small statured white man stood beside the auctioneer scribbling notes. Then a woman, arms bound behind her back and legs kicking, was hoisted on the platform. The crowd pressed forward for a closer look, not backing away even as she spit and cursed them.

"Keep your head down," Romaine called out to Mary

from the wagon. Glancing behind her, Mary noticed Romaine did not heed her own advice. The Prophetess was watching the scene at the courthouse with intense interest. The air around her seemed unnaturally still as the wagon jostled James beside her. Even without her white turban, Romaine emanated power. She repeated her command, and Mary did as instructed.

Eyes on her horse's mane, Mary could feel herself being studied by the men and women below. Mary guessed at the work of the mechanics' shops by what she could glimpse through their opened doors: bricklayer, cooper, carpenter, shoemaker, brass founder, rope maker. In one, a white woman sat upright and still, as if for a portrait. Indeed, the man opposite her peered intently at an easel, brush held aloft. The smells of offal and meat, from fresh to nearly rancid, mixed with the wet brackish smell of the harbor, announcing a meat market nearby. A pair of enormous black buzzards stood at the entrance, shoulder high to the humans, beaks lifted in haughty patience. Mary could not help but look up, counting the buzzards perched along the roofs of the market houses. Behind them was the water, blocked from Mary's view. She turned to Red Eagle. "My sister is here."

"In the market?"

"In Charleston, somewhere."

"Where do you think?"

Mary was pleased Red Eagle believed her. James would have contradicted her. Romaine would have humored her. "Nearby, I know it." The stronger her belief, the more certain it was to come true.

Red Eagle abruptly pulled his horse to a stop and told Mary to do so as well. He dismounted and leapt to Mary's side, nearly pulling her off her horse when she did not move quickly enough. With one hand on her elbow and his other at the small of her back, he walked her quickly behind the wagon and then hoisted her up.

Mary stared at Red Eagle as he pushed her inside the wagon, his face blackened by the brightness of the light behind him. She was too astonished to resist.

"You and your sister are the same look."

Mary nodded, annoyed. Red Eagle knew this already, having seen both of them.

"We should not risk you being recognized, by someone thinking you are her."

"That's not so likely," Mary protested.

"They keep a very close watch here," Red Eagle said. "On everything." He muttered a few angry Muskogee words to himself. Then back to English, "We should have had you hidden—it was careless to ride out in the open."

"I'm not one to hide."

"Only until I find your sister."

Mary started. Red Eagle intended her to remain hidden in the back of the wagon, tucked in like a snail. It could be days, or more. There was nothing in the world that scared Mary, with a single exception: small dark spaces sent her heart pounding in panic. She looked around to remind herself this was James's catering wagon, not the little half cave she'd crawled into when her mother had sent her and her sister off to go hide on the day she was sold away. Her mother's face floated before her, a blur. The possibility of being entombed in this blackened wagon for another single minute was terrifying. Mary made a feint to escape. She was fast, but Red Eagle was faster. He had her by her shoulders and pressed her back under the sail cover.

"I will be quick about it," Red Eagle said. Behind him, a white boy sucked his thumb and tried to look around Red Eagle to see what the Indian was struggling to push back into the wagon.

Mary tried to calm herself. "I believe you," she finally managed.

"I know."

"But hurry." Mary wished she did not sound so afraid. Her fear, an unfamiliar creature, spooked her. She wanted to run.

The last dash of sunlight disappeared as Red Eagle tied the flaps together from the outside. Mary wondered whether Jonah had been surprised at the darkness when he was swallowed by the whale. A few motes of light drifted up from the cracks in the floorboard, but otherwise it was black as a bucket of pine tar. Jonah made it three days and three nights. Mary struggled against the panic that rose in her chest.

The wagon pulled forward, and Mary forced herself to lie down in the stretch of floor space between the trunks and cabinets. There was something horribly wrong in this city by the sea. She felt it the instant they rode inside its walls, and now, undistracted by the sights, she felt it all the more powerfully. This was a place of death and suffering, where traders tossed people overboard into the harbor to avoid being taxed on property too damaged to sell.

It was difficult to breathe. Her sister could have been re-sold already by Pinckney, at the race course between heats of the races, or in the public Negro yard, or at any of the importing merchants' wholesale warehouses along the wharfs. The gentlemen and ladies she'd glimpsed, gliding along in neatly tailored waistcoats, fluttering delicately painted fans, any of them might have been a Pinckney, or worse. She prayed for Red Eagle to find her sister quickly, before the weight of a place so accursed crushed the life out of her.

Chapter 8

It was dusk when they arrived, the governor's wife waiting for them at the portico.

"You are here for the banquet," she said, lifting her hand to Red Eagle.

Red Eagle took her hand and smiled as if he were the Duke of Somerset. "Mrs. Pinckney. They are here to cook. I am here to race."

The governor's wife pointed Red Eagle to the racetrack, then escorted James, Mary, and Romaine to the kitchen.

"I hope it's adequate," Mrs. Pinckney said. She meant it as a joke. None of the governor's six other plantations had half as elaborate a kitchen.

"It's small," James said. In Chantilly, the kitchen had been ten times this size. Mrs. Pinckney looked pained. James added, "It's perfect."

Mrs. Pinckney followed behind James as he ran his hands over the chopping blocks and took stock of the bowls. Mary Eleanor Laurens was very young to be a governor's wife. With the astonished eyes of a tree frog set deep in cheeks still plump with baby fat, she was everywhere at once, yet always somewhere else. Her father, Henry Laurens, was partner in the largest slave trading house in North America. So she was no stranger to the trade. Still, the day-to-day work of enslaving hundreds of people spread over so many plantations, and the effort of keeping veiled the unpleasantries inherent in slavery, was a duty that carved away at her.

"Your servants will be at my disposal?"

Mrs. Pinckney affirmed they would be. "There are five in this kitchen, though Luisa is only good for washing the pots. Rose is the cook, she will do your bidding. I can bring in more if you need them."

James assured her that, though a small army of servers would be needed at the banquet itself, there was no need for more hands to assist in the preparations. He instructed Romaine, "Rice and flour to the rear, keep these two counters clear, and see if the oven can be made hot enough for a crusty bread." Romaine rolled her eyes as James gave young Mrs. Pinckney an easy smile, to let her know he understood the heavy burden she carried in having to specify in detail even the most basic tasks. It was a well-honed skill, helping white people feel comfortable around him.

"My father did so much more than import slaves, you know. He brought in limes and ginger. Olives too. Capers. You must find that interesting as a cook."

"Your father." James kept his voice neutral, holding close the approval she seemed desperate to get from him. "Olives. Thank you. If you send a cask of water, we have everything we need."

Mary pulled sauce pots out of soup pots, setting them according to size along the stovetops. "This kitchen is too small."

"What are you doing out of the wagon?" James asked, alarmed.

"Who's going to see me?" Mary continued unloading the crates at her feet. "No white person has set foot in this kitchen since it was built."

James pointed out that Mrs. Pinckney had been standing by the stoves just a few moments earlier, and she was certainly white.

Mary waved her hand as if shooing off a fly. "Don't be so worried, James. There is nothing to be afraid of here." It was a gesture she made frequently, and every time it made James think of Sally.

"You can't be here." James grabbed Mary's wrist and took away the mixing bowl. "You need to get back into the wagon before someone sees you."

Mary glared up at James and yanked her arm out of his grip. She squashed her instinct to slap him. "You don't tell me what to do, James Hemings."

Romaine appeared quick as a sneeze and stepped between the two. "You're right the chances are low, but it is a risk," she said soothingly to Mary. "One we might be safer not to take."

"I can't hide forever," Mary said. The thought of being forced back into the dark belly of the wagon nauseated her.

"Pinckney's six other plantations are all within a day's ride from here. Red Eagle will find your sister very quickly." The Prophetess cocked her head to get a longer look at Mary's face. "Is there something about the wagon that scares you?"

"Of course not," Mary snapped. "I just don't like hiding."

"It's not only for your sake," Romaine said. "We're all in danger if you're recognized."

Romaine was right, of course. Mary well knew she was a threat to the group. As children, even their own mother sometimes had trouble knowing which twin was which. These white owners pretended the men and women they enslaved were invisible, but in truth the owners enjoyed nothing more than to gaze upon their riches. They knew the skin tone, eye shape, jaw set, earlobe, hairline, shoulder width, hip spread and foot size of every last person they owned. If one of them who'd seen her sister spotted Mary, it would raise enough questions to put them all in danger.

"I'll be careful," Mary said. She bent down to finish unloading the crate at her feet. She could feel Romaine's eyes boring into her back, but she ignored them until the

Prophetess sighed in defeat and turned back to the tasks at hand.

The three set to work. The guest list for the banquet to dedicate the new racetrack stood at a 150. James examined the stoves and made the final grocery list. Mary sharpened the knives. Romaine's task, to make the stocks, required a few hours more tending. The Prophetess shooed James and Mary off to the wagon to sleep.

Alone at the stoves, Romaine stirred the stockpots and said her prayers to the Virgin Mary. *Thank you for your grace. Please, a sign so I know how to serve you.*

She received no response but the cicadas.

It was past midnight when a man pushed through the kitchen's side door, and crossed the room, confident and quick. He was thick-shouldered, with hair cropped close to his broad, copper brown face. A fine coat, buttoned high, stretched across his compact frame. He smoothed the front of his coat as he approached.

"You are the Prophetess," the man said in Twi. His dark brown eyes were nearly black. Part of an ear was missing. "We come seeking your guidance."

Romaine could understand Twi, the language of her mother, but speaking it was more difficult. She tried a mix of Twi and English. "We? There are more of you?"

"There are thousands. I am Ellison." He switched to English.

"Thousands where?"

"Here and on the plantations up both rivers."

Romaine studied the man's stance—feet wide, head drawn back. She told him to continue, but, please, quietly.

"There are twenty captains in agreement, that we will start the rebellion at...."

Romaine held up her hand and told the man to stop.

"You are the general or only the messenger?"

"I am the general," Ellison said, straightening to his full height. He was not tall, and his voice had a reedy whinge.

"You want to end the rebellion before it starts?" Romaine asked.

Ellison looked confused.

"If I decide to betray you," Romaine said, "do you know what will happen to each of the captains you were about to name?" Even with less than a year of English, Romaine had all the words she needed. "They will have their hands and testicles cut away. The lucky ones will be hung by the neck, the unlucky ones will be burned. They will be gibbeted for crows to eat."

"But you will not betray us!" Ellison said, vehement. "You are the Prophetess."

"You do not know who I am. Why do you think I am the Prophetess?"

"You were seen riding into town. I got word you are here for the banquet."

"And when you saw me you hoped that I was, indeed, the person you sought."

Ellison stared at Romaine. Finally, he asked, "Are you the Prophetess?"

"I am," said Romaine. "I will help you, and this is your first lesson: be careful who you trust."

"I know who to trust," Ellison said. "I know every slave on this plantation. I'm the driver here."

"You are Pinckney's commandeur? His … overseer?" Romaine was unsure of the word. Every place with large numbers of enslaved had a different word for the enslaved man who rode the horse cracking the whip to enforce the will of white master.

Ellison shook his head. "Only whites are overseers here. I am the driver. For this plantation, not the others."

"How many of the—you called them captains? How many are drivers?"

"Half, at least," Ellison said. He smiled proudly at Romaine's surprised look. "And another two are free men."

Romaine checked all the doors before leaning back against the chopping block, arms folded. "Tell me your plan."

Ellison pulled a soot pan from the bottom of the stoves and set it on the table in front of Romaine. "Here," he said, using the handle of a spoon to draw a long line in the ash. "The coast." A series of wavering lines were the rivers that flowed into the ocean. He poked a series of holes along two of the rivers, the plantations. At each plantation along the Ashley and Cooper Rivers was at least one captain ready to call the others to arms. At the signal, they would kill the owners and seize their guns, calling out for others to join the march to Charleston. Ellison slashed a downstroke with his spoon from the Cooper River, an upstroke from the Ashley. Once in town, those enslaved would join the column, and together they would set fire to the city. Once they seized the cannons at forts overlooking the harbor they would demand and receive—Ellison smacked the soot pan with the back of the spoon—a full surrender.

Romaine waited for Ellison to continue.

"That is all?"

Ellison's silence confirmed it was.

Romaine eyed Ellison, searching for a reason to believe this plan might work. Courage seemed in good supply. People were roused by courage. A good number would fling down their shovels and fall in behind Ellison's cocky strut. But thousands? Romaine doubted thousands, unless there were indeed twenty other captains spread across the plantations.

"That is not a particularly good plan. How long has it been in discussion?"

"Two years, ever since we heard of the uprising in

Saint-Domingue and of your success along the southern coast," Ellison said.

"You said thousands are ready to march." Romaine asked. "How many are you sure of?"

"When they hear the Prophetess is here they will not hesitate."

So there were not thousands. Romaine wondered whether there were even hundreds. "How do you know they will follow you?"

"They follow me now."

"Because you wield a whip."

Ellison bit his bottom lip to keep from reacting to Romaine's jab. "We have been ready to take Charleston since we heard of your victory in Léogâne. And now you are here. How can it be anything but a sign that it is finally time to take action?"

"You have a gift for flattery, Ellison."

Ellison blinked. He was not trying to flatter. It was the last thing he knew how to do. This was simply the truth.

"Do the owners here grant manumission papers to anyone who exposes a plot of insurrection?"

"There is a new rumor every week," Ellison said. "They can't free everyone who talks."

"But they still talk."

Ellison grimaced and nodded. "It is why we must move quickly. You are here! We can call the attack this Sunday."

"I might help you gather your troops, but I have no muskets," Romaine said. "Knives, but no guns."

"There are three batteries along the Ashley River and another two along the Cooper. We will be well armed before we reach the city."

Romaine picked up a knife and started sharpening. The sound of steel against stone calmed her as she studied this commandeur seeking her help. A man of action, seeking freedom, sure, but more than that. He lorded over other enslaved men and women. But he wanted something more. He wanted glory.

"How many of your people know how to load and fire a musket? To clean out a jammed weapon? Can they do it crouched in the mud with cannon fire all around?" When Ellison did not respond, Romaine continued. "Do you have horses and horsemen who can fire a pistol from the saddle? Do you know how we won in the south of Domingo?"

"Léogâne was won because men with the courage to act took the city from the whites," Ellison said.

"We won Léogâne because we had a camp at my coffee plantation. We had Trou Coffy," Romaine said. "A camp allows you to gather forces, train them. To prepare."

Ellison shook his head with the vigor of a dog shaking off water. "We must be simple and quick," he said. "If it is too complicated, no one will come. You cannot give these men time to weigh and balance their options."

"There is some truth to what you say," Romaine admitted. "But you will need more than an army ready to fight. You need one that is ready to win."

"I know these men," Ellison said curtly. "I am with them every day. I know what it takes to compel men into action."

"And the women?"

"What of them?"

"A third of those in Trou Coffy were women," Romaine said.

Ellison looked skeptical. "It was the men who marched on Léogâne."

"The women marched. With arms."

That was not quite true. There had been plenty of men like Ellison in the Trou Coffy camp. At first, at least. They did not think of the women as comrades-in-arms, and ordered the women to make the coffee and do the wash. For a while, Romaine did not interfere, but then one Sunday when she laid her head on the tabernacle to receive the word of her godmother, the Virgin Mary made plain her displeasure. Romaine quickly redistributed the tasks at the insurgent camp, basing the assignments by skill rather than sex. Still, when it came time to march on Léogâne, the muskets were all given to the men. With sticks and hoes sharpened into lances, the women fought like banshees. But they had not been armed. The memory pained Romaine.

"It was the men the people of Léogâne were afraid of. That is why the mayor signed the treaty with you."

Romaine laughed. "I have to remind you that you were not there."

Ellison grew impatient. "Enough of these questions. You will help us or not," he said to Romaine. "That is up to you."

"You are brave," Romaine said, her hand on his arm. She tried to sound conciliatory. "But you must establish a camp."

"Building a camp will only slow us down. The men are ready to fight now."

Ellison turned to leave. His hand was on the door when Romaine called out behind him.

"You are ready to fight. You are not ready to win."

Ellison turned back to face Romaine. "The Prophetess is here in Charleston, but will not lead us into battle."

"I will not lead you into slaughter."

The two watched each other across the kitchen, Romaine at the stoves, Ellison at the door. Inside, Romaine felt herself wavering. Was this cautiousness on her part born out of experience or fear?

"Your pot is boiling, Prophetess." Ellison pushed open the kitchen door. "You should tend to it."

The day of the banquet, church bells rang along the waterfront to announce the start of Race Week. The scions of the

Rice Coast stepped from their carriages at Charles Pinckney's plantation mansion and sniffed the air.

"Pinckney has hired an interesting cook, Negro from Orleans," said one young white woman to another, hand on her hat to keep the feathered thing from flying away in the sudden wind. "Trained in Paris, they say. What a sense of humor the governor has."

From plantations up the Cooper and Ashley Rivers came General William Washington and his wife, Jane Elliot of Sandy Hill. There was General William Moultrie, the former governor, and his slew of sons; and General Jacob Read, a lone daughter holding his elbow. There were more than a dozen Balls—all of the same generation—first cousins and spouses all at once; this Ball married to that Ball in order to keep their estates intact. And the Smiths and Hamptons, and Joseph Lawton, whose hair turned white as cotton one winter afternoon for an execution gone awry. The insurrectionist who had poisoned her master would not die, and when the flame petered out and Lawton stepped in to relight it, a charred hand closed around his ankle. It took an ax to the wrist to save Lawton from being consumed himself by the blaze.

William Alston was from Halifax County, upcountry, but together with his brother, Willis, was as wealthy as any low country planter of Charleston or Beaufort. From far down the coast, some with sons spread well into Georgia, came William Stephen Bull and the Bulows, Joseph Calhoun and the Chisholms, the Cuthberts, the Pringles, and Thomas Drayton. Gabriel Manigault, the tender-hearted architect, once tried to slip away to the North, but returned to bear the burden of tending to the family fortune—456 humans and fifty thousand acres of land amassed by his grandfather. The Hamiltons arrived as well, and the Colemans, and the Maybanks.

From west of Stono came the Stoneys and Colonel Prioleau, Philip Prioleau, John Boone and his son John Boone and his grandson John Boone, and old Lucretia Radcliffe, her crumpled face a cancelled bill of a sale, who controlled the Almonbur, Cockfield and Harrison plantations; and John Pyne and the Rhetts, all still connected with rice in one way or another. And Arnoldus Bonneau and the Broughtons and James Sinkler, who called his plantation the Wampee, after a fruit tree from the East Indies he could not coax to grow. Isaac Fickling, Joshua Ward, Benjamin Fuller, Thomas Gadsden, Theodore Samuel Gaillard, Gilbert Geddes, the young Paul T. "The Good Reverend" Gervais, John Gibbes's son, Adelaide and Theordore Gordan, A. D. Graves and Jacob Guerard—they came to court one another's sisters and Elizabeth Cook, as well, and when Joshua wandered with Elizabeth into the garden it was clear the match was his to lose.

Benjamin Allston Jr. from Waccamaw Neck arrived with his wife, Charlotte Anne, and his brothers, Robert and Francis Withers. There was Henry Laurens in his dotage, eager to talk about his nursery—how the hyacinths had made it through the winter. Later on, with the rest of the arrivals already deep into their third glass of punch, Joseph Blake came with Daniel and William Blake and their patriarch, Joseph Black, who must have been a hundred years old. There were more, their last names the ones of the great American capitalists whose descendants, if pressed, will claim were gentle botanists one and all, who loved, more than anything, flowers and gardens.

All these people came to Governor Pinckney's Charleston house for the day's festivities. It was the start of Race Week. After the luncheon at Pinckney's, there was to be a four-mile race to christen the new racecourse, after which they would return to Pinckney's for a banquet the governor promised to be as grand as anything ever served at Versailles.

The men compared notes about their yields and congratulated one another on their good luck with the weather this winter. The women complimented each other on their hats and shoes and exchanged advice about the management of insolent servants. At noon, Mrs. Pinckney had her servants gather up the guests and herd them into the great hall, where they admired the sculpture of an alligator composed of nuts and cleverly carved chunks of cheese. The conversations turned to whether to allow their slaves to hunt, the alligators having become particularly troublesome these last few years. Allston allowed it, the quality of meat being a good source of energy. The elder Hamilton went further, sending a pair of hunters armed with his best guns to clear the marshes behind his fields. At this, General Moultrie slapped his thigh and called the elderly man a fool. The alligators helped keep the slaves from running away, Moultrie exclaimed. Why would you do anything to lessen such a useful fear?

They ate their lunch with more speed than appreciation, picking apart the alligator but leaving the eel soaking in its mushroom sauce. The table was cleared in fifteen minutes.

"They eat like Germans," James said to Romaine as the servants carried platters back into the kitchen.

"Some are," said Romaine.

"They should remember to chew."

James took the dough down from the shelf where it had been resting and called Mary over to help him form the loaves. Romaine examined the side of lamb laid out on the chopping table. It was too heavy for the spit, a thin lance intended for roasting birds, but there was no time to make a substitute. Romaine inserted the sharp end of the spit into the thickest part of the saddle and pushed. In an instant, James was at her side.

"Stop, you'll break it." James made a twisting motion with his wrist. "Skewer, don't force it."

Romaine tried the screwing motion, but the metal was stuck against a rib. James eyed the side of lamb and returned to his loaves. "You'll have to force the spit."

"You would make a good field general," said Romaine

through gritted teeth as she pushed. "You're a natural at giving orders and then retracting them."

With a grunt, Romaine forced the spit through the bone. She grabbed the slab of meat and tossed it over the coals.

"This kitchen was never meant it to be cooked in," said James. The lack of ventilation had him in a sour mood. Romaine wiped dry the chopping block and then selected two platters for the duck. She tilted the silver trays in the light to check their shine. The one with brass laced into its handles needed polishing. Romaine snapped open her cleaning towel and was giving the tray its first swipe when the door crashed open.

Reflected on the silver surface, Romaine saw three hazy figures squeezing through the doorway carrying something. A deer, perhaps, field-dressed and still bleeding. Romaine frowned. If one of the Pinckney boys had had a successful hunt and now wanted his trophy incorporated into the banquet, it would mean extra work. Romaine turned around to tell them to please leave the kitchen at once.

But they were not white boys with a deer.

It was Ellison and two other Black men. And what they carried was not at all a deer but a boy.

Ellison held the limp weight against his chest. The other two men carried parts of the boy that were no longer attached to the main of him.

"You can fix this," Ellison said, raising up the body as if to present an offering. "My son." His voice cracked with desperation. "Please. Prophetess."

Romaine scooped the boy up and laid him on the chopping block. Red washed over the wood. At one end of the block two thin waterfalls formed and became rivulets that crept forward for a few inches until one found the other and the blood trickled on together in search of the lowest ground.

Draped over the wooden planks, the boy's torso was twisted, and a strip of cloth was tied near where a knee must be. The boy's upper limbs had too many joints, sending his arms this way and that away from his chest.

"The mill caught him."

The man speaking was tall and thin, with eyes set far apart on a narrow face. A shirt blotched with stains hung on his shoulders. In his hand he had a short, thick stick. It was the lower part of the boy's leg. The man held it carefully at the ankle.

"He was not careful," the man said. He said it like an apology.

Romaine touched the boy's neck, the only part of him that appeared unharmed. It was warmer than she expected, but she could find no pulse. There was so much blood already lost. There might be some way to—

Someone screamed.

Romaine turned to see two white women at the door, hands up to their mouths. They were dressed in ball gowns. The one who was held upright by a brilliant blue bodice was screaming. She screeched out one lungful after another after another. Romaine looked around for someone able to make her stop. Then the screaming woman was roughly shoved aside, and Governor Pinckney and another white man strode into the kitchen.

Pinckney held a riding crop, the other man a whip. They crossed the kitchen to the chopping block and pushed Romaine away. Pinckney used the handle of his riding crop to lift the boy's arms, first one and then the other. The white man's face puckered in disgust. He raised an eyebrow. The man with the whip scanned the kitchen.

"How did this happen?"

Ellison did not answer—the blood in his ears roared too loud for him to hear. The man with the whip repeated the question. Pinckney pushed his riding crop against the bottom of the boy's chin, closing his mouth. The blood spilling off the edge of the table, *tink, tink, tink* onto the floor, was the only sound.

Pinckney swung his riding crop against the chopping block. The crack of wood breaking wood was loud as a gunshot.

"Ellison, answer me!" Pinckney demanded. "Two in a week! How did this happen?"

Ellison stared at his master. A rage rushed through this body, consuming every bit of him. "This is my son." Each word was drawn out along the edge of a steel razor, ice cold.

tink tink...tink

tink...tink...

tink

Silence stole in and waited, patient on its haunches.

tink

Pinckney roused himself. He looked around the kitchen. "Take him away," the governor said. His eyes skimmed past Ellison. It was James he addressed. "An unfortunate mess. Don't let it delay your preparations for the banquet."

Chapter 9

The two white women who had come to the kitchen could not recover their appetites and insisted their husbands depart with them at once. Such bad luck to have been exposed to such unpleasantness. They begged the pardon of Mrs. Pinckney for leaving before the banquet, but really there was no way they could unsee what they had seen.

The rest of the guests heard of the incident as they returned from the racetrack. "It is unfortunate," General Washington said to O'Brien Smith, ashen from having lost three horses and a good deal of honor when the horse he chose to win had failed to finish at all. "But these things happen to the best of us."

In the kitchen, Romaine and James each took an end of the spit and heaved the lamb from the roasting pit to the chopping block. Someone had cleaned the heavy slab of wood, but not well. There remained a glimmer of fresh blood over the older stains. The lamb landed with a thud. Servants streamed in and out of the kitchen carrying wine bottles and plates.

"Let it rest before you cut it," James said.

Romaine sharpened her knives as she waited.

The night's wine steward came into the kitchen searching for another bottle of Madeira. "Add a dash of brandy to each glass!" James instructed as the man hurried out under the archway.

Romaine watched the movement swirling around her. James was preparing a ten-course dinner involving 126 ingredients, where each entremet was balanced fore and aft and every dish would arrive precisely on time at the perfect temperature, char, and garnish. Within James lived the kind of genius the rebellion needed. History's greatest military tacticians, whether Alexander the Great or Ghengis Khan, could not carry off such a feat of coordination.

Memories of her children bubbled up unbidden from whatever small cove they had gone to hide this past year. Pierre-Marie, grabbing for a ray of light. Marie-Jeanne, running with long, sure strides to jump a fence. A sparkling laugh that could have been either Louise-Marie or her mother, the two so alike in every way. Romaine switched her grip on the knife, from a handle grip for slicing to a reverse grip for stabbing, and brought the knife down hard into the chopping block. Two inches of the blade disappeared into the wood. Romaine unfurled her fingers, leaving the knife upright and quivering in the chopping block. The planks of chestnut wood bled red as she walked away.

Servants flowed among the tables in the great hall, replacing empty glasses with full ones. None had ever served such a vast, complicated meal, but they all had the primary requisite skill: the ability to pass within a hair's breadth of the white guests without ever making contact, all while balancing platters piled high with meats or breads or tarts.

The members of the Jockey Club sat at an enormous oak table at the front of the room. One complained of being ignored earlier that week when he'd asked a Negro to water his horse. "He claimed to be a free man and just walked away!"

Next to the complainant, a gaunt-faced man stroked his carefully tended red mustache and said, "Bring him to me and I'll fine him ten dollars. The sheriff can auction him off to pay the fine."

"You're the law," the man laughed.

The judge turned his red mustache back to his conversation with the lady to his left, a refugee from Saint-Domingue. Her plantation had been burned to the ground, poor thing. The Judge leaned in as if to tell a secret. "We had our own uprising, you know, in 1739. It taught us to take precautions."

The lady asked of what sort. O'Brien Smith on her left answered into her bosom. "Patrols, madame. In fact, I am a police officer tomorrow night."

"Good for you," the judge said. He tapped his palm against the table, insistent. The chatter around him faded. "Governor Pinckney! Tell our guest here how you protected us from too much liberty."

The Judge's prompt delighted the governor, who felt his contributions to the creation of the new nation were quite underappreciated. "The northern merchants know their fortunes rely on our willingness to manage the necessary labor, but their representatives pretend otherwise."

"Fools!" O'Brien Smith called out, cheeks ruddy with punch. Already slumped in his chair, he slid another few inches down.

"And so I made certain our nation's new constitution includes a fugitive slave clause. Should my man run off to Pennsylvania, our countrymen are obligated to return to me my own property."

The governor was ready to continue his lecture, but the lady from Saint-Domingue had a question.

"But why did those who want to end slavery agree to it?"

"I let the northerners know South Carolina was ready to go it alone. So the northerners folded. Because what is the United States without South Carolina?"

"Shhhhmaller!" O'Brien slurred.

The judge jabbed a finger towards the governor. "That man right there is the reason the United States exists at all.

And he is the reason our sacred way of life will persist long after we are dead and gone." The judge grabbed his glass of wine from the table and raised it high. "To Governor Pinckney!"

The men around the judge's table laughed and lifted their own glasses. The judge was, as usual, both drunk and right. From a nearby table, someone yelled, "May our sons surpass us!"

The guests all raised their glasses and shouted their agreement. "To Governor Pinckney!" "Governor Pinckney!"

It was hours past midnight when the last of the guests departed. Governor and Mrs. Pinckney waved good night to John Boone Sr. and John Boone Jr. as the son helped the father, head slumped to chest, into their carriage. Mr. Pinckney pried the judge's fingers from the stem of the wine glass and, with a firm grasp of his elbow, eased him off the porch. Exhausted, the party over and their duties done, the Pinckneys climbed the winding staircase in silence and retired to their respective bedrooms.

Dozens of women circulated around James as he directed them in reassembling the kitchen. They cleared the tables, washed the wares and utensils, loaded the crates, and divided up what remained of the meal. The work lagged behind James's commands, the women dillydallying. They came from all seven of Pinckney's plantations, and, now that they were in a room without white people around, there was news to be exchanged. The worst of the news was the most recent, about Thomas, the boy killed in the new rice mill just hours earlier, a sleeve caught between grinding stones.

There was more bad news from the upriver plantation. A group scrubbing the pots gathered around Ana to hear about the young woman, a new acquisition, who two nights ago drowned herself in the river. The woman had asked for Ana's help carrying out the dreadful deed. "I refused," Ana told the group. Her voice dropped low. Her audience stopped pretending to scrub and leaned in to hear. The young woman was pregnant, Ana told them, her hand palming an imaginary pumpkin jutting from her stomach, nearly ready to give birth.

"I am not one to judge," Ana said, her eyes sweeping the circle of faces crowded around her, "but you have to—" Across the kitchen, a familiar face caught Ana's attention. Her mind stuttered at the impossibility of what she was seeing. A cannonball of terror exploded up her spine.

At the far side of the kitchen, Mary felt herself being looked at. She turned to see who was staring. It was one of the pot scrubbers. Mary grabbed the last of the dirty pots off the stove and walked towards the group.

Ana nearly screamed. Her hands flew to her mouth to stuff the shout back down her own throat. Her eyes bulged as Mary approached. Everyone turned to stare.

"Impossible." Ana's voice was a terrified hiss. Ana gawked at Mary's face, then looked at Mary's flat belly and reached out to touch it. In an instant, fear overwhelmed her wonder and she snatched her hand back. She looked back up, eyes wide. "I dressed you myself."

Ana kept talking, mumbling. She was saying words about a new arrival, a young pregnant woman. Mary's ears could not catch the jumble of syllable as one after another fell like knucklebones to the kitchen floor. She managed two steps back, and she felt James's hand on her back.

"Talk sense," Mary said. "Tell me who is dead. You be careful what you say."

Ana's voice shook. There was no doubt this was Sarah, the new acquisition—her face, the way she walked, the chalky timbre of her voice. "Jacob's mule almost couldn't pull you out. Snagged on something under the water. I dressed you, a good cotton dress, a real dress. Someone will go without this summer, but I didn't care." What a struggle it had been to dress her body. She had had to cut the dress up the back and drape it over, tucking and smoothing it around Sarah for her long sleep. Ana's words came faster and faster, racing ahead of panic. "Master Pinckney said to just bury you straight in the dirt, but we did you right. You and your baby. Randolph tore up his own steps to build you a real coffin. Wasn't that enough? We still have to draw water from the bend where you did it."

Mary's hand flew to grab what she could from the chopping block. A paring knife. Her hand wrapped around the handle, and she stepped towards the talking woman. James grabbed Mary's wrist and wrenched it back.

The women around Ana seized her and pushed her back behind them, beyond Mary's reach. They formed a wall and put up their hands, some in anticipation of Mary's knife, some to fend off whatever devil had been bribed to bring a dead woman back to life. Had she given the devil her baby in the deal?

"You are done here. You are all done." James stepped into the rift between the women and Mary. "The work here is done." He turned his back to Mary and commanded everyone out of the kitchen. "Go. Go, go. Quickly now, go."

One of the women grabbed Ana's arm and pulled her away from the cook and the phantom he was protecting. Ana resisted, but her legs were weak with terror, and she let herself be carried off by the group out the door into the cool night air.

Mary stared at the miniature face reflected in the flat of the knife. She was vaguely aware it was James who was prying her fingers one by one from the knife's handle. The eyes watching Mary from the steel blade's shining grey were pulled close by fear and worry. It soothed Mary to see her sister's familiar, stricken face reflected in the blade. Mary closed her fingers back around the handle but too late—James snatched the knife away. The face disappeared, and with a desperate yelp Mary lunged to grab it back. Her hands found only air as she stumbled to the floor.

"Sarah," Mary said. Drowned? How could this be? When they were children, Sarah refused to go near water, afraid of snakes. She only went in when they were older because Mary insisted, and then only if Mary went in first and made a show of beating the water with a stick to chase away any danger. Mary examined her palms, as if they might hold better answers.

At the kitchen door, Romaine watched the women slip off into the night. They were quickly swallowed by the pitch. In the distance, a dog howled. A bit of orange light caught Romaine's attention—Race Week festivities, maybe a bonfire.

Something moved, very quickly, out from the dark. The Prophetess counted three, four, six figures as they burst out of the blackness and ran towards her. Within seconds, they were close enough for Romaine to see that at the front of the group was Ellison. The man's face was slick with perspiration. He seemed startled to find Romaine in the doorway and was barely able to stop himself and the others before they hurtled into her.

Ellison struggled to catch his breath. "Step aside," he said.

Romaine looked up behind Ellison and the men at the orange smudge off in the distance. It was now larger, too wide across to be a bonfire. Something substantial was burning at the mouth of the river.

"You cannot stop it," Ellison said. "It is already begun." His eyes bulged from his skull. Swamp muck climbed up his legs. His right hand grasped an axe. His left hand opened and closed into a fist again and again like a fish gulping the air. The man was half crazed, that was easy to see. He closed the distance between himself and Romaine.

"You are not ready," Romaine said.

"Look!" Ellison roared. He spun around and pointed his axe at the flames in the distance. "It is not up to you, Prophetess. My son was killed."

The blaze in the distance threw a halo upwards into the night sky. It glimmered in silence. Romaine heard inside her head the shouts and bedlam such a fire produced. She knew well the sounds that were not carrying across the river and through the curtains of moss that hung from the oaks. There were horses whinnying to be let out of their stables. Commands to stop. Screams and yelling. Gunshots.

"It is the signal," Ellison said. "The captains will know what to do when they see the flame."

Romaine turned her attention back on Ellison. "Your plan was to start from the plantations furthest from the city."

Ellison shook his head in furious denial. "It doesn't matter."

Romaine did not say the obvious. It mattered a great deal. Starting from the farthest plantation, as they had done in Saint-Domingue, would have allowed them to sweep up new recruits along the way, swelling the ranks of the new army. By setting fire to the plantation closest to the city, Ellison had undercut his only chance of success.

"Are there others?"

"They are on the way," Ellison said.

"How many?"

Ellison did not answer. He looked upwards to where the wall met the ceiling. Governor Pinckney was just beyond there, in the bedroom closest to the back staircase, tucked between freshly laundered sheets, head on a down feather pillow, peacefully asleep.

Romaine wished for time to pray. There was no time. Ellison said a word to his group and jerked his head to the door that opened into the hallway. He ran out, and, after a moment's hesitation, his men followed.

Mary bolted for the door. Romaine stepped in, blocking

her way. The two women stared at one another. "You can't stop it," Mary said.

"We can't win," Romaine answered.

Mary spotted the meat cleaver and pushed past Romaine to snatch it up. The heavy knife in hand, she looked around for an ally, but there was only James, his head drawn back in dread. Mary turned to Romaine. "His son, my sister. You've been praying for a sign, here it is. How can you not see it?" Without waiting for a response, Mary rushed out of the kitchen after Ellison, bounding up the stairs three at a time. Romaine cursed under her breath and ran after her, pausing to pick up a knife of her own. The two arrived at the top of the staircase to see, down the hall, a bedroom door kicked wide open.

Within the chamber, Ellison charged the bed. Governor Pinckney scrambled up out of the sheets, eyes wide. Ellison planted his foot and reared back as if he intended to throw the axe. The men behind him crouched, their bodies reacting to this familiar posture of Ellison raising his whip. It took an instant for Ellison to realize his mistake—that what he held was not a whip but an axe, and his intention was not to enforce the wishes of his master but to kill him. In the moment's hesitation, Pinckney leapt out of the bed towards the door. The whites of Pinckney's thighs startled Ellison out of his pause, and in three soaring strides Ellison was upon the older man. But the habits of his body intervened yet again at the critical instant. Instead of swinging the axe as required, Ellison flicked it as if it were a whip. The flat of the blade struck Pinckney on the shoulder and bounced harmlessly away. The governor twisted away from Ellison and spun around, making a dash for the hallway. One of Ellison's men grabbed Pinckney's arm as he ran past but could not hold on.

Pinckney glanced behind him to see Ellison and the men scrambling over one another in a vicious scrum to get to him.

In front of Pinckney, at the end of the hallway near the stairs, were two figures. Two women, Pinckney saw, and rushed towards them to escape.

Mary raised up her cleaver.

The governor could not stop his forward momentum and ducked under Mary's upraised arm. The cleaver split the air a fraction of an inch behind the white man's neck, burying itself into the banister. In the time it took Mary to wrench the knife free, Pinckney turned back the way he'd come and ran back towards the men. They had scythes and staffs. A few held only rocks in their hands. Some had nothing but fists. One wielded a tree branch.

Pinckney did not slow. With impressive agility, he stepped to the left, then changed direction and tried to slip against the wall to the right. But Mary was quicker still. She caught a handful of Pinckney's nightshirt and yanked the white man to a halt. With the handle of her cleaver, Mary struck a hard blow to the space between the governor's eyes. He fell to the ground, stunned into a daze of slow blinks.

Romaine held back the men as Mary knelt beside the governor.

"You know my sister," Mary said. She smelled the sour on Pinckney's breath. "Tell me what you did to her."

Pinckney looked up at the face looming above him. It was the face of Sarah, who had dared to struggle when he went to take what was his. Who stupidly went and drowned in the river. Who was back from the dead.

"You cost me," Pinckney mumbled. It was hard to breathe. Perhaps he was already dead. "You are here to kill me," he gasped, startled by the inevitability of his death.

Mary pulled the governor's chin up and back with her left hand, and with her right raised up her cleaver.

"I am here to save your goddamned soul,"

Mary brought the cleaver down in a short, hard arc.

Romaine stepped aside, and the fountain of blood doused

the men behind her. The one carrying the tree branch dropped his weapon and snatched at the head of Pinckney. It was still attached to the body by a strand of muscle. Mary detached it with a quick chop.

The sight of the slave master's head, held like an unlit lantern and now just as useless, produced a moment of silence.

Mrs. Pinckney peered out of her bedchamber.

With a yell, the small army gathered around their new totem and escorted it towards the governor's young wife.

James appeared at the top of the stairs, between the men and Mrs. Pinckney. Emitting a high, thin wail, the young wife collapsed into a crouch and scuttled to the stairstep behind James. She curled herself down tight and grabbed the bannister with one hand, James's ankle with the other. Ellison pushed his way to the front of the group and snatched away the head from the man carrying it. He rushed to the top of the stairs, shaking the bloody prize.

Unable to comprehend the scene before him, James discovered himself utterly frozen, unable to move a muscle.

A noise drifted up from below, near the front door. "Governor Pinckney!" someone shouted up the stairs. "Is everything alright here?" There was the loud mumble of men talking, disagreeing. A commanding voice rose above the chatter. "You five go upstairs and take a look."

As a single entity, the group behind Ellison turned to the front end of the hallway. Romaine was now at their fore.

Their best chance, Romaine knew from experience, was to surprise the men downstairs and overwhelm them before they could react. She raised her knife and swept her arm forward. It was a silent command, *Follow me*, and the men did, falling in behind Romaine as she ran the length of the hall and down the winding stairs.

As the group disappeared down the steps, James looked down to see what was whimpering at his feet.

"Mrs. Pinckney."

The young woman's hand tightened around his ankle as she ducked her face into the cave of her arm. Whatever she was saying disappeared into the hole she'd made of herself.

James shook his leg to try to break free as the sounds of battle drifted up from below. Romaine was shouting something. A gun barked, followed immediately by a vicious howl. Doors slammed shut. The shouting spread, flowing from the front of the house to the back, mixed into the din of metal clashed against stone against wood, things breaking.

"Mrs. Pinckney," James said again. He reached down to pry himself loose of her grip. "This would be a good time for you to hide." When she did not respond, James hauled her up to her feet. "Somewhere more effective than behind me."

Mrs. Pinkney squeezed her eyes tightly shut. How such a volume of tears managed to escape was beyond James's understanding. All of this was beyond James's understanding. Those must be patrollers downstairs, or the militia, even. The crashes and cries gave no clue as to who held the advantage. The one thing James knew for sure was that at some point the fighting would be done, and having a white woman hanging off his arm would not endear him to the victor, whoever that might be.

"Open your eyes, Mrs. Pinckney."

She opened one, barely. "There is nowhere to go!" she wailed, clutching James's arm with surprising strength. "Help me, what should I do?"

"Please, Mrs. Pinckney, you cannot stay here." The force of the white woman's grip on his arm was astounding. It took both hands and a great deal of effort to pry himself loose. He backed away and was ready to bolt, when a child appeared at the bedroom door, Mrs. Pinckney's daughter.

"Make a rope of the sheets and let yourself down the window." When Mrs. Pinckney did not budge, James repeated his instructions. "Hurry! Before they come and cut off your head too."

Her hands flew to her neck. James quickly turned her around by the shoulders and pushed her towards the bedroom. Inside the bedchamber, James helped pull tight the knot on the bedsheets, then wrapped mother and child together. At the window, Mrs. Pinckney hesitated, but a scream from downstairs loosened her grip on the windowsill and James lowered them down.

The sounds of the battle downstairs slowed. There was a yell of triumph. Then the voices all fell silent. There remained in the fresh quiet only a muffled *thack...*, *thack...*, *thack....*, slow and rhythmic.

James turned from the window and made his way to the edge of the stairs. Reluctantly, he peered down.

The sound was being produced by Ellison, knelt atop his foe. Romaine approached from behind and laid her hand on the back of Ellison's neck, careful to stay out of the way of his arm that drove a knife into the white man's chest, pulled it back out, drove it back in, pulled it out, drove it back in. "You can stop now," she said.

Ellison did not stop. Mary, the front of her dress splattered red, went to Romaine's side, and the rest of the men drifted into a semicircle around them. Strewn across the foyer were eight dead white men, plus the one Ellison was not done killing.

"Ellison, how many others are behind you?" Romaine caught his arm, and Ellison, exhausted, let drop the knife. He could not answer, his chin against his chest heaving for air. Romaine instructed the others to gather up the weapons, and they set before her feet a sorry pile: two muskets, a few pistols, and a half-empty cartridge box. Romaine repeated the question but got from Ellison only a blank stare.

It was the man armed with the tree branch who answered for Ellison. "It's only us, Prophetess." He pointed to one of the muskets, asking permission to take it.

"Do you know how to load it?" Romaine asked.

"Show us," he said.

"What's your name?"

He told her "Jeremiah." Romaine smiled. "Sent to tell the rulers of Israel their God has turned against them." Outside, a church bell tolled. Romaine counted the peals and at six realized it was not tolling the time. "They are calling out the militia."

As if summoned by Romaine's declaration, the *clop clop* of horseshoes on cobblestone drifted through the mansion's front door. There were thirty or more horses approaching.

"Douse the lights," Romaine ordered. She grabbed a musket and loaded it before handing it off to Jeremiah and starting on the second musket. She had the ramrod back into its channel when she heard the horses being pulled to a stop. They were in front of the mansion. Romaine scanned the group around her. They were not enough, but they were all there was.

"Don't fire until I do," she instructed Jeremiah. "You have one shot. Don't miss."

The Prophetess made her way to the window flanking the front door and lifted the curtain the barest bit, just enough to peer outside. Romaine could see only the marble steps that glowed pink from the light of a distant fire. The street beyond was erased by a thick blanket of mist. But, from inside the fog, the sharp strike of horseshoes against cobblestone rang out clear as bells. Mary and the men gathered behind Romaine, waiting for her signal. The silence inside the foyer was complete. They had all, as a single body, stopped breathing.

Who emerged from the fog was Red Eagle, astride an enormous palomino. Behind them came a heavy-chested bay, a saddle cinched around its belly but without a rider. Behind the bay trotted a black horse, also saddled but without a rider. Another horse stepped out of the fog, then another, and another.

"Mary, mother of God," Romaine muttered as she

counted thirty, thirty-three, thirty-seven horses behind Red Eagle, each one more magnificent than the one before. Setting down her gun, she relit the lantern and went outside to greet Red Eagle.

Atop the palomino, the horse that less than a day ago had won the four-mile, Red Eagle tensed as the mansion's front door swung open. He was riding a very valuable horse, leading a string of even more valuable horses. Champions, all of them, the fastest horses in the new United States, stolen from the gilded stables of Charleston's new racecourse.

Red Eagle dismounted, hitched the palomino, and made his way quickly up the front steps. "The militia is on the way."

Romaine nodded. "Do you know how many there are?"

Twenty bells plus twenty bells meant the full militia was being summoned. Every white man with a gun. Hundreds upon hundreds, he guessed. A thousand or more, even.

Red Eagle glanced at the foyer that opened behind Romaine. It was strewn with the bodies of white men. Three of them wore the sash of night patrolmen. "You will come with me to Muskogee country," he said to Mary and Romaine.

Romaine counted the crowd around her. A dozen, herself and Mary included. "We all go."

From the edge of the group, a man growled, "We stay and fight."

"Ellison, if we stay we die." Romaine spoke as calmly as if she was telling a friend her opinion on the weather. "We must go. We will make ourselves a rebel camp, as we did in Trou Coffy. We can recruit and train. It is how we won in Saint-Domingue."

Ellison was unconvinced. "If we run now, we'll be caught before we get to the Ashley River. I'll take my chances here."

Romaine made her way to Ellison and set her hands on his shoulders. "We will return, I promise you."

"We have horses, many," Red Eagle said. "We can make it out, but we have to go now."

Mary picked something off the floor. Red Eagle blinked twice to make sure his eyes were not playing tricks on him and it was, indeed, a white man's head she held by the hair. She walked off away from the group to the door. At the edge of the marble steps, Mary turned back around to address the group.

"If you don't know how to ride, I'll show you. I'm not dying. Not today."

Mary started down the steps. The sky was dark. The night was new.

"This is not how it ends."

Chapter 10

Red Eagle led the way. There was a back trail through Stono swamp that would soon turn them westward to connect with the Cherokee Path. Mary brought up the rear, to soothe the horses carrying the two men most afraid of the hulking animals. She took up, as well, the string of horses that remained without riders. She left the last horse for Romaine, conferring with James at the base of the front steps.

The Prophetess gave James a fierce hug. "Goodbye, my friend."

James's face showed no emotion. "Good luck," he intoned. He did not shake off Romaine's embrace, nor did he return it.

Romaine smiled, surprised by the tenderness she felt for James. An hour earlier, he was well on his way to becoming a celebrated chef. Now everything was upside down. Would the whites believe James's claim that he had nothing to do with this bloodshed? The church bells repeated their twenty peals, followed by another twenty. Romaine had no time left to wonder what would become of James. She swung her leg over the roan and, without a glance back, rode off to join the group.

James turned back to the mansion, his heart beating a panicked tattoo. He considered his chances of not being killed when the militia arrived. He made his way to the kitchen to finish loading his wagon, skirting the pools of blood spreading over the floor. After loading his pots, James found the mansion's cask of salt and hoisted it up into the wagon. A quick run upstairs through the study rewarded the chef with a large well of ink and stack of paper. These he secured under the front seat, out of sight.

The faint glow of first light was on the horizon when the militia found their way to the governor's mansion. They came striding up the street four and five abreast, waistcoats and court suits thrown over night clothes. James finished hitching the third and fourth horses and climbed up onto the driver's seat. From the tone of the shouts, he knew they had found the bodies in the foyer and made their count. James smoothed the front of his shirt as he waited. He pulled up his socks and squared his shoulders under his fine coat. He neatened his eyebrows. He needed to look too expensive to shoot.

The man who spotted him immediately turned tail and ran. A minute later, he was back with a dozen other men, guns bristling. Every man had one eye on James and the other on their leader, a squat fellow whose cautious approach exaggerated the bow of his legs. None of the men fired out of panic and James gave a quick thanks this militia was well regulated. Careful not to move too quickly, James bent at the waist to give a slight bow.

"Sir," James said in his most British English, "I must thank providence you have finally arrived."

The bowlegged man stopped and lowered his gun. "Boy, whadya know about this?"

James cleared his throat and enunciated like his life depended on it. "They came in after the banquet, while we were cleaning up."

"Who? How many?"

"I don't know, sir. A dozen, maybe."

"Can you count?"

James resisted the urge to respond with an insult. His silence was rewarded with a musket barrel shoved under his ribs. With deliberate care, James raised his hands to show he was unarmed.

A woman's voice cut through the air. "Put that gun down,

Tommy!" James recognized the voice before he made out her face.

"Mrs. Pinckney," he said.

She grabbed the gun and pushed it away. "He saved my life. I'd be dead if he hadn't saved me from those … those … monsters!" Mrs. Pinckney's eyes as she looked up at James glistened with emotion.

"Tell us what you know," Tommy demanded of James. He did not like being told what to do by a woman, even if it was the governor's wife. The *former* governor, if her story was accurate. There was no reason to doubt it—they had indeed found a headless body upstairs in the place she described—but it was also too stunning to believe. The governor of South Carolina, killed by a band of murderous slaves. It was what every slave-owner feared most, but for it to be the Governor himself was unthinkable. Tommy focused his ire on the fancy Negro sitting atop the wagon. "Answer me! What happened here?"

"They came in looking for something to steal, I think," James said. "I hid in the pantry, and, when I came out, they were on their way out."

"Which way did they go?"

"I overheard them saying they would go south, to Florida. They said it very clearly: south to Florida. They knew they would be safe once they crossed the border into Spanish Florida." James pointed to the street that led into town. "They went that way, south."

"We would have seen them."

James paused. He had not thought through this part of the story. "They said they knew to avoid the main streets. One of them must have been from here and knew what to avoid. He was the one who kept repeating: Florida, we will be free in Florida."

Tommy squinted at James, skeptical. He instructed his men to search the wagon. "If you are telling us a tale we'll tie you up like a pig and roast you good."

Mrs. Pinckney, a hand on her hip, shook her finger at Tommy. "This was the chef, of course he wasn't part of it," she said. "If he was part of the plan, he could have just poisoned all of us. Easy as pie. A poison pie." Mrs. Pinckney laughed at her own joke, a chortling that rose in pitch than dove into a sobbing cry.

A man stuck his head out of the wagon to make his report. "Nothing in there, just pots and flour and kitchen things."

Tommy looked at Mrs. Pinckney and decided to believe her. "Blockade the harbor, seal off the Ashepoo bridge," the militia leader commanded. His mouth winched tighter with each syllable. "Get word to Beaufort. They are running south."

Ten days later, far to the west, Red Eagle brought home with him to Hickory Ground a caravan unlike any the town had ever seen. Riding next to him was Romaine, light flashing from crystals embedded in her turban. Behind them were thirty or more handsome horses, a third of them with riders. Mary rode farthest to the rear, pushing forward the laggards.

As the forest gave way to town, the path widened and was soon filled with townspeople raising their hands in greeting. The children who came to welcome Red Eagle home were initially shy but became emboldened by one another's presence and pressed in close. Red Eagle reached down to tap the tops of their heads and laughed, calling each child by name. The bravest of them reached up to grab at the horse's mane.

The noise drew people out of their homes, and, by the time they reached the center of town, a hundred children ran alongside, waving sticks and shouting. The street opened up into the town square, where the smell of cooking fires and boiled corn hung in the air. A handsome log building stretched along each side of the square. The perimeter created by the windowless walls of the four buildings glowed an orange brown in the noonday sun. A rocky-faced woman appeared, and the children fell silent as she strode across the square. Red Eagle's heart seized with the crushing mix of fear and adoration he always felt in seeing his mother after a long absence.

"You brought friends," said Red Eagle's mother in the Muskogee spoken between women. The lines tracing her face were deeper and darker than Red Eagle remembered. "They have white owners?"

Red Eagle nodded yes. "Some." That did not seem right. He added, "No longer. They fought against their owners. These are who escaped."

"They are simanoles," his mother said, using the Muskogee variation of what the Spanish called cimarrones and the English called maroons. His mother looked over his shoulder at the group on horseback. Her eyes turned back to Red Eagle's, boring in. She cupped his face in her hands. "You have a talent for forcing an argument, my child. Having simanoles here is a danger, a provocation."

"I don't mean to bring trouble," Red Eagle said.

"You have always made things more difficult for me. That is a fact, not a complaint."

His mother's brusqueness made Red Eagle smile. "You have every reason to make it a complaint."

The barest of smiles tugged at her mouth. "It is far too late to bother."

Red Eagle had, indeed, always made things more difficult for his mother, the mighty Sehoy. The unsmiling, much-loved, greatly feared, colossal and immovable, unflinching Sehoy. Or, as she sometimes referred to herself, as an invocation of her lineage, Sehoy Sehoy Sehoy.

Red Eagle had come into the world as a baby girl, and so had been named Sehoy as well. Sehoy Sehoy Sehoy Sehoy.

As the first daughter from a long line of first daughters, there were great expectations for baby Sehoy: the namesake of the Wind Clan, she would one day take her mother's place as the leader of the Muskogee Confederacy's most powerful clan. Good-natured and uncomplaining, baby Sehoy had a talent for getting what she wanted. At age four, when she insisted on spending all day and night at the stables with Charles Wetherford's horses, no one thought to say no.

Charles Wetherford was the girl Sehoy's father. He was also a double-dealing gambler and drunkard of the worst sort. That is, he was English. The powerful Wind Clan women took on white men as husbands to enhance their trade positions with the British, the Catholics and the French, but sometimes the white husbands misunderstood their place in the town, a common belief being that the marriage made them a king or chief of some sort. The mistaken men had to be sent away to fend for themselves. Wetherford had been so banished, soon after baby Sehoy's birth, to a narrow strip of high ground across the Tallapoosa River.

After he got over the shock of his reduced status, Wetherford built a racetrack and a boxing ring, in which his brother-in-law, the nearly famous French boxer Ben Durant, tried to knock down all comers in bare-knuckle fisticuffs. It was a raucous place, smelly and full of bad characters with low morals. Curses were shouted in fifteen languages. The Catholics hated the Scots, the Choctaws could not tolerate the Hitichis, and every few days Durant the nearly famous French boxer had to use his boxing skills outside the ring to restore order. It was a dangerous place for children, and the girl Sehoy loved every bit of it. She could not be coaxed to leave.

By the age of nine, Sehoy was close to adult height, with unusually broad shoulders and a love for all forms of sport. The boys of Hickory Ground broke their toes and sprained their ankles trying to outdo her. When the boys practiced for stickball by flinging balls at a target, everyone wanted Sehoy on their team. They created contests—hanging from a branch, catching lizards, pulling a hair from the Spaniard's moustache—to test themselves, and Sehoy won them all. Most of all, Sehoy loved horse racing. This delighted Wetherford to no end, both as a matter of paternal pride and as a matter of business. He won enough pesos, francs, pounds, and dollars in bets placed against his child to keep himself in fine Indian cotton during the summers and thick Scottish woolens through the winters.

At the end of childhood, to no one's great surprise, Sehoy insisted on being initiated into manhood alongside the roustabouts at the racetrack. At first, Sehoy's mother would not permit such a thing, but the mother understood a few months into the quarrel that she had met her match. Obstinate determination was a trait passed down from mother to child as surely as the name Sehoy. The younger Sehoy wore down the elder Sehoy's resistance, and at the end of the five-day-long ceremony capping the yearlong process, the child who had been named Sehoy emerged from the water as Red Eagle.

Following custom, Red Eagle turned not to his father but to his uncle for direction. His uncle, Alexander McGillivray, was Sehoy's older brother. Having been sent as a boy to live among the whites in the town of Augusta on the Savannah River, McGillivray came of age in Charleston, returning to Hickory Ground only once a year to attend the green corn festival. Whenever McGillivray was home, young Red Eagle was by his side.

His uncle talked with Red Eagle only in the Muskogee spoken between men. Instead of giving commands, as his mother did, McGillivray asked Red Eagle questions and listened closely to his answers. When McGillivray's Muskogee faltered, or something about Muskogee custom puzzled him, Red Eagle's uncle asked Red Eagle for help to understand it. "It's different in Charleston," McGillivray often said, "The British believe…" or "White people think…"

In this way, Red Eagle learned a great deal about the society of white people who lived in Charleston. They built ships and traded in rice and indigo. To live in the port city, they accepted cockroaches, mosquitoes, plagues, stifling heat, and sour water. They had a strong preference for sons. Red Eagle learned that some in Charleston lived in opulence while others wore rags. This was not only tolerated, it was part of their God's design. At the bottom of God's Chain of Being were those enslaved to grow the indigo and rice that made those at the top fantastically rich. To maintain this Chain of Being, the whites at the top committed spectacular acts of cruelty. Those enslaved who poisoned their masters or destroyed their property were hung in an iron cage for the crows to eat or burned alive in the town square. The lords of the low country, McGillivray explained to Red Eagle, sincerely believed this arrangement to be the pinnacle of civilization. By bringing Africans to Charleston, the plantation owners were turning savages into Christians.

"While ensuring the prosperity of their own sons," his mother Sehoy spat, "who then steal Muskogee land to carry on this plan of civilization." Through the years, McGillivray's conversations with Red Eagle oftentimes became arguments with Sehoy as the three of them sat in the shade of Sehoy's courtyard and puzzled out what to make of the Americans, as they now called themselves. These Americans were forming a *United States* and laying claim to Muskogee land. If the Muskogees wanted to maintain rights to their own land, McGillivray told Sehoy, they had to form a nation as well.

Red Eagle listened as his mother and his uncle argued back and forth through the night. When his uncle spoke, Red Eagle agreed with him, that the British king had given Muskogee land away to the Americans at the end of their war because the Muskogees were a confederacy of towns along the rivers, with no central authority to claim the hunting grounds they held in common. When his mother spoke, Red Eagle agreed with her, that forming a central council and naming a chief of all Muskogees in order to deal with the Americans was acquiescence, a submission to their view of the world. It was too late to quibble over worldviews, McGillivray countered. The Americans were here to stay, and the Muskogees had to consolidate their own power to better negotiate the distributions of land. At this, Sehoy calmly took off her shoe and slapped her brother across the face with it. You *always* quibble over worldviews, she said as McGillivray rubbed his jaw where he'd been struck, when your neighbor's worldview believes *people* and *land* can be bought and sold.

From one year to the next, as McGillivray returned to Hickory Ground with news from the coast, it seemed to Red Eagle this difference between Muskogee and Charlestonian became more pronounced. The whites in Charleston bought and sold people with increasing intensity, and they pressed farther and farther into Muskogee and Cherokee territory, claiming lands for the enslaved to work.

"We must learn to negotiate with them," McGillivray pleaded with Sehoy the year Red Eagle turned eighteen. "They believe land has a price, and if we don't give them a price, they will simply take it in order to place a price upon it." He took care to remain out of range of Sehoy's shoe.

"How do you make agreements with such people?" Sehoy demanded. "They have no common obligations. They hoard cows and land and humans and pass them on to their sons. Do you intend to negotiate with them one by one?" McGillivray started to respond, but Sehoy was not done. "They agree on a boundary and then ignore it." She suddenly turned to Red Eagle. "What should we do about the Americans?"

Red Eagle stammered, knowing he was being tested more than he was being asked. He got as far as, "Perhaps we can try..." before his mother turned back to her brother and resumed her litany of defects. "These Charleston whites put themselves at the top of a hierarchy. This is not natural; this is out of balance. Their hierarchy can be maintained only by violence. These Charleston whites will forever be terrified of all they subjugate. Tell me, brother, in their world are we Muskogees among the lords or the slaves?"

"I'd rather us be on top, wouldn't you?" McGillivray said. He ducked at the shoe that came flying, but not in time.

That was the year his uncle left for good and fenced in a plantation on the Tensaw River, near the town of Mobile. The next year, he bought two strong young Black men from a merchant in Augusta.

For a few years, Sehoy refused to receive her brother at Hickory Ground, and Red Eagle had to ride down to the Tensaw to see his uncle. One year, Red Eagle brought news back to his mother that McGillivray was being invited by President Washington to New York alongside other leaders of the Muskogee Confederacy. The American president claimed he could put a stop to the Georgians and Carolinians infringing on Muskogee territory.

Sehoy and McGillivray came to a compromise, that McGillivray would take the mantle as the Muskogee's supreme micco, chief of all the Muskogees, but only to negotiate with the U.S. president for the purpose of keeping the Americans out of Muskogee land. When McGillivray traveled north, he took with him Red Eagle, whose ostensible task was to translate for his uncle among the Muskogee leaders who spoke Hitchiti and Yuchi. Red Eagle's real work was to act as a lookout for his mother. He traveled for the first time in a coach, pulled by eight horses, then on a schooner, ten times the length of Hickory Ground's largest canoe. In New York City, Red Eagle was the only one among the group to accept the invitation to the President's Birthnight Ball and, with the help of three glasses of wine, was a favorite among the ladies dancing the minuet.

The treaty they signed made the Oconee River the boundary between the state of Georgia and Muskogee territory. The United States conceded that Muskogees would be free to punish trespassers as they saw fit. In exchange, McGillivray agreed on behalf of the Muskogees to turn maroons and new runaways over to federal agents. Unknown to all but Red Eagle, McGillivray received on the side an envelope stuffed with cash, and a commission in the U.S. Army that paid a generous yearly stipend.

Sehoy listened to her child's recounting of their success and understood immediately what her brother had done. "Your uncle signed a terrible deal," she told Red Eagle. "There is no worse mistake he could have made. Agreeing to return runaways—" The grim set of Sehoy's face turned somehow grimmer. "He has turned us against our most natural friends."

Red Eagle was flush with the victory of a successful negotiation and paid little attention to his mother's words. But now, a decade later, the number of settlers crossing westward past solemnly sworn borders had turned from a trickle to stream. They ignored Muskogees' demands to turn back, and, when pressed, American governors used debts and deeds to justify the seizure of Muskogee land. More runaways appeared in Muskogee towns each year, and disagreements over whether to return them was turning Muskogees against Muskogees. With each passing year, Red Eagle better understood his mother's warning.

In the grey light that filled the roundhouse, Alexander McGillivray's mix of Muskogee and English words jammed up against one another in a rush to be heard. He was at Hickory Ground for the one visit he was permitted each year, the terms of a truce with Sehoy. It was a way for the two to keep an eye on one another, to see firsthand outrages such as this one.

"They are slaves, with masters who will be looking for them; we need to return them to their owners. Or if they want to be simanoles, we should send them south immediately. It is too dangerous for them to remain here. We are already in a poor position. Having them here puts us in even more danger."

Red Eagle kept his eyes on his mother and tamped down the urge to correct his uncle's Muskogee.

"This is not your decision," Sehoy said to her brother.

McGillivray gave a curt nod of acknowledgement. "Of course. I am a visitor here. I am only offering my thoughts."

"Nor is it my decision alone," Sehoy continued. She turned to Red Eagle. "The woman with the white cloth wrapped around her head. Bring her here so we can have a word."

"A woman," McGillivray said, trying to hide a grimace. "Is there another leader among them? To keep things in good balance?"

By balance, his uncle meant a man. Someone more likely to take his side in the Muskogee-wide quarrel between the old women who favored tradition and the young men who chafed at its restrictions. Red Eagle pretended not to understand him and answered truthfully, "There is also Mary. The men follow her without question. Mary is the best horseman." He liked saying her name. "Mary is the fastest rider I've ever met. Other than myself."

Understanding crept across his mother Sehoy's face. "Mary is the one whose sister was sold for losing to you," she said slowly. Red Eagle guessed by the way his mother went completely still that she was piecing together a much larger story than he had ever told her about Mary and the horse race that bound him to her. Where other people saw a corn stalk, Sehoy saw the whole of creation. "Bring Mary as well, then. We can see what kind of people you have brought home."

In the time it took Red Eagle to find Romaine and Mary and bring them back to the roundhouse, the embers at the center fire were stoked and a pot of cornmeal stew bubbled over the fire. Sehoy waited for them on a high wooden perch, McGillivray at her side.

"Welcome to Hickory Ground, friends," said Sehoy in Muskogee. Red Eagle repeated her words in English. His mother spoke English as well as he did, but when she pretended otherwise, it was to encourage plain speech and to give herself time to think before responding. McGillivray glanced at his sister, annoyed at her choice. Sehoy addressed Romaine. "Why are you here?"

Romaine glanced at Red Eagle, puzzled by the question. "We came at Red Eagle's invitation," she answered carefully.

"Red Eagle tells me you murdered your owners in their sleep," Sehoy said. Red Eagle flushed red and dutifully translated word for word, despite having not ever having said such a thing.

"I have no owner," Romaine responded, glaring at Red Eagle. "If you will indulge me, I will tell you who I am."

Sehoy nodded and sat back to listen as Romaine described for her the uprising in Saint-Domingue and how she had turned over her body and coffee plantation to carry out the commands of the Virgin Mary. How Trou Coffy became a rebel camp, how they won Léogâne and then lost it. How she came to be in Nuevo Orleans, then Charleston, and now here.

"The men you brought here," Sehoy said at Romaine's conclusion, "*they* murdered their owners in their sleep."

Red Eagle tensed as he translated, expecting a rebuke from Romaine. Instead, the Prophetess smiled and, amazingly, the famously unsmiling Sehoy smiled back. The two seemed to be sharing a joke.

"Mary did the murdering," Romaine said, pulling Mary to her side. "But it wasn't her owner, and he wasn't asleep."

"A mistake," McGillivray growled at Red Eagle. "You shouldn't have brought them here."

"Yet here they are," Sehoy responded to her brother in English. "What would you have us do?"

"If they want to be simanoles, send them south to join the others along the lower Chattahoochee. They are eager for more runaways. These men will be welcome if you send them south with your blessing."

Sehoy turned back to Romaine. "You wish to make Hickory Ground your, what did you call it? Trou Coffy. Your camp."

"It can be here or south among the simanoles," Romaine said diplomatically.

"Two miles down and across the river is an old racetrack," Sehoy said. "There are stables for your horses. There is land suitable for planting when the time comes to plant. You will remain on that land. You will not go beyond one day's ride to hunt. You will clear the land and fence the fields. When we plant our fields, you will plant as well. Then you will tend to the crops until the corn is in the common bins."

"You are inviting an attack," McGillivray said, his voice rising. "The whites will be well within their rights to come reclaim their property."

Sehoy ignored her brother's interruption. "You will be of the Wind Clan, under my protection. No slave catcher will be allowed to steal you, so long as you remain within a day's ride. If you dishonor or disgrace me, you will be banished."

McGillivray pointed an angry finger at Mary. "Her, at least. She must go. Having her here puts all us in danger."

"This girl is not the danger," Sehoy said.

"She stole herself away from her master and now has killed the governor of South Carolina." McGillivray struggled not to yell. "Allowing her to stay here will bring ruin to Hickory Ground."

"I can go," Mary offered, stepping forward. "I do not want to be a curse on your people."

"No, no," Sehoy said, shaking her head. She stepped down

from her seat and took Mary's hands in her own. "You are the opposite of a curse, my child. You are the universe trying to set itself back into balance." Sehoy turned to Romaine. "You will stay and build your army here."

It was an easy ride to the racetrack. The Coosa River ran to their right, a canebrake grew to their left. The canebrake ended where the river turned, and then where the river narrowed, a rope strung above a line of rocks made up the crossing to the open fields on the other side. The group continued along the river until it widened again and slowed to a flow that the horses could swim across. Next to the stables, a lean-to sheltered a long stack of firewood and a few rotting barrels.

Mary surveyed the land. "Not much to get us started," she said.

The stables were quickly put into good enough repair for the horses. The task of shelter for themselves proved more difficult. There were only a dozen of them, and each had a different memory of home. They bickered about what to build and in what order. They drew pictures in the dirt and explained the advantage of circular walls or a particular kind of thatched roof. Jeremiah proposed a line of cabins. Ellison wanted to first build a fortified guardhouse. Romaine argued for a single large bunkhouse. With the chill serving as encouragement, they agreed to start simple. Out of the river cane and mud, the hut they formed was crooked and ugly but large enough for all the men to lie down to sleep, nearly warm.

Mary and Romaine claimed for themselves the bit of shelter that jutted out from the stable's far stalls. The shack was barely larger than the square stage that took up the middle of the floor, the place nearly swallowed by the weeds.

"Durant's boxing ring," Red Eagle said to Mary, holding his fists up in front of his face and shuffling his feet. He watched Mary as she picked through the rubble. For the duration of the ride from Charleston, he had watched Mary. She rode with a startling simplicity of movement. Red Eagle watched how she let her horse decide how best to cross the roughest terrain. When he had seen her ride as a jockey in the four-milers years ago, Red Eagle suspected Mary might be the best horseman he would ever encounter in his travels. On the ride west, watching her work her way through a stretch of overgrown brush and fallen branches, Red Eagle had no doubts. Each night after dinner, when Red Eagle had sat close to her at the cooking fire and offered her half of his blanket, she did not refuse it.

Red Eagle waited until late in the day to press his advantage. The four walls and bed of his house back in Hickory Ground, he pointed out, made for a far warmer and more comfortable night than sleeping in this yet unfinished shack. Did Mary care to join him?

She did.

The distance from the edge of town to Red Eagle's home was filled with townspeople calling out greetings and exclamations and reminders to visit. After determining the woman with him did not speak Muskogee, there were also teases and encouragements.

"This does not make me one of your seven wives does it?" Mary said.

"Only my sixth," Red Eagle said. "What kind of man do you think I am?"

He'd decided he would let her find the way, as she had allowed her horse to pick their way through the brambles. So when she made a sound of delight at the plush warmth of his bed and fell promptly asleep, he sighed and accepted his fate. He looked up at the ceiling and counted fifty slow breaths to slow his heart. He was patient, he could wait another few days. But then she turned over into the crook of his arm and with a small sound of great contentment settled her hand on his belly and he could not wait another minute. He rolled up on his elbow above her. When she hooked her leg around and pulled him to her, he went to kiss her but misjudged the distance between them. It was very dark. "Can I still be your wife if I have a chipped tooth?" she said, her hand examining her mouth.

"Always," he said. He had her face in his hands and tried again. When she opened her mouth to him, the wolf rose up along his back, and he felt he might devour her whole. He meant to be restrained, then quickly discovered she had no need for restraint. He had known since he was a child that his gifts were all physical, that his blessings were in his body. Mary, he concluded many hours later as they lay panting on the floor, was someone with talents as simple and great. The bed would have to be repaired.

That was last night. It was now far past mid-morning as Mary lay asleep on his chest. A pang of guilt shot through Red Eagle's happy heart: what kind of host was he to have left his guests on their own this morning, their first day in their new home? Had the newly thatched roof kept out the night's rain? Had anyone gone to gather them for the morning bath? Red Eagle scolded himself as he scrambled to his feet and searched for his breeches.

They returned to the other side of the river with a stack of blankets. Red Eagle carried them to the men as an offering, his eyes barely clearing the top of the stack. Ellison gave him a hard look and kept his distance, but the others eagerly took the blankets. Some wrapped them around their shoulders, cursing the cold.

At the stables, Red Eagle rested his back against a stall wall, and Mary leaned up against him. He pulled her closer. He could feel his own heart beating against her back.

"The horses like having you around," Mary said.

"I cannot stay here with you," Red Eagle said. "My mother will not approve."

"No one was asking you to stay," Mary said.

Red Eagle laughed. "You can come back with me, then."

Mary rested her head on Red Eagle's arm for an instant before shaking herself loose. "Your mother would not approve." Mary gave him the barest hint of a smile. "She expects us to raise an army."

"My mother did not mean *immediately*," Red Eagle said. Surely there was time to spend a few slow evenings at the river's edge, some more nights like the one just past. The look Mary shot him made clear she disagreed. "Alright then, I'll stay to help build the cooking space."

"Do you think he will come?" Mary asked as they put the last stones into place to make a fair-sized stove. Romaine's design was as close an approximation as she could manage of what she imagined James would want.

Romaine lit the fire in a pan fashioned from an upturned turtle shell. This morning, she was certain James would soon arrive. Now she was just as certain he'd already decided otherwise. Why would someone with as many advantages as James choose to throw them away?

"We will put this kitchen to good use either way," Romaine said.

Mary nodded and squatted down to examine the shell, as if she cared that it was proving to be a good substitute for a coal pan. She and Romaine both knew that what they needed from James was not just his skills as a cook. To raise an army, what they needed was James's exquisite penmanship.

Chapter 11

At the fork in the path, the lead horses paused for instruction. James tugged on the right rein to direct them to the right, northward. After a moment's hesitation, he tugged left, to head south. Then right again. Finally, he pulled back to bring the horses to a halt.

His present indecision annoyed him, having already decided immediately after setting out from Charleston to take the right fork at this place in the journey. Going north would, Red Eagle had told him, send him on to Hickory Ground, to be reunited with Romaine and Mary. But somewhere between the second and third day, another plan had taken form in James's mind. Left at the fork put him on the path back to Nuevo Orleans. He could ride back into town triumphant, his reputation enhanced by the dramatic turn of events at Governor Pinckney's banquet. He was a bystander, surprised by the violence, who had risked his own life to save an innocent young white woman and her child from certain slaughter. He could find another sous chef to replace Romaine. The restaurant would prosper even more than before. His increased fame would shorten, perhaps quite dramatically, the amount of time it would take to save enough to buy his family from Thomas Jefferson.

James had gone over the numbers again and again as the miles rolled by under his wagon's wheels. With a modest increase in the restaurant's profit, he could make a fair market offer to Jefferson in seven years rather than the ten he'd previously calculated. If providence smiled more broadly on him and he doubled his profits at the restaurant and then doubled them again by catering, it would take only five years to buy his sister Sally. In another three he could retrieve his mother as well. Robert would take another three or four years, even though he was worth far more, since his brother presumably had some credit amassed towards his own freedom. Together in Nuevo Orleans, working as free men, James and Robert could together eventually buy all their siblings into freedom.

That was if he chose to turn left. To the right lay a future with Romaine and Mary, uncertain in the details but likely to include a fourth revolution. James stared down each path as the horses stamped at the ground, impatient at the delay. A sound rumbled inside his head. It was Denmark, laughing at James for believing Jefferson would ever sell Sally or any of the others.

It was that maddening, raging river again. He could see on the other side his triumph: Sally and their mother, their siblings and their children, all bought fair and square at market value. It was a river not his to cross.

Yet had he not crossed this last one? He'd thought there was no way to take the commission in Charleston, but, with Romaine and Mary, he'd gone. He considered the lesson. He'd made it across, yes, but with Romaine and Mary.

James slapped the reins and tugged right.

When he arrived three days later at Hickory Ground, a welcome party met him at the edge of town. At its fore were Mary and Romaine. A mix of relief and affection flooded through James as Romaine walked out to greet him, an enormous smile spreading across her face.

"You seem surprised to see me, Prophetess," James said, climbing down from the driver's seat.

Romaine laughed and admitted she had hoped James would take the right turn and join them in Muskogee country, but when the group took bets on whether he would, she had bet against him. "There was a better future waiting for you in Nuevo Orleans," Romaine said. "No one would have faulted you for taking the easier route."

James felt the doubt rise in his throat, burning like bile. Forgoing his restaurant might prove to be, in the end, the wrong choice. "I could have…" James started to tell Romaine about his calculations for buying first Sally, then his mother, and then the rest of his family, but stopped at the futility of it. What he could have done differently seemed suddenly superfluous. He'd taken the right turn rather than the left one, and whatever future unfolded from that choice would forever feel like the only possibility. He looked away from Romaine to keep her from seeing the dread that threatened to overtake him. "How could I not come? " James said as casually as he could manage. "You are my family now."

"*I* knew you would come," Mary said. She stretched up to kiss his cheek. "Did you bring paper and ink?"

"Under the seat, as much as I could find." James could not help but smile at Mary's yelp of joy when she pulled out ream after ream of paper. In Romaine's hurried departure from Charleston, she had asked James to bring as much paper as he could find but had not told him the reason. He turned to ask Mary, but she was already gone.

There was much to be done as James and the others settled into their new life. For housing, the group settled on cabins of the sort found in Hickory Ground. They eagerly accepted the lessons offered by the townspeople on how to weave the long lengths of cane, then cover the wattle with mud daub to form sturdy walls. Mary took charge of the horses. She declared herself captain of the cavalry and asked for volunteers. Half the men shrank back, their backsides still in pain,

but the other half eagerly followed her into the fields to become horsemen. Red Eagle brought them cudgels made of
hardened wood, and a ball the size of the human head. Mary
kicked her horse into a gallop and, in a half crouch over of her
saddle, walloped the ball off a post as she thundered by.

One morning Mary asked James to come with her and
Romaine across the river to Hickory Ground. Mary hooked
her arm to James's elbow and led him down the neatly swept
dirt street that ran through the middle of town. People came
outside and watched silently as the group passed by. Glancing
at their faces, James sensed their mix of curiosity and unease.
When they arrived at the roundhouse, Romaine pushed open
the door. "Go on in. We got things ready for you."

In this dim light, James saw Red Eagle and counted five
women sitting along the curve of the wall. Romaine led him
to a seat close to the door, where the light was brightest, and
gestured for him to take a seat. Mary pulled out a single sheet
of paper and set it down on a smooth slab of wood placed
between two stumps. James found himself behind a desk of
sorts.

Red Eagle handed him a pen. "What's this?" James asked.
The handle, shaped much like a pencil, held a metal nib.

"The latest invention," Red Eagle said proudly. "The tip
stays sharp. Better than a quill—and a lot more expensive."

James took the pen and examined it while Romaine introduced the women. They were the town's best artists, ready
to draw up maps to lead runaways to Hickory Ground.

James set the pen down slowly and stared at Romaine,
incredulous.

"Runaways to Hickory Ground," James repeated, testing
the phrase.

His job, Romaine continued, was to write out documents.
She needed him to put his beautiful penmanship to good use
and forge papers that the runaways could show any patrolman demanding them.

"You must think I'm a magician," James said. "I can't draw up something convincing enough to save their skin if they're stopped."

"Of course you can," Romaine replied. "And anyway, that's not what matters. The paper has to be good enough to convince someone to run. *That's* the magic."

Romaine explained the plan. The maps and freedom papers were to be distributed by the men from Pinckney's plantations. They were all in agreement that whether courageous or cautious, a person was more likely to run if the recruiter was themself a runaway. The men—and Mary and Romaine herself—would each ride with someone from Hickory Ground. In case of trouble, their guides would claim to be their Muskogee owner. Half the Black and Muskogee pairs would ride through Muskogee country into Cherokee land and fan up and down along the coast. The others would ride north through Tennessee country on across to North Carolina.

"That's insanity," James managed. "Do you have any idea how dangerous this is?"

As Romaine coolly listed the various ways there might be more losses (increased patrols, poor horsemanship, slave catchers, bad luck) or less (inclement weather, good luck), Mary produced a bottle of ink and set it atop the blank sheet of paper. She plucked the pen from between James's fingers and dipped it into the ink. Handing it back to James, she asked, "Should we start with a deed of manumission or a certificate of freedom?"

"A letter of purchase," Romaine said. "Or a free person of color registration."

"Any of the freedom papers will work," Mary said. "And a general description—female, average height; male, average build. It might not match up. Just make it look like a rich white man wrote it."

James looked around at the dozen or more people who now formed a tight semicircle before him, jostling shoulder to shoulder to get a better view. A feeling of excitement and expectation pulsed through the air as his audience waited for James to perform his magic trick. His back pressed up against the wall of the roundhouse, James realized he was trapped.

James blotted the pen on a piece of cloth. "A deed of manumission, then," he said. "Let's have it be from Thomas Jefferson himself." James leaned over the paper and wrote out a long sentence in a flowing script.

As James worked, Red Eagle read aloud for Mary and the others: "…to manumit and set free my Negro woman Betty Jones Davies, forty years of age of average height. And I do hereby declare the said Negro woman liberated and set free to all instance and purposes. In witness whereof I have hereunto set my hand on this 4th day of July 1793." Mary slapped James on the back, sending his elaborate flourish at the end of Thomas Jefferson's signature wobbling off in the wrong direction. She shouted, "The great liberator, James Hemings!"

James leaned back and admired his completed forgery. "Pretty convincing, I have to admit," he said.

"Oh it's beautiful," Mary exclaimed. She and the rest of the group leaned in even closer to watch the next paper being produced. The only sounds in the roundhouse were their breathing and the scratch of James's pen. Mary felt she might burst into flames. "Can you write faster?"

"Don't rush me."

"Yes, let James take the time he needs with each one," Romaine said. "He knows, I'm sure, that the moment the South Carolina militia returns from Florida empty-handed, they will start searching the interior."

James, knowing no such thing, grumbled and bent back over his free person of color registration. He made the holder of the paper *a free mulatto of medium build, age thirty or there-abouts*, and signed it as the clerk of Spotsylvania County, Virginia. Reviewing his work, James fell under the spell of his own script for a moment and wondered what a free mulatto from Virginia was doing so far south.

As James labored over more deeds and certificates, the group of women gathered around Red Eagle and dripped water into their color pots. With great care, they drew as Red Eagle instructed. The mighty rivers flowed down and across the page: the Chattahoochee, the Ocmulgee, the Coosa, the Tallapoosa, the Alabama. Along each river, the mapmakers dropped dots of ink to show the Muskogee towns where runaways could hope for a meal and a night's rest, then drew thin x's to show the Muskogee towns to avoid.

The maps reached beyond the borders of Muskogee hunting grounds and then farther still, beyond Cherokee territory. Red Eagle grew worried at the expanses on the maps that contained nothing but a line of dashes, the marks being the days needed to traverse the blank space where he could offer no guidance. Ten days worth of blank space seemed to Red Eagle the limit of what someone would be willing to risk, but Mary and Romaine wanted to extend the maps all the way to Virginia. The three went outside to discuss the matter.

Across the square, the ground painted red by the setting sun, Red Eagle spotted his uncle. When he waved for McGillivray to join them, a scowl flickered across Romaine's brow.

"He's been talking against us ever since we arrived," Romaine said.

"He is worried for our people," Red Eagle said. "He will soon agree with my mother that an alliance with the runaways is the best course."

Romaine looked skeptical. "He has conceded before to Sehoy?"

"Everyone always concedes to Sehoy," Red Eagle said, pulling his uncle in by the elbow. "Isn't that right, uncle? We can have all the words we want in between, but the first and last word is Sehoy's."

"That has always been the case, but the world is changing," McGillivray said. He scanned the group and offered up a tight smile.

"And we can use your help keeping it on the right path." Red Eagle draped his arm around his uncle's shoulders. "Tell us about the plantations in Virginia. Given a map and papers, will people steal themselves away?"

McGillivray snorted. "It's too treacherous to send our riders that far beyond Muskogee borders. And no runaway will come this far—it is impossible on foot. Philadelphia is a fifth the distance."

"They can still be returned to their owners from Philadelphia," said Romaine. "Here they know they would be safe." Romaine gave McGillivray a long look. "Isn't that right?"

"Slave catchers are not welcome here, if that's what you mean," McGillivray said. His eyes neither met Romaine's, nor did he look away.

"And unlike in Philadelphia, here they will be able to fight alongside the fearsome Muskogees," Romaine continued.

"You'll need more than the Muskogees to win a war against the Americans," McGillivray said. "They are ambitious."

"All the more reason to act quickly," Romaine suggested.

McGillivray shook his head vigorously and shrugged Red Eagle's arm off his shoulder. "We are too fragmented. Every nation is dealing with the Americans in their own way. With Dragging Canoe dead, the Cherokee are ready to end their fighting. The Chickasaw are playing Spain against the United States. The Choctaw..." McGillivray's litany drifted off as he looked off into the distance, lost in thought.

"And what is the Muskogee's way?" Romaine prompted.

McGillivray's eyes refocused, and his arm shot out, pointing to the roundhouse. "Not what you're doing in there." He suddenly grabbed Red Eagle's shoulders and pulled the young man around to face him. "We made a promise to the Americans to return runaways." McGillivray's voice rose as he addressed his nephew. "It is one thing for the mico of a daughter town to ignore our obligations, but it is quite another if Sehoy herself is encouraging and harboring fugitives."

"They've not kept their side of the agreement..." Red Eagle started. He meant to reassure his uncle that bringing runaways into the fold would only strengthen their bargaining position with the whites, but the sight of Mary's face stopped him. That frown made clear she certainly had no interest in being part of anyone's bargain. What kind of negotiation was possible with people who believed they should own you? "I will talk with my mother," Red Eagle managed.

"Sehoy." McGillivray rubbed his face with both hands, like he was trying to scrub off a layer of grime. "How much longer are you going to hide behind your mother, Red Eagle? She's not who brought these people here. She is not the one riding out tomorrow. This is your doing as much as it is hers."

Red Eagle felt trapped by his uncle's accusation and looked instinctively to Romaine for help. The Prophetess thankfully understood his silent plea.

"*Chief* McGillivray," Romaine said, her voice honey-coated. "You have such good relationships. Not only with the Americans, but the British and Spanish as well. You are clearly un hombre *extremadamente* talentoso. Tell more how you do it."

Red Eagle slipped away as his uncle leaned back to start his soliloquy. Back inside the roundhouse, Red Eagle delivered a fresh set of paints to the women drawing the maps. "Virginia is too far," he said, settling in on the bench. "Let's head west to the Mississippi. Here is Natchez. Draw a boat here and around it, from here to here, the cross marks to show a swamp."

As Red Eagle and Mary and the others prepared the horses to ride out, a messenger for Sehoy came running into the stables to find Red Eagle. A white surveyor had been captured at the Tallapoosa, the messenger panted. He had been hauled in late last night and was at this moment being brought to the roundhouse for questioning.

Sehoy was already well into her inquisition when Red Eagle arrived. "This paper proves that you are a surveyor," she said. "It does not prove your innocence."

"It does if you can read." The white man's beady green eyes threatened to slide down the sharp planes of his cheeks and land in the curl of his sneer.

Sehoy read from the paper. "… *each plat of at least 2000 acres containing sufficient quality farmland and streams …* you are admitting then that you are a surveyor."

"Keep reading. I'm acting under authority of the Georgia-Mississippi Company. It is all legal."

"Not to me."

Immobilized by Sehoy's silent glare, the contempt on the white man's face slowly changed, turning first to comprehension, then to worry.

"Look, you can take it up with the company. I'm just doing my job."

"Tell me about this map." Sehoy pointed to the paper unrolled on the floor at the surveyor's feet.

The surveyor took a more cautious tone. "Georgia runs to the Mississippi River. That was the original land grant."

"That is a lot of land for one man to survey."

"I'm only marking the best thirty."

"For what purpose?"

The white man stared at his hands and did not answer.

"I can have those removed," Sehoy said, nodding to his hands. "We are savages here, as you know. You will be tied to the pole at the center of the square, and after your hands we will move on to your feet. Better to just answer honestly. It is a simple question. Why are you marking out the thirty best plats of land?"

"They are for the senators." Seeing this did not satisfy Sehoy, the surveyor reluctantly continued. "So they will vote to sell the rest of it to the Georgia-Mississippi Company."

"Which will then…" Red Eagle said.

"Resell."

"For a large profit."

"Of course. They're a land company."

"Selling land that is not theirs."

"It will be theirs once the Georgia legislature sells it to them." The surveyor no longer sounded confident in his argument.

"The senators will vote to sell this land after they each receive their two thousand acres. It's a bribe," said Red Eagle. The anger that throbbed inside his skull made him speak slowly, to keep from shouting. "The British gave away land that was not theirs to give. Now your company wants the Georgia legislature to do the same. You're here to mark the boundaries of gifts that are not yours to give."

Sehoy leaned forward from her perch, looming over the white man. "This is Muskogee land. Tell me why I should not roast you after your hands and feet are gone and feed your char to the wolves."

The surveyor looked wildly around him, eyes wide. "I am only marking the land. I have nothing to do with giving it away."

Sehoy turned to Red Eagle and spoke to him in Muskogee. "Your beloved uncle believes land can be sold. He believes people can be sold. So this is what happens. Land is stolen to be sold, then people are bought to work it. Do you understand me?"

Red Eagle nodded. He understood.

"This is why we will welcome runaways when they come," Sehoy said, an accusatory finger jabbing at the map at their feet. "May Hesegedamesse ride with you and send back the fiercest warriors." Satisfied by the obedient bow of Red Eagle's head, Sehoy abruptly dismissed him with a lift of her chin. Red Eagle stood and embraced his mother, trampling the surveyor's map on the way out of the roundhouse. At the door, he heard the surveyor's pleas rise in volume and pitch and wondered what fate his mother had just promised the white man.

Chapter 12

The stables were empty by the time Red Eagle returned, the horses and their riders already amassed under the canopy of dogwoods that stretched between the cornfields and the cabins. The dogwoods' blossoms formed a billowing white cloud over the commotion of townspeople milling around the loose formation of riders, handing up packets and bidding each other good-bye and good luck. Red Eagle passed a pair of dogs that barked their protest at being tied to a tree away from the excitement.

Among the riders, Red Eagle nearly did not recognize Romaine when she passed by, riding a sturdy chestnut bay. In a rough calico dress and a tattered cord bonnet, Romaine wore her disguise convincingly. If he were to meet her on the path, riding alongside a young Muskogee, Red Eagle would assume the Muskogee to be one of those with a plantation along the Tensaw, and this woman his slave.

"That is a mighty fine horse for a slave woman," Red Eagle called out as she approached.

Romaine pulled her horse to a stop. "Did your mother have any advice to give?"

"No advice. Only her—what do you Catholics call it?— her blessing."

"Even better." Romaine adjusted her bonnet, somehow making the floppy piece of cloth stand at attention. "You better hurry. Mary was ready to ride off without you."

Red Eagle thanked Romaine and scanned the group for Mary. "For this, she needs me." They were tasked with the largest of the rice plantations down the Savannah River and then south along the seaboard. It was the most dangerous route, but Red Eagle was known by the innkeepers and ferrymen along much of the route and would be able to talk their way out of trouble. The runaways whose escorts spoke only a bit of English and had few connections were the ones in the greatest danger of being snatched up and taken to a magistrate. Some would not return.

Now delayed by half a day, Red Eagle wanted to wait until the next morning, but Mary insisted they ride out immediately. Mary was on a spotted appaloosa, built more for distance than speed, and Red Eagle on a larger roan. They had two horses trailing, allowing them to swap in a fresh horse whenever one of their mounts flagged. Mary's stamina surprised Red Eagle, then thrilled him. Here, finally, was someone who could keep up with him on the paths. By the fourth day, they were already at the Bowsman crossing on the Etowah River. The ferryman tilted his head to one side and looked the pair up and down as they dismounted. Red Eagle pulled Mary close to him and held a silver coin in front of the ferryman's eye. "Twice the fare for your trouble," Red Eagle said. He waited until they were on the other side and safely out of earshot before teasing Mary.

"He just wanted to make sure you belonged to someone."

"Don't get any ideas."

Over the next five days, Red Eagle and Mary fell into a rhythm. Upon rising each morning they went down to the water and bathed as was Muskogee custom, then ate a breakfast of cornmeal and whatever greens and berries they could gather. Then they rode, side by side whenever the path widened. Red Eagle learned that Mary and Sarah were too young when they were sold away from their mother to remember her, but they told stories about her anyway. Mary would say,

Our mother had a big head, remember?, and Sarah would say *Yes, and a big mouth that sang so loud.* Between them, they created a mother who sang, danced the calenda and spun candy out of cobwebs. "When I see our mother, I will recognize her," Mary said, certain that one of the freedom papers being distributed up near the Tennessee River would find its way to her.

On the days when Red Eagle knew of a tavern or inn where they could safely stay, it was usually well past dark when they arrived. Days when he knew there would be no inn available, Red Eagle would have preferred to stop while there was still daylight, improving the odds of shooting some game for dinner.

"We have plenty of salt meat still," Mary said. "There's no need to stop now."

"We should save our provisions when we can."

"You'll never let us go hungry. You're too good a shot for that."

That was true. Red Eagle with his bow could hit a turkey at a hundred paces. "We'll be on the run once we cross Roanoke River and start giving out papers. It'll be harder to hunt when we can only ride at night."

Unexpectedly, Mary turned her horse in towards Red Eagle's and leaned out of her saddle to kiss him. The horses snorted at the near collision. "You will do it easily. How far to Savannah?"

Red Eagle told her two days, but by riding through much of the night they were at water's edge by the next evening. They swam the horses across, careful to keep the papers dry, and tied them in a copse of elms. His heart pounding, Red Eagle led the way around the stone wall that lined the lawn.

A plantation house rose from the green glade, a stolid box of limestone blocks lightened by three rows of windows. They found a double line of small cabins behind the main house. Red Eagle hung back as Mary selected one and crept inside. For what felt like hours Mary crisscrossed the lane from one cabin to another, skipping some, lingering at others. She was grinning ear to ear when she returned to him. Without a word, taking care not to break a single twig, they made their way back to the horses and continued north.

Mary directed them to a plantation twelve miles away. "They said there is a man there who's been making plans." The two reprised their roles, Red Eagle on watch and Mary as the enlistment officer of an army that did not yet exist. In the second cabin Mary found the man scheming escape and left him extra papers for the three others he claimed were also ready to run. Satisfied by their night's work, Mary acquiesced to using the remaining hours of darkness to find a place to hide and sleep.

Five nights and sixteen plantations later, they arrived at a small rice plantation. Red Eagle dismounted to examine the path snaking its way from the back swamp into the rice paddies.

"This place is not worth the danger, no more than a hundred people," Red Eagle said. "We should pass over this place."

"A hundred hardly seems small," Mary said.

"Further on, we'll have larger schools of fish."

"Don't these hundred deserve a chance as well?"

Red Eagle swung himself back up into the saddle and turned his horse back towards the road. "We have no leads here. I'm being careful."

"I'm not." Mary untied the follow horse from her mount and squeezed her legs. Her horse sprang forward along the levee towards the plantation house visible in the distance.

Mary urged her horse into a cantor. She wasn't trying to lose Red Eagle, but she also did not want to waste any time discussing whether this plantation or that one was large enough to look for recruits. At the field's edge, Mary paused to consider her next move. There were only two small cabins in the row near the main house, too few to house the number of people necessary to work even the small fields behind her. Another of the buildings must be quarters for those without favored status. One had a chimney from which a wisp of smoke curled. Mary decided to start there.

She listened outside the door and was glad to hear voices talking. Recent experience taught her it was better to walk in on people talking than on people sleeping—the nick on her arm from the woman who sprang up from her bed with a long nail still smarted. Mary pushed open the door and stepped inside to find a single room, sleeping pallets arranged in six tightly spaced rows that ran the length of the floor.

"I am looking for Romaine the Prophetess," Mary said. This was the opening line of a gambit perfected over the last few days. "I have come a great distance to find her. Does anyone here know where to find the Prophetess from the revolution in Domingo?"

As she guessed he would, the largest of the men seated in the small open space at the front of the room rose and beckoned she come in and close the door behind her. "What brings you here? Speak low. There is no need to wake the children."

Mary waited until a group gathered around her. "Have you not heard? The Prophetess is here. She is raising a battalion to join her forces to the west."

A murmur shot through the crowd. "What forces?" someone asked. "Where in the west? Tell us!"

Mary told her tale of Romaine the Prophetess, here to spread the slave rebellion from the sugarcane fields of Saint-Domingue to the rice plantations in South Carolina. She was seven feet tall, swinging a sword personally blessed by the Virgin Mary. The rebel camp she was building in the middle of Muskogee country was stocked with a thousand stand of muskets and an endless supply of powder and shot. Mary swelled her own cavalry numbers to two hundred and gave all the cavalrymen pitch black stallions that snorted fire. Mary watched the faces around her as she talked. Some were excited, others skeptical, still others alarmed. Mary paused when she found what she was looking for: one of the young women had her chin drawn back in a mix of fear and disgust, her eyes shifting left to right as she calculated what she might gain.

"The Prophetess has placed a curse," Mary said, her eyes boring into the young woman. "Should you speak a word of this to your master, you will die in childbirth and all your children will be sold away, your name forever forgotten." Mary swept her attention back over the crowd. "Who is ready?"

A young man with slight, sloping shoulders stood at once. Hands immediately reached up to pull him back down. "Sit down, fool," the man to his right hissed. "It can be a trick." A hubbub erupted, voices arguing whether Mary's sudden appearance was a trick or a chance.

"She's a witch, don't listen to her."

"Who's she with? We've never seen her before."

"We'll be caught before we even reach the river."

"Even if there *is* an army, they have cannons? I don't think so."

"Worst of the patrollers are Indians. How do you know those Muskogees won't turn around and sell you?"

"We need some time." This was an older woman with grey speckled hair and a broad, windswept face. "To gather provisions, get a compass, say our good-byes. There are dozens of things to do before we set out." She sounded calm, like she was already sorting the list in her head and assigning people to tasks.

Mary swung around and jabbed a finger at the older woman. "You! Yes, you're the one. You will lead the way."

The older woman raised her left eyebrow. "Is that so?" she said slowly.

"How many will follow you?"

The woman said without pause, as if she had been thinking on the question for years, "Six."

Mary took the woman by the hand and walked her out of the workmen's house to the edge of the woods where Mary's horse waited. Red Eagle waited alongside his own horse. He pulled a map out of his saddlebag and explained its markings.

When Red Eagle was satisfied the woman understood how important it was to destroy the map if they were caught, he selected freedom papers to match the woman's description of her six person group. "This one says Abraham, from Charleston," Red Eagle said, pointing to the 'A' in the name. He was manumitted by Neil Alston."

"Abraham from Charleston, freed by Master Alston," the woman repeated, her brow furrowed in concentration. "And where is Abraham going?"

"He is headed north to Baltimore, to start a new life there."

"He's a bit off course. And with five others, all free as well?" The woman grinned at Red Eagle's pained silence. "Be not afraid—I won't let us be caught. The patrollers are still searching the roads leading south. The slaves who killed the governor are headed to Florida." The woman peered closely at Mary, a bit of her grin still on her lips. "You don't know anything about that, do you?"

Mary smiled back at the woman and shook her head. "Maybe I've heard a rumor. The governor was killed by a slave?"

"By his own driver, can you believe it? He was known for being loyal to his master. Finally turned on him, they say. You think that's true?"

"Almost true but not quite," Mary said. "I hope you get to meet him and ask him in person. Someday soon."

The woman gave a slight, careful nod. "Someday soon." She stood motionless as Mary and Red Eagle mounted their horses to leave.

At the end of the levee, Mary turned around in her saddle and saw the woman was still there, no bigger than Mary's thumb. "Godspeed," Mary said under her breath, and turned her horse downriver to find the next plantation.

Ellison was hard at work alongside Jeremiah and others skinning a felled pine of its bark when the first runaway appeared at the edge of town. He was a strong-looking young man named Albert, with unusually large ears and hands. He told of having been marched down from Virginia to Savannah two years ago to a dealer who then sold him sight unseen to a planter in the Southwest Territory near Knoxville. There, a week ago, a free Black man appeared at their sleeping quarters in the dead of night and offered a map and papers to anyone willing to run south, to *here*, a dot on the paper. He was told there would be a musket and a meal waiting for him.

The next morning another runaway appeared, huffing as if she had in fact run the entire distance from Fancy Buff. Her name was Sara, and she reported there were nine others half a day behind her. She had the thin handsome face of a fox, her eyes darting all around her in disbelief. "Nine others," she repeated. "The child's ankle might be broken." She had to be coaxed to eat a meal before she turned around to go bring them in. Three of the townspeople from Hickory Ground set off with her on horseback.

When Sara reappeared with her nine fellow runaways, they were greeted by the triumphant smell of charred meat. Four large hogs hung over the pits, two sisters chattering away in Muskogee as they turned and basted the meat with a new sauce created by James. The concoction of tomatoes, vinegar, and sugar molasses coated the meat in a sticky sweetness that melted into the seared edges of the slow-roasted pig. James prepared a plate for each of the newcomers, setting the food before them as if they were royalty. Of the nine, Romaine noted with some consternation, only two were of fighting age.

But then more runaways arrived at a greater clip, some-times alone but more often in groups of three or seven or a dozen. On a cool and drizzling day, forty-six men and women appeared out of the mist. They were an entire coffle from Virginia, sold as a lot in Richmond and shipped by boat to Wilmington. From there, they were headed inland when the coffle was ambushed. The men and women decided as a group to follow the map one of the ambushers had, and here they were.

"There were three drivers?" Red Eagle asked. "You are certain they are dead?"

The older man who stood at the front of the group nod-ded, confident. "We weighted them with stones and rolled them into the river. Two of them."

"And the third?" Red Eagle asked.

"Escaped but wounded. No way he made it back. Too much blood gone out of him."

"If he made it back the entire South Carolina militia will be here in half a day. You did not cover your tracks, did you?"

"We did what we could," the man said, chastened.

As the numbers swelled, Romaine conferred with Ote Emathla, Hickory Ground's swaggering war chief, about which of the runaways should be given instruction in the fighting arts. Anyone who desired to learn, Romaine argued. Ote Emathla hesitated, worried the warriors of Hickory Ground, already wary of joining forces with strangers, might balk if the group included women. Romaine raised an eye-brow, very high. At that instant, Mary rode up, pointing a pistol at Romaine and Ote Emathla.

"You don't even flinch," she said, pulling her horse around, "because you know I have no powder."

Romaine's raised eyebrow fell into a furrowed brow. She reached up and pushed down the barrel of Mary's pistol.

"People are getting impatient," Mary protested. "We need to practice loading and shooting if you want a cavalry that can do more than wave an empty gun around."

"The runaways are already eating their way through the corn bins," Romaine said. "We can't do the same to the gunpowder. Deerskin does not bring as much in trade as it once did. It's taken Hickory Ground years to build up this store of ammunition." At Sehoy's insistence, most provisions at Hickory Ground were held in common. This included the corn, as it was in all Muskogee towns, but also salt and ammunition. Romaine knew from experience how closely the runaways were being watched by the townspeople, calculating whether these newcomers were adding or subtracting from the common stores.

So when the first group of ten runaways—seven men and three women—presented themselves to Ote Emathla for training, Romaine was glad that the grizzled warrior sent them into the fields and directed them to tend the emerging stalks of corn, turning wood ash into the soil and scouting for signs of earworms.

The next day, Fanny arrived with her ten-year old twins, the broadside advertisement announcing their auction folded in behind the map that had passed from hand to hand three times before reaching hers. Jack from the Holloway plantation in Georgia braved the dangers of the vast and dark Okefenokee Swamp. At the King plantation on the Flint River, Edmund, Frank, Jack and James made a pact of mutual aid and, on the next moonless night, ran together west. From outside of Natchez, the same pact was made by Sancho, Frank, Martin, Abram, Absalom, and Gabriel. All six survived their journey east, though Absalom who suffered dysentery, survived only barely. From North Carolina, it was the woman Chastity who insisted three others from the Jernegan farm risk an escape. The foursome arrived the same day as Fanny Goode, who rode in on a hag nearly as old as her.

A month after Romaine returned from her distributions along the Gulf of Mexico coast, a group of men and women enslaved by the corporation of Panton, Leslie & Company made their way from Pensacola. They numbered thirty-five adults, five children, one babe in arms, and sixteen horses. The horses were in exceedingly fine condition; the humans' general condition was only fair. Red Eagle took the string of sixteen new horses and presented them to Mary.

"I thought your cavalry might have some use for these."

Mary's eyes widened at the string of horses. "Which plantation is missing their horses?"

"Not a plantation, exactly, a trading house. The largest one, Panton." Red Eagle stopped himself before he revealed his uncle McGillivray's role as a partner in the firm. "Come to the ball field. My cousin is giving a lesson in ground fighting today."

"Which cousin? You have a hundred cousins," Mary said, only half listening as she examined the teeth of a dark bay. She performed drills with her cavalry every day, and the sight of fifty horses wheeling in unison under the morning sky brought many recruits to the stables asking to join. She now had three times as many would-be riders as she had mounts. These horses from Pensacola looked healthy and strong, and she was eager to see how they rode.

"Ote Emathla."

This caught Mary's attention. "You think he'll open the powder magazine today?"

"Come make the case yourself. My cousin likes your spirit."

Ote Emathla, tall and lean, demonstrated how to swing a war club into position as a defensive block. Well-built young Muskogees ran onto the field to demonstrate first a leg lock, then a shoulder throw. Ote Emathla had the strongest of them stay, pairing them up with runaways of equal size. The runaways had moves of their own to teach—a sweep to bring down a larger man, a quick move to slip out from being straddled. The wrestling turned serious enough to leave blood on the ground. Edmond, who ran from a plantation on the Flint River, nearly lost an eye to an overenthusiastic eye gouge. The injury thrilled him, his enormous hand covering an eye and a grin as he howled in pain.

When the group paused their exercises to eat lunch, Ote Emathla joined Mary and Red Eagle at the side of the field.

"You've come to ask again for powder," Ote Emathla said to Mary through Red Eagle.

Mary smiled her acknowledgement. "For the horsemen, at least."

"It's not the guns that win a battle," Ote Emathla said.

"But they certainly help," Mary replied.

Ote Emathla laughed. "When we can win without guns, then the gun is a help, yes. Otherwise, it's a crutch."

When Ote Emathla finally allowed the first barrel of powder to be opened, a large crowd of both runaways and townspeople gathered for the occasion. They stomped the ground and sang an upbeat chant. Ote Emathla invited Romaine to take the first shot.

"This is your powder," Romaine said.

"A gift," Ote Emathla said. "Can you hit that tree?" He pointed to a pine marking the far corner of the field.

"I can try," Romaine said. The tree was tall and straight, with a thick trunk three armspans around. "For that, I prefer a cannon."

Ote Emathla laughed. "No need to fell it. You need only hit it, to give us something to cheer."

Romaine accepted the musket presented her. It was worn

but well kept, with gouges in the stock and a polished lock. Romaine half-cocked the piece, doing her best to ignore the crowd as they murmured, some of them seeming to negotiate bets. Loading and swinging the gun to her shoulder, Romaine pulled it to full cock. She looked down the barrel for the tree.

To her surprise, Red Eagle stood between her and the tree, grinning. He held something the size of a man's head.

"Romaine!" Red Eagle shouted. Using both hands and bending his knees, Red Eagle heaved the melon skyward. Romaine pointed the gun upwards and pulled the trigger.

The melon hung in the air, paused in the moment between ascent and descent. Romaine knew instantly her shot had gone far to the right. She scolded herself for allowing Red Eagle to distract her. Her target was the tree, not the melon. She should have—

The melon exploded.

The crowd went wild with delight.

In the joy of the live fire exercises that ensued, only three people blasted off bodily digits. Four if Thomas's little toe lost under the rim of a barrel of powder was counted. Taking after Mary's example, the horsemen leaned low and shot their pistols at full gallop. Red Eagle's heart hammered with excitement whenever Mary and the rest of the horsemen rode by, balanced over their saddles in a half-standing crouch, sighting down an outstretched arm.

Every other night, the runaways made their way across the river to Hickory Ground's town square, where the townspeople called them *simanoles* and challenged them to wrestling and throwing contests. There was a horse race in the twilight, along a dangerous course Red Eagle created around the square and through the town. There was a great deal of singing, each clan taking a turn. Jeremiah and the other men who came from Governor Pinckney's plantation took a round as well, prompting the group from a plantation on the Savannah River to offer up a work song. When dinner was served, it was once again pots of sofky, the cornmeal stew burbling softly over the common fire. James threw down his bowl and declared he would perish if forced to eat another spoonful.

Romaine recovered the bowl as it clattered on the ground. "Not to your taste, my friend?"

"There *is* no taste is the problem," James said.

"Let's prepare them something with taste, then," Romaine said. "We can return some hospitality. I don't think Red Eagle expected quite so many runaways would make their way back." They were now up to nearly three hundred, according to the palm-sized notebook Romaine carried around with her, taking notes with a pencil stub the way her daughter Louise-Marie did once upon a time when Trou Coffy had still been a coffee plantation.

James scowled and listed all the implements and ingredients he lacked to make a proper banquet.

"Sofky it is, then," Romaine said, returning her attention to the axe-throwing contest. Red Eagle was winning, to no one's surprise, but a slender, solemn-faced man who'd recently arrived from near Knoxville was closing in on the lead with a string of bullseye throws. "Sofky forever."

James made a face. "We would need to first build me a better kitchen."

Romaine noted there was more than enough talent among the new arrivals to make light work of such a thing. At Trou Coffy, the regularity of the evening meals eased tensions among the recruits, but it was the special feasts that made them all feel part of the same revolution. Might a banquet of some sort help bring together the Muskogees and runaways into common cause? Romaine warmed to the idea. A feast to celebrate the arrival of the thousandth runaway, she decided. A roar went up from the crowd at another bullseye and the solemn faced thrower raised his arms in triumph.

"Any cook can make brulee in Chantilly," Romaine said. "Only a true genius can do so here. How many stoves do you need? Twelve? Fifteen?"

The runaways—the simanoles—were glad for the challenge. Jeremiah in a flash of ingenuity rejiggered the turkey traps in a way that hauled in nine birds where before they had caught only one. Not to be outdone, the young men of Hickory Ground sharpened their arrowheads and disappeared into the forest. They returned with rabbits and ducks of all sorts. Fishing nets and dozens of hook poles brought in rainbow trout and walleye. There were leeks and sage, rosemary and onions. Mushrooms abounded. The children filled their baskets with the dark pungent wood ears, black trumpets and mushrooms James had never seen before, leathery waves stacked in dense layers one atop the other. One of the smallest children came back with the largest prize: enormous morels that smelled like a deep, deep cave. The next evening, Ellison rode back whooping like he had won a high stakes mile. He leaned down from his horse and held out a crabapple. James gave him such a joyous slap on the shoulder the man fell off his horse and twisted his ankle.

Young Opothleyahola came with an offer from his father, who had a few years before left the town to fence off his own plantation: there was milk from his cows if they wanted it.

"Crème fraise!" Mary yelled. She ran to get a jug.

The day of the feast, James made whisks, a dozen delicate instruments made of bent strips of river cane, and recruited an energetic young warrior to work this strange new instrument at the appointed hour much later in the day. A series of long tables covered the square in an arrangement new to the town. Elders raised their eyebrows at the design, unlike anything done for a green corn dance or penance feast or even a war feast.

When the first dishes were set on the tables, the townspeople paid them little heed. Red Eagle tried to ease James's glowering displeasure by explaining that the food was not the primary purpose of a Muskogee feast. The purposes of a feast, in descending order of importance, were to flirt, to dance, to gossip, to honor whatever was the excuse of the gathering, to recover the pot borrowed by your cousin last month and never returned, to complain to friends about your family members, to complain to friends about their family members, and then, finally, to eat.

James snorted at the explanation and ordered his sous chefs to overturn the largest kettle. He banged on its side with a spatula, then sent out the rabbits, each stuffed with mushroom cornbread and drenched in a scorched leek sauce, and the turkeys, smoked and sliced, laid in a black apple and morel broth, topped with crisps of white sage. The men and women of Hickory Ground stopped their chattering and sampled the meats. A murmur of surprise rippled down the tables. Then out came the bowls of strawberries topped with crème fraise. Sehoy's sister, Sophia, scooped up the crème with her fingers and laughed as she tasted it. A shout went up, and someone started a song. It grew loud, a joyful sound.

Sehoy finished her berries, leaving the crème untouched in her bowl, and turned to Red Eagle. "No matter how delicious your friends make their milk, don't allow the hoarding of cows when you take my place as the beloved grandmother."

Red Eagle grinned and pat his mother on the shoulder. "It will be a long time before that happens," he said. A long time meaning never, he thought. He had no intention of taking his mother's place.

"Alexander would have enjoyed this feast," Sehoy said. Her face took on the look it always did when she said her brother's name, one eye tender, the other glaring. "When I pass on, Hickory Ground cannot come under his influence."

"It will not," Red Eagle said. "I promise."

"A promise you can keep only if you take my place."

"I am not…" Red Eagle swallowed his fear and forced

himself to finish the sentence. "I am not going to take your place as the beloved grandmother." He had never declared his refusal so plainly.

"You will," Sehoy said.

"You have nieces," Red Eagle said. Even as he said it he knew the argument was worthless. He was the one born Sehoy. He was the one gifted with the temperament and talents of the Sehoys before. Most important, he was the one the town expected to take the place of his mother.

"It is your obligation." Sehoy stated the fact simply.

"We have done well like this," Red Eagle said, voice rising. "You are not dying for many years. We can discuss it later, when we are closer to the time."

Before his mother could respond, a bell rang to announce the arrival of another runaway. Red Eagle touched his mother's shoulder again, this time in silent apology, and made his way to the freshly built welcome cabins where new arrivals spent their first days and nights.

Romaine was already there, standing beside the table where new arrivals were served a bowl of sofky, turning then from runaways to simanoles. The man seated at the table tonight was enormous, with thighs thick as a regular man's waist. His face was hidden by the bowl tipped up to shake loose every last drop. When he lowered the bowl, still slurping, Red Eagle saw he was dark-skinned but not African.

"I welcome you to Hickory Ground," Red Eagle said. When the man stared at him without returning the greeting, Red Eagle turned to Romaine.

"Where's he from?"

"He won't say."

"I did say," the man said. Switching from English to a peculiar-sounding Spanish, he continued, "I'm from everywhere and nowhere. What is this woman's name?" He spoke very fast.

"This is Romaine," Red Eagle said.

"Had to make sure, always check twice, as Denmark says. Trust nobody. Find Romaine. And here you are." The man stuck out his hand and offered a broad, gap toothed grin. "I am Nikola the Giant."

"As Denmark says," Romaine repeated, a grin spreading over her face. "You know our friend the first mate of the *Golden Dragon.*"

"Oh, first mate no more," Nikola said, pumping Romaine's hand. "It's *Captain* Denmark now. And golden no more—it's the *Black Dragon* now." Nikola finally let go of Romaine's hand. "He got wind of your camp and sent me to find you."

Denmark, Nikola the Giant reported in his scattershot Spanish, took the helm when Mai took her profits and bought a handsome mansion on the Ashley River, half a day's ride upriver from the town. In return for a share of future profits, she gave the ship to Denmark, who renamed it and ran up the skull and crossbones. The first ship he chased down was a British merchantman, where Nikola was a midshipman. Given the chance to join the *Black Dragon* crew, Nikola did not hesitate.

The British ship produced trunks of pearls and ivory tusks, barrels of gunpowder, and chests packed full of guns. From the next ship, a French brig, they liberated casks of wine and wheels of cheese, then turned the vessel into a man-of-war, switching out the four-pounders for eighteen-pounders. The captain of the next unlucky ship took one look at those eighteen-pounders and surrendered without a fight. A straggler of the treasure fleets, its hold was stuffed with silver and gold. In this way, one ship became two, two became five, five became a squadron. Word spread quick as a school of minnows and now men (and a few fearsome women) of every nation, tribe, sultanate, and kingdom had been clamoring to quit their posts to join the crew of the dreaded pirate Denmark.

Nikola completed his tale with a dramatic sweep of his ham-sized hand and waited for applause.

"Denmark has found a way to build us a navy," said Romaine, laughing. Nikola's news lifted Romaine clear off the ground. She had not been so filled with faith since the Virgin Mary stopped talking to her. "Is there more to the message he sent you all this way to deliver?"

"Yes, yes, madame, yes," Nikola said. "Not to you. A message to James. James Hemings. If he is here."

"He is here," Romaine said, "but busy cooking at the moment. Can I take the message to him?"

Nikola shook his big head no. "To James only. Captain Denmark said."

"Let's take Nikola to find James, then," Romaine asked Red Eagle. "There's much to celebrate tonight." An army of simanoles and Muskogees, a navy of pirates, and perhaps even love as well. Romaine prayed silently for all of it to be so as she led Nikola outside. Let it all be abundantly true.

Chapter 13

The morning after the feast, James sat hunkered on a stool and watched with bleary eyes as crows picked through the bits of food fallen to the dirt. His head, stuffed full with cotton from too much rum, throbbed and spun from the message an enormous Russian had delivered a few hours earlier. *Captain Denmark*, the man had recited from memory, one English word placed carefully after another, *was in control of a fleet of ships. The captain very much desired to treat his crew to a good meal. Would James please follow him*—Nikola, the man called himself—*back to satisfy the captain's deep and persistent craving for the great chef's talents?*

"You must be a very good cook," Nikola said, moved by the passion of his own performance.

"The best," James replied. The message made him at once furious and ecstatic. How dare Denmark ask James to drop his affairs and follow an abnormally large, pock-faced man, a complete stranger, to who knows where, to cook for a bunch of *pirates*? The nerve of the man. So cocksure of everything. So willing to demand, so insistent on getting exactly what he wanted. In this instance, for James to come to him. Why in the world would James do such a thing?

He asked Nikola when he intended to leave.

"As soon as you are ready," Nikola said.

James kicked at the dirt, his head in his hands. This was him getting ready.

At the far end of the square, Romaine appeared, covering ground in long, fast strides. A slightly built young Muskogee man that James did not recognize walked with her, hustling to keep up.

"Good banquet, James." Romaine did not break stride. "Come with us. We've been discovered."

James managed to rock a bit up from the stool, but could not work up the momentum to stand. He watched as Romaine and her companion veered off towards Red Eagle's compound. A moment later, Ote Emathla rushed into the square, rubbing the sleep from his eyes. He paused in front of James. "Trouble," he said. "You come." He offered a hand and pulled James up.

James and Ote Emathla entered Red Eagle's cabin as the Muskogee scout, his hands and unusually long legs trembling in the way exhaustion gives way to excitement, stumbled through his report. Two weeks ago, a pair of runaways had been caught crossing the Cumberland River carrying papers and a map. They were taken to Nashville, where they were held at the workhouse and whipped until they confessed before the magistrate they were not the people named in the deeds of manumission they carried. The pair had tried to destroy the map but enough bits of it were recovered to give one of the runaways a spot to point to when, after eighty lashes, he was given the opportunity to avoid the next ten.

The Muskogee scout had a source inside the courtroom. This source described for the scout how the magistrate rustled through the *General Advertiser*, counting twenty pages of runaway notices where normally there was one. The magistrate first ordered the pair of runaways returned to their owners, who were better situated than the court to mete out appropriate punishment, then ordered the printing and delivery of militia muster notices. The judge advocate of the district militia, a tall and aggressive man named Jackson, volunteered to lead the contingent. He promised to march out before the end of the month.

"Together with the simanoles, we will destroy them," Ote

Emthla said. "We will meet them at the Tennessee and turn the river red with their blood."

Red Eagle translated for Romaine, and the Prophetess shook her head. "Surprise and momentum are our best weapons. If we reveal ourselves at the Tennessee River, we lose both."

"Hickory Ground must be protected," Ote Emathla said, stepping up to Romaine. "We are being attacked because of the simanoles."

"And we will fight alongside you, without hesitation," Romaine responded. "But we have only one chance to mount a surprise attack. We cannot waste it on a mere district militia."

"Defending Hickory Ground is not a waste," Ote Emathla growled.

Romaine nodded and touched Ote Emathla's shoulder. "I did not mean that," she said. The Trou Coffy camp had been hosted at her own coffee plantation. When it fell, her wife and children were killed. It was too much to ask that Hickory Ground, an entire town, risk the same fate. Still, what Romaine needed to bring the Saint-Domingue uprising onto the mainland was a port city. And she could not see a way to overtake one—whether Charleston, Nuevo Orleans, or Philadelphia—without the shock and chaos that comes with the element of surprise.

Mary emerged from the back room. "You said Jackson. The man leading the militia. Say his full name."

The scout jumped a bit, startled by Mary's sudden appearance. "An-diyu Jackson."

"It's him," Mary said. She turned to Ote Emathla. "I'll go with you."

Romaine's hand on Ote Emathla's shoulder squeezed tight, to steady herself. She felt the room suddenly cool and exhale, the way the mountain air of her coffee farm lightened ahead of a storm.

"There is much to consider," Romaine said to Mary.

"Andrew Jackson is on his way to Hickory Ground. We can stop him. What is there to consider?"

Romaine looked to the scout. "Do you know how large a force he will have?"

The scout shook his head no, looking dismayed at not being able to give an answer.

Red Eagle spoke up. "If they are coming to recover their runaways, it will be only a few people, just enough to carry back their property. At most, they will send thirty men."

"We are not turning anyone over when they arrive," Mary said.

"Of course not," Red Eagle replied.

"But nor will Jackson leave here empty-handed."

Red Eagle scratched his nose. "They will leave when they see they are outnumbered a hundred to one."

"He will come with more than thirty men," Mary said.

"He may come with less," Red Eagle replied. "I will ride up to the Tennessee to see. I may be able to turn him around there, convince him the map is a fake. He knows me as an honest horse trader—he may trust me enough to believe me."

"If Jackson does come with enough men to stage an attack, we will need more ammunition," Romaine said slowly as she ran a dozen scenarios through in her mind's eye. "Can you secure more powder from Wewocau?"

"They do not hold powder in common."

"Coosada?"

Ote Emathla shook his head.

"Tuskegee?"

"Perhaps, but not without a long negotiation. This is not their concern," Ote Emathla said.

James spoke up. "Denmark probably has powder." He picked at a fingernail as all eyes turned to him. "Pirates tend to have that sort of thing, don't they?"

"Our friend Denmark." Romaine suppressed a smile.

"Was this his message to you, that he has gunpowder? Is he ready to give it over to defend a Muskogee town?"

"You can come ask him yourself," James said. "That oversized Russian is taking me to see him."

"It's decided, then," Mary said. "Red Eagle and I go to meet Jackson at the Tennessee River. Romaine and James go get from Denmark a wagonload of powder."

Red Eagle started to correct Mary—no one said she was coming, and he was going up to take a look, not "meet" him, which he imagined to Mary meant "behead" him—but stopped. He looked around the semicircle crowded in his cabin. They seemed to all be waiting for him to give some kind of affirmation that was not his to give.

"I will go bring my mother."

Sehoy, alas, could not get out of bed.

When Red Eagle propped his mother up into a sitting position, her breathing eased only a bit.

"You must *breathe*," Red Eagle said.

Sehoy shot a look to let him know she was in need of air, not useless advice. She turned her attention back to gathering up the strength for her next gasping breath. It was as arduous and tricky as pulling in a monster catfish on too thin a line. Sometimes she caught a breath; other times it skimmed away. Red Eagle knelt next to his mother, miserable for being useless.

For the last few years, Red Eagle had noticed some difficulty in his mother's breathing, but when did it become so bad? How long did these bouts last? Red Eagle sank back on his heels. He had never seen his mother in such a state—he had only known her to be sturdy as an oak, indomitable.

The door opened, and three of Red Eagle's nieces tumbled in. Tallassee cried out "grandma grandma grandma!" in a happy way that let Red Eagle know it was not an unusual occurrence for the girl to find her grandmother sick in bed. The oldest, Millie, carried in a small leather cask of water and handed it solemnly to Red Eagle.

Sehoy shook her head, and Red Eagle set down the cask. Her breathing was easier, and some color crept back into the folds of her cheeks. She smiled at Tallassee, who was now sitting on the edge of the bed squeezing Sehoy's toes one by one, yelling "grandma!" with each squeeze. And it was working! A speck of life seemed to enter the old woman with each squeeze of her toe.

After accepting a sip of water, Sehoy waved her hand and said to the room, "Go now." Tallassee gave one last pump and scrambled up to kiss Sehoy, then the sisters filed out as abruptly as they had come in. Alone again with his mother, Red Eagle told her the scout's report.

"You will do well," Sehoy said. She spoke so low Red Eagle had to lean in to hear her. "Has Alexander come?"

"No. Do you expect him?"

"He will feel I am weak. His great talent, sensing opportunity."

"He is at his Tensaw plantation," said Red Eagle. "He will not have…"

"Do not let him take it." Sehoy paused to gather her breath.

"Uncle McGillivray is only doing what is best for the Muskogees."

"He believes this, but he is wrong."

Red Eagle felt a wisp of panic start to swirl in his gut. "We will have time to discuss this later."

Sehoy folded her hands around Red Eagle's. "This battle will not be done for a long time. I will not be here to tell you how to fight it. I can only tell you who to fight alongside."

"You believe in Romaine," Red Eagle said.

Sehoy nodded. "And Mary. You have a gifted heart, my

child. It is pulling you down the right path." Sehoy pushed Red Eagle's hands gently away, releasing him. "Be not worried, Red Eagle. You will know what to do. You have already won."

Chapter 14

Aboard the *Black Dragon*, Denmark's quarters glowed like the inside of a well-cut ruby. Light from the skylight and stern windows bounced off the mahogany table's broad expanse. Around the room, every wood and metal surface was oiled and cleaned to a high shine. The light green walls, trimmed at the ceiling with gold beaded molding, gave the room an airy feel despite the heavy bookcase that ran the length of the wall opposite the windows, its shelves lined with leather bound books. The door to the sleeping chamber stood open. Visible inside was the bed, luxuriant in Witney blankets and a silk covering filled with down collected—according to the merchant ship captain who wept as Denmark's men carried off his furnishings—from the nests of Norwegian eider ducks. Madras chintz curtains hung from the bed's four posts.

"You've come into the life of a French Duke," Romaine said, looking around. "You are still a Jacobin at heart, I hope."

Denmark gave a salute to Nikola the Giant and indicated with a push of his hand it was time to leave. As the Giant pulled the door closed behind him, the stern planes of Denmark's face broke into an enormous grin. Here were James and Romaine both. Denmark did not know who to greet first, or how. With an awkward nod of his head, he invited them to sit.

James strode past the offered chair and took Denmark's face in his hands, planting a kiss on the captain's lips. "You fool," James said. "Sending that ugly behemoth to fetch me, like I'm some chaise longue you want for your collection."

"No one would mistake you for a chaise longue, James Hemings," Denmark said, "whatever that is." Glad but also embarrassed by the display of affection, Denmark broke free and turned to Romaine. "I hear you have an army."

"And you a navy," Romaine responded.

"Of sorts. Discipline is a bit lax."

"And my army is not quite one yet. We are low on ammunition."

A look of understanding passed over Denmark's face. "You've come to the right place, my friend."

At that moment, equidistant north of Hickory Ground, Red Eagle and Mary were belly down in the mud of a low bluff overlooking the Tennessee River, peering through a curtain of cattail. Across the water, white militiamen tramped up and down the riverbank, looking for a good place to make camp for the night.

"How many?"

Mary counted nineteen and Red Eagle added another six for stragglers still to come into camp. The men themselves were not impressive, dressed in tattered shirts and ill-fitting breeches, but they were well armed. Each man carried a long-gun, and some carried two. All had pistols strapped to their legs and stuck in their belts.

At the edge of the river a tall man on horseback watched over the activity. Mary recognized her former master by the way he sat in the saddle, crooked and favoring his right hip. She had an urge to leap up but Red Eagle's hand on her arm reminded her to stay hidden. If she was alone, she thought, she would swim across, pull Jackson down from his horse with her bare hands, and drown him in the river before anyone could stop her. But she was here with Red Eagle, to make a count, so Ote Emathla could know how many warriors to assemble at Hickory Ground to convince Jackson to return to Nashville. Also, the river was wide, and she did not know how to swim.

"You really think ten to one?"

Mary nodded. "Bringing out two hundred fifty warriors to greet his twenty-five is the only way he'll leave empty handed."

Mary shifted her weight onto her elbows and pulled herself closer to the edge. She could not take her eyes off the ugly curve of Jackson's back. He sat with such arrogance atop his horse, as if the magnificent creature would not even exist if he was not there to ride it. She watched him move back and forth along the river, directing his men by pointing his pistol to where he wanted the fire made and the horses watered.

Her sister's laugh suddenly filled her head, a birdlike trill that Mary had found ridiculous in life. Sarah laughed at how mockingbirds on a branch flicked their tails up and down, as if they were losing their balance. She laughed when a noise in the night frightened her. Whenever Mary won a race and recounted her victory to her sister, letting her know she was safe until the next contest, Sarah should have sighed with relief but laughed instead. How many times had she snapped at her sister to stop that twittering, there was nothing to laugh at? What would she do to hear it again? Mary reached behind her and touched the small of her back where her own pistol was stowed. It was too long a shot across the river.

One of the stragglers came out of the woods and made a beeline to Jackson, covering the distance between them in long, easy strides. Jackson leaned down from his horse, and the two men talked. When Jackson gestured across the river, the new man turned to consider the ferry crossing where Jackson pointed. Mary squinted for a better look. Next to her, Red Eagle made a startled noise and started to stand up. Mary instinctively reached up and dragged him back down.

"What is it?"

Red Eagle felt all the blood rush out of his head, leaving an empty cavern swept clean by a cool wind.

Mary stared at Red Eagle, not understanding the look of horror on his face.

Red Eagle struggled to find words. "That's my uncle. McGillivray."

"What's he doing with Andrew Jackson?" Mary demanded.

Red Eagle shook his head, trying to coax forth a coherent thought. Was his uncle here to intercept Jackson? Was he trying to dissuade Jackson from continuing on, or to distract him by sending him down a different path? Or was McGillivray helping Jackson find his way to Hickory Ground? Red Eagle tried to glean some clue from how the two talked with one another, but the men now had their backs turned and Red Eagle could not see their faces.

Mary repeated her question, more insistently, an edge of anger in her voice.

"I do not know," Red Eagle managed. He watched McGillivray leave Jackson's side and disappear back into the forest. "It could be anything. He might be trying to…" Red Eagle stopped as McGillivray reappeared. This time, there were two white men with him. Behind the trio, another five appeared. Then another five. Then another four. Then a cluster of twenty. Then another twenty-two or three. Then dozens more. Among them, four horses pulled a wagon, where a pair of cannons glistened side by side. Behind the cannons, more men streamed out of the forest. They made their way down the long riverbank, a swarm of ants, too many to count.

Captain Denmark unrolled a map that covered nearly the entire table. *La Louisiane et Pays Voisins* was six beautifully printed broadsheets pieced together to form a seamless representation of the New World. The rivers, ports, and towns were colored in by hand; more roughly sketched annotations noted errors, new discoveries, and changes in populations and governance.

Romaine and James looked on as Denmark placed a Bristol green wine glass on the corner of the table, off the map in the direction Florida pointed. "The island of Domingo," he said, "where the uprising has become a revolution." On the northern corner, past the edge showing Wilmington, Denmark put another glass. "Philadelphia, capital of the United States of America." A third glass he set atop Nuevo Orleans. "Whoever controls Orleans controls the Mississippi, and so the continent." The final glass went over Charles Town. "Now called Charleston. The Holy Land of slavery."

"If the choice was yours, Romaine."

"Spain is weak, and a base in Nuevo Orleans will encourage Cuba," Romaine said.

Denmark jumped in, "Yes, but with Charleston there is rice. If we secure Charleston, the rebels in Saint-Domingue will no longer be beholden to France for food..." He and Romaine quickly fell into their familiar banter practiced at a more modest table, at James's restaurant. They debated back and forth for twenty minutes about which of the port cities to attack before James interrupted.

"The pot's already boiling," James said from the depths of an armchair that sulked by the door to the bedchamber.

Romaine and Denmark looked over. "What pot?"

"Do you remember the time the governor demanded a banquet for the pardo militia?"

"We had five hours to make it, when we needed five days," Romaine said.

James nodded. "The camp at Hickory Ground has been discovered. You don't have time to decide on the perfect dish."

Denmark cocked his head. "And so instead...?"

"You lay the best ingredients you have on hand and use your skills to make what you can out of it."

"Denmark laughed. "And sometimes it turns out to be ngombo, magic."

"Other times it's inedible," Romaine said.

"Have I ever made anything that was anything less than good?"

Romaine laughed, then immediately sobered. "I may not be as good a general as you are a chef. I lost Leógâne in the end, you remember."

"My first soufflé fell too. But it taught me yes, it *is* necessary to beat the eggs to the end of human endurance." James's eyes went soft with longing. "My second soufflé was perfection."

Captain Denmark folded his arms and leaned back, a bemused smile flickering on his face. "Tell us then, James, what are our finest ingredients?"

"That is a question for Romaine. I'm just a chef."

Romaine considered the map. "Where are the rest of your ships?"

Denmark pointed to a curving cove not far south of Charleston. "Port Royal, here."

"And the simanole army is here, with the Muskogees at Hickory Ground." Romaine drew a line westward across the map and laid her finger at the convergence of the Tallapoosa and Coosa Rivers.

"Charleston, then," Denmark and Romaine said at the same instant.

Romaine looked more closely at the map around Charleston. "We have runaways from all these rivers. Cooper, Ashley, Edisto, Savannah. These are rice plantations."

"The numbers?"

"Four, five hundred enslaved on the bigger ones. It's the same as Saint-Domingue's sugar plantations—the numbers are far in our favor. They need only be rallied."

"Are these ingredients good enough, James?" Denmark tapped the tabletop, smiling.

"It never hurts to add something unexpected. A spice of some sort, a dash of something strong."

Romaine found the Cooper River and followed it inland three inches until it became the Congaree. "The maroons of Congaree camp, here. Or here, the Savannah River maroons, if we can find them."

Denmark jumped in. "The swamps around the Santee River are full of maroon camps."

"Which is why Charleston's defenses are so strong," Romaine said.

"So what we need to do is…"

James leaned back and sank into the plush of his armchair, half listening, half dozing as Denmark and Romaine planned their attack. His work was done. He thought suddenly of his sister Sally, as a little girl, sitting on her heels in Ursula's kitchen. Her face was serious as she picked through a bowl of dried beans, doing her best to help. "Thank you," James said quietly. "Let's get your children free another way."

At the Tennessee River, Red Eagle forced himself to continue counting as the light dimmed with the setting sun. He made a mark in the ground for every twenty men. He stopped only when the string of supply wagons rolled in and it came clear: this was why it had taken them so long to make the trip from Nashville to the Tennessee. They were not twenty men travelling extraordinarily slowly. They were two thousand men travelling at the pace of the supply wagons, laden with a month's worth of food, an enormous cache of ammunition and nine cannons.

"We have to hurry." Red Eagle crawled back off the bluff, pulling Mary with him. She came reluctantly, keeping her eyes on Jackson as long as she could. "Stop trying to figure out how to get across the river to shoot him, you can't do it. We have to get back home." Once in the cover of the trees, Red Eagle broke into a run, and Mary followed without a word. Andrew Jackson was not headed to Hickory Ground to demand the return of a few runaways. No, Jackson had with him a full-sized militia, ready to lay a siege. They intended to make an example of the town, send a warning to any Muskogee town that dared to harbor fugitives. They intended to destroy Hickory Ground, utterly and completely. Red Eagle untied his horse and leapt into his saddle like a man possessed. His horse felt his urgency and sprang forward, trot to cantor to gallop. Whether Mary was following him or not, he did not know, nor did he wonder. A single phrase beat along to the rhythm of the hooves as Red Eagle raced down the trail—*get home get home get home.*

Chapter 15

The setting sun covered the walls of Sehoy's meeting room in a wash of orange-yellow. In the center of the room, Hickory Ground's beloved grandmother leaned back in a reclining chair, with Romaine, Ote Emathla, and Mary seated before her. Red Eagle stood beside his mother, holding her hand and willing her to breathe.

"Your war council," Sehoy said to Ote Emathla. Her voice was thin as onionskin.

The war chief nodded his acceptance.

"Tell us what you know, my child."

Red Eagle recounted what they saw at the Tennessee. Two thousand men, two hundred horses. Nine cannons, a dozen supply wagons. A full complement of arms and an unknown quantity of ammunition. He estimated they were at this point ten days away.

Sehoy turned to Ote Emathla. "And our defenses?"

"We can build a palisade," he started.

Sehoy interrupted. "In ten days?"

"The simanoles will help," Ote Emathla said. He glanced at Romaine and waited for the Prophetess to nod at Red Eagle's translation before continuing. "The warriors and simanoles combined, we can match them in numbers. If we strike out tomorrow morning, we can meet them at Tallassee."

"Leaving Hickory Ground defenseless."

"He will not attack a town of women and children," Ote Emathla said.

Mary did not wait for a translation. She understood enough Muskogee to be able to respond, "He will. I know him—he does not see the world like you, or me. He has no..." Mary looked to Red Eagle for help finding the right word.

"Soul," Red Eagle tried.

At Sehoy's suggestion, they went around the room, and each person said what they considered the best course of action. Ote Emathla wanted to set out immediately and attack as far north of Hickory Ground as possible. A successful ambush would break the militia and send them scurrying back to Nashville. Mary quickly agreed with Ote Emathla.

Red Eagle pointed out that an aggressive ambush, if unsuccessful, left Hickory Ground in too much danger. He thought it was better to build a palisade around Hickory Ground and, with the help of the simanoles, defend the town. If Jackson was forced to lay a siege, he would eventually lose, since neighboring towns were sure to come to Hickory Ground's aid.

"And you, Romaine?" Sehoy asked.

Romaine forced herself to hold Sehoy's silent gaze as she considered her response. When Red Eagle brought them to Hickory Ground, Sehoy could have sent them away to Florida. Instead, Sehoy had welcomed Romaine and the others, stretching the town's provisions to keep everyone fed. As the runaways came in, it was Sehoy who insisted Ote Emathla help Romaine train those of fighting age alongside his Muskogee warriors. The beloved grandmother of Hickory Ground did not waver even as the trickle of runaways turned into a flood, exposing her town to the risk of attack by white slave-owners. Now the risk was coming to pass. How could Romaine do anything but help protect the men, women and children of Hickory Ground from attack? An attack brought on by Romaine's own actions?

Yet, in the captain's quarters of the *Black Dragon*, she and Denmark had devised a plan to march on Charleston and secure the port city's surrender. Such a plan required those enslaved on the rice plantations along the rivers near Charleston to pick up their scythes and join the march. It required good timing with Denmark's pirates, and good luck in general. Most of all, it required surprise. That surprise would be gone if they revealed themselves by fighting Andrew Jackson's militia here in Muskogee country. In Charleston, there was a chance to spread the uprising from Saint-Domingue to the United States, and from there through all of the West Indies and perhaps even South America, wherever Africans and Indians were being held in bondage.

"Our fight is not here in Hickory Ground," Romaine finally said. "We are commanded by the greater spirits to march on Charleston."

Sehoy struggled to sit up in her chair. Red Eagle helped with a hand on her back. "Your greater spirits have come to you, Prophetess?"

The Virgin Mary had not once visited Romaine since she sailed away from Saint-Domingue. Not as a possession, certainly. Nor as a voice inside her head giving instructions of what to say and what to do. Not even as a flicker of the supernatural in a copse of trees or the morning light. But she had come to Romaine in other ways, had she not?

"She has," Romaine replied. "When I was defeated in Saint-Domingue, she came to me in my prison cell, in the form of Denmark at the grate. In New Orleans, she came to me in the form of young Mary, a girl with the courage of a lion. But she has spoken most clearly here in Hickory Ground, in the form of a beloved grandmother, who sees how the river here flows to the whole of the world."

Romaine focused all her attention on Sehoy and continued. "For months now, we have eaten your corn and taken shelter on your land. You offered us sanctuary, at great risk to your own security. There are those among your people who ask why you have put them in such peril. Why offer refuge to runaways? Why provoke the Americans?" Romaine stood and started to pace the floor.

"They are right to ask such questions. Is it because we command a navy vast as Spain's armada, or a Mongol army of a million men? We do not. Is it because we are envoys of a powerful empire beyond the sea, one that will come to the Muskogee's aid in this time of trouble? We are not. We have no empire behind us. We have no king, no chief, no army beyond what you have helped us make here.

"We are a nation yet unborn. We are a people not yet made, and already we are in great debt to you. We will repay this debt, in blood and in full. But let us repay it in Charleston. The Tennessee militia is a fist, meant to deal a killing blow to any threat to slavery. It is a powerful fist. But it is only a fist. Let us slip under it and strike at the heart." Romaine stopped her pacing and looked around the room.

"If we win in Charleston, it will be to finish the battle the Muskogees started eighty years ago, alongside the Yamassee, to return the land to its rightful keepers. In Charleston, we will take the harbor that has received a thousand slave ships and make it our own, to send rice to Saint-Domingue. To send warriors to Cuba. To send children home to Accra."

Romaine knelt beside Sehoy, to address her eye to eye. "My people in Saint-Domingue are in rebellion," Romaine said. "It is a rebellion that the greater spirits—yours and mine alike—wish to spread."

"You believe our people are in common cause." Underneath Sehoy's labored breath was a hum of high regard.

Romaine nodded. "Not only in this time of uprise, but after as well, in peace."

"It will be a long time to peace," Sehoy said.

"We will fight one day longer than them. Your people and mine together."

"A more perfect union." Sehoy could not smile but her eyes shone. She leaned back against Red Eagle's hand. Her weight against his hand was no more than a bird's nest. She seemed ready to fly away. Sehoy turned to Mary. "What do you desire?"

"I have a score to settle with the general from Nashville," Mary said quietly.

"Andrew Jackson will give chase," Romaine said. "In Charleston, you can avenge your sister and a hundred more like her." Even as she said a hundred, Romaine knew she was far off the mark. An image formed in her mind, the years rolling out before her like a ribbon unspooling into the distant future. On the ribbon were inscribed the names of enslaved men and women one after another, year after year, too many to count. "Ten thousand more," Romaine guessed. "A hundred thousand." Surely it could not be too many more than that, but the ribbon continued to unspool, every name a life, every life a joy crumpled by suffering.

Sehoy turned to Red Eagle. "This is how the universe wishes to bend." She closed her eyes, and the room went silent. After a long while Red Eagle leaned in to assure himself she was still breathing. As his ear came close to her mouth, she spoke.

"Ote Emathla, go with Romaine. The warriors and simanoles are a single force. Charleston is our destination."

The furrow of Ote Emathla's brow deepened, but he nodded his assent. He unfolded his arms and clutched his thighs. "And what of the women and children of Hickory Ground?"

"We walk into the cane and disappear," Sehoy said. "South to Coweta, Chehaw, Oconee, Eufaula. Our kin will take us in." She opened her eyes and looked around the room, pausing at each person to confirm they were in accord. "It is time, then. We have none to waste."

The war council dispersed and spread the word. There was a lull of quiet disbelief as neighbors visited on silent feet to gape at one another to confirm the news. Was it true? It was. Even the mockingbirds fell silent. Then Hickory Ground erupted in an explosion of activity. By nightfall, every family had their utensils, clothes, and bedding packed. Which treasures to bring and which to leave. Some scraped a bit of dirt from their home square into a jar. Through the night, the townspeople scooped what corn and flour remained in the common bins into sacks, gathered the animals, loaded the tools, and said their good-byes the best they could to ancestors buried in the earth beneath their homes.

Red Eagle waited until all were ready to leave before going to wake Sehoy. A bit more sleep would let her rest for the upcoming journey. They had a bed prepared for her in James's wagon, facing backwards and arranged so she could get one last look at Hickory Ground as they rolled out of the town.

Red Eagle was proud of how quickly and well the town had carried out Sehoy's command to evacuate. He bent to wake his mother. She was very, very still.

"I will not go." She spoke without opening her eyes. "This is my home."

"This is home for all of us." Red Eagle felt a wisp of panic ride his breath to slip into his skull. "You have ordered everyone else to leave it."

Sehoy shook her head, a tiny movement left and right. "Too weak."

"We have James's wagon."

"Wagon—for the powder."

"The wagon is waiting for you. Everyone is waiting for you."

Sehoy's eyes flew open. "Tell them *go*—you—" The strain was too much. Sehoy's eyes fell back into her head.

Red Eagle resisted the urge to grab his mother's shoulders and shake her. She was the one ordering the dispersal of the town. She was the one sending him to Charleston. This was not the time for her to die. However badly she felt, she could not leave him now. This was an argument Red Eagle was determined to win.

"Your wagon is at the front of the—" He fell silent as his mother struggled to lift a finger. Red Eagle reached out and folded her one hand between his two.

"They will not go without you," he said, more gruffly than he intended. He pressed his hands into hers, afraid his heart might shatter if he let go.

"You say—you are—"

Red Eagle understood his mother's command as perfectly as if she had said them aloud. He was to see the evacuation through. He was to go to Charleston and lay siege if necessary, then lay claim to the town. He was to take her name and position. He was to become again a Sehoy. The fourth. The most beloved.

Outside, a woman yelled out for someone to get her water bladder back from her nephew. A child cried to be picked up. Head down, Red Eagle listened to the noise of a town preparing to disappear. They were waiting, he knew, not for Sehoy, but for him.

The sun threw a sudden slice of light onto the far wall. The day was nearly done. "I will," Red Eagle finally said. He raised his head. This was one last bargain he would make with his mother. "But not as Sehoy. You are the last of the Sehoys." Red Eagle squeezed his hands together to make clear this was his final position. He expected acquiescence from his mother—wasn't she dying, after all?—but instead felt her redouble her effort to speak.

Summoning the last of her strength, Sehoy somehow lifted her head and turned to face her most troublesome child.

"Sehoy is *in* you," she managed. She fell back on the pillow and smiled, just barely.

The beloved grandmother of Hickory Ground was satisfied at her victory.

By nightfall, the women and children of Hickory Ground were gone, a vanishing as sudden and complete as a flock of blackbirds scattering into the midnight sky. One scout raced eastward to find Denmark at his ships. Another went to find the maroons. They urged their horses faster and faster yet.

All those who remained gathered in the square, warriors and simanoles shoulder to shoulder in a densely packed circle around the central fire. Somewhere near the fire, hidden from Romaine's view, a set of drums started a rhythm. Romaine felt every ear turned to the sound of the drums, waiting for a signal. Shoulders rubbed against shoulders. Hands sought out their neighbors' backs and elbows. A group of young men rested their hands on the shoulders of the people in front of them and bounced up and down, the bangle of shells around their ankles clinking in time with the drums. A crag-faced woman nodded and mouthed a chant. The drums grew suddenly louder and a shout went up.

This war chant led by Ote Emathla was unknown to Romaine. Yet it was also as familiar as a smell from childhood, forgotten until now. In Trou Coffy, the uprising had started with a night like this one, everyone gathered near a bonfire to transform themselves from slave to avenger, to join themselves from many into one. Romaine had preached from the tabernacle under an inverted cross, shouting assurances from the Virgin Mary that they were chosen and beloved, on their way to certain victory. Here in Hickory Ground, Romaine was a foreigner, with no prophesy to offer. She watched and listened from the outside edge, glad to see the simanoles hanging back as she was, respectful of the Muskogees' gods and traditions.

But then the drums increased their tempo, and a woman's voice shouted to the heavens and started a prayer. Romaine recognized the voice as belonging to a woman—Betsy or Rebecca was her name, from a Carolina plantation—who a month ago had started leading songs among the simanoles.

Her voice rolled and tumbled with the power of a rain-swollen river, one refrain sung after another, calling to the beat of the deepest drum. There was an answering shout in Muskogee, then another. Romaine caught a glimpse of Ote Emathla in a low crouch around the fire, gesturing to his warriors to answer the woman's shouts, to join him as he adjusted his song to her rhythm.

Romaine plunged into the assembly. Bodies turned to make way, hands slapping her back and shoulders as she made her way through the crowd. Romaine recognized the mood that the multitude of hands seemed to be passing on to her—it was a feeling both somber and elated. They moved to the pulsing of the drum as a single animal, ferocious, throbbing with life. Romaine knew this feeling. Their powder horns were full. They were warriors, every one, overflowing with courage. They were ready to march.

Two days later, there remained in Hickory Ground only Red Eagle. The funeral pyre he built at the center of the round-house stood waist-high above the embers of the common fire. He hummed a mourning song as he covered the body of Sehoy with a blanket of kindling. After he laid the last of the sticks across her neck, Red Eagle examined his handiwork. His mother seemed to be taking a nap to escape the afternoon heat. Red Eagle moved a lock of hair off her forehead. Grief closed in on him like a cave.

He knelt with a bundle of old war clubs, some cracked from use, some from age. The handles he placed into the embers. The heads, red with paint, some with blood as well, he leaned against the pyre. There was a long pause, then the crackle of wood catching fire. It was time to go.

Red Eagle was at the roundhouse door, waiting for his eyes to adjust to the daylight, when a figure appeared at the edge of the square. The solitary figure cut through the empty square and, spotting Red Eagle, quickened their pace. Red Eagle recognized the lumbering gait of his uncle McGillivray.

Alexander McGillivray yelled something as he approached, thrashing his arms around like a drowning man, both slow and frantic, gesturing this way and that around the square. Red Eagle made no movement even as McGillivray grabbed him by the shoulders and demanded to know where everyone was. He wanted to know what Red Eagle was doing in the roundhouse. He wanted to know what was going on.

"Sehoy," Red Eagle said. He pulled himself loose from McGillivray's grip and backed away two steps.

"Sehoy what?"

"Is dead." Red Eagle felt the edges of his thinking sharpen and take shape. "Why are you here, uncle?"

McGillivray stared as if he'd been punched in the nose. His sister. His eyes ricocheted wildly around the square until they settled back on Red Eagle. "Impossible. How can...? Why is there no one here?"

Rather than answer his uncle's sputtering questions, Red Eagle repeated his own. Displeasure bubbled up as he asked it. "What are you doing here?"

"The whole town is empty," McGillivray said. "And the runaways' camp, gone. Did they turn on the town?"

"You are riding with the white militia."

McGillivray stared at Red Eagle.

"Tell me why," Red Eagle demanded.

McGillivray clenched his jaw and shook his head. "I am my own man. I do not ride with any militia."

"I saw you at the Tennessee. You were friendly with the general."

This time it was McGillivray who backed away, cautious of his nephew's uncharacteristic ire. "I spoke with Jackson, yes." Red Eagle's scowl prompted McGillivray to take another step back. "I came to prevent an attack on Hickory Ground."

"How do you intend to do that?"

"The militia will leave peacefully if Sehoy returns the runaways."

"You know she will never do that."

"They are on their way with two thousand men. She will do it when she knows their strength. She will do it to save Hickory Ground." McGillivray's voice faded as he realized he was talking as if Sehoy was still alive. His sister was dead. She will not be the one to save Hickory Ground. Hickory Ground was already gone. Sehoy, immortal, was dead. He looked around, still searching for an explanation. "Did the runaways do this? I warned you slaves away from their masters are dangerous."

"The simanoles are not the danger," Red Eagle growled. He wondered whether his uncle could hear his heart hammering in his chest.

"I came to warn you," McGillivray insisted.

"You thought there was a deal to be brokered. How much did Jackson pay you for your services?"

McGillivray tried to hide his surprise at the accuracy of Red Eagle's accusation. "Hickory Ground is my home too," he stammered. "I am doing what I can to save it."

"You chose the wrong side."

"This is not about choosing sides. This is not..." McGillivray seemed suddenly exhausted. "Sehoy." How he called his sister's name was, in turn and all at once, bewildered, disdainful and despairing. "Where is she?"

Red Eagle tilted his head towards the center of the roundhouse. McGillivray looked in, struggling to understand the contraption built atop the common fire. "This is not how—" McGillivray did not complete his thought, pushing roughly past Red Eagle into the roundhouse. The crackling turned into a low roar as the fire climbed. McGillivray glanced down at the body of his sister and then craned his head back to watch the smoke as it rose out of the opening.

He looked up in exactly the same way he had looked up at Andrew Jackson as the two talked on the riverbank. That day, Jackson had leaned down off his horse towards McGillivray like they were old friends. Red Eagle's rage at his uncle's deals suddenly exploded.

Without thought, Red Eagle sprinted into a vicious tackle that sent McGillivray crashing to the ground. McGillivray tried to roll away, but Red Eagle was on top of him in an instant, swinging a fist into his uncle's face. Knucklebone cracked against jawbone. The pain of it sent Red Eagle's other fist flying. McGillivray turned his head, and Red Eagle's blow bounced off his skull. McGillivray pulled the rest of his body over to the side, taking Red Eagle with him. As the two slammed back into the dirt, McGillivray scrambled to secure his fifty-pound advantage. Red Eagle found himself pinned to ground, one arm trapped beneath him. With his free arm, it took all his strength to push himself out from under his uncle. Red Eagle jumped to his feet and, in a single motion, turned and kicked McGillivray hard in the gut.

McGillivray grunted, and Red Eagle waited for his uncle to pull himself off the ground. Instead, McGillivray put up a hand in surrender. The gesture incensed Red Eagle. He looked around for a stick, a rock, anything with heft enough to split open his uncle's skull. There were the war clubs under the pyre, but they were all in flames. Except one. Red Eagle dropped to the ground and thrust his arm into the fire to retrieve the one. A noise behind him prompted him to spin around and swing the club up in defense. It struck his uncle's hand, wielding a hunting knife. Red Eagle scrambled back and fell into a crouch. The piece of wood in his hand felt dried out, too light to strike a killing blow.

"Come now, Red Eagle." McGillivray stood bent at the waist as if wounded.

"You tried to stab me in the back."

"To keep you from killing me." McGillivray squinted

at Red Eagle and then at the knife in his hand, calculating. He made a show of placing the blade back into the sheath strapped to his leg. "I did not come here to fight you, Red Eagle."

Behind McGillivray, the flames finally reached the funeral pyre, and in a flash the whole pallet exploded. Red Eagle watched the spire of flames shoot upwards, a creature from another world seeking the air to breathe in this one. A blanket of rain clouds threw a grey shadow across the opening in the roundhouse, and a low grumble of thunder rolled across the far sky. It started to rain in slow, fat drops. Red Eagle stood from his crouch and looked up at the water coming through the smoke hole. But it was too late. The fire burned in full. No amount of rain would quench it now. Red Eagle tossed his fighting stick into the fire.

Red Eagle closed the space between him and McGillivray and lay his palm on his uncle's cheek. Blood was already purpling under the skin. "You are right, uncle. My fight is not with you." When did his uncle grow so old, the grey hairs on his proud head overrunning the black, the lines in his face etched so deep? He watched McGillivray's eyes soften a bit, though behind them the weighing and measuring continued. Red Eagle rubbed his thumb along the edge of the brightening bruise before turning to leave. He was out of the roundhouse and in the square when he heard his uncle call after him.

"Red Eagle—"

Red Eagle turned to respond. This was his uncle, still, who raised and loved him as much as his mother had. His mother's brother had chosen one path, and Red Eagle was now far down a different one.

"I will see you in the next world, uncle. I pray there you and I will be at peace."

"Red Eagle—"

"You, uncle, you will call me Sehoy."

Chapter 16

It was the grey hour before dawn when Romaine and her contingent arrived at the Congaree River. The Prophetess sat astride her dark bay horse, her hair loose in a halo around her head. Beside her rode Mary, with two dozen horsemen in formation behind them. It took a long while for the remainder of the simanoles and warriors to amass at the river's edge. James brought up the rear, leading a pair of horses loaded down with pots and provisions.

"They understand the dangers of welcoming us?" Romaine asked the scout, a young man named Little Warrior, thin as a stick, eyes too big for this head, head too big for his body. Little Warrior struggled to find the English words until his fellow rider Samson, a simanole run away just a month ago from this very part of South Carolina, nodded yes and pushed forward to answer Romaine.

"The king of the maroons has a message for you: come without delay. They want to join our army."

Little Warrior pantomimed raising a gun. Samson nodded and added, "They want you to know they have guns of their own."

Romaine hesitated. The swamps that protected the maroons were more water than solid land, filled with panthers and poisonous snakes. There were tales of mud pits that grabbed the unlucky traveler and sucked them underground, horse and all. The mosquitoes came in hordes thick enough to kill a deer. But it offered a path to Charleston that the paddyrollers were loath to frequent. And the Congaree maroons knew their way around not only these cypress swamps but all the swamps that stretched up and down the coast. Romaine leaned down from her horse to lay a hand on Little Warrior's head, then Samson's. It was as likely as not one or both of them would be dead by week's end. They were brave young men eager to fight, because they saw only victory. They knew of no other possibility. "Lead the way, then."

The way was slow going. The trail that wound along the sliver of higher ground started out well but soon shrank to the width of a footpath, forcing the horses to step gingerly into the sucking muck off to the side. They came to a wide lake. It was shallow enough to walk across, a terrifying journey as one alligator after another slipped down from the water's edge and disappeared under the surface. At the other side there was no path to guide them. Samson and Little Warrior used the tangles of roots and branches to zigzag from one soggy patch of land to the next. Twice they paused the procession to confer with one another, assuring themselves they were still on the right path.

When the contingent finally arrived at the maroons' camp, Samson and Little Warrior were greeted like returning heroes by the group waiting at the island's edge. Romaine's army stamped at the solid ground beneath their feet, giving thanks and cursing with relief. Before them were thirty or so structures, handsomely built and elevated a few feet off the ground, with porches and shingled roofs. The cabins formed a perimeter around what seemed to be a field of sweet potatoes and squashes. There were drying racks draped with strips of venison. A pair of guitars leaned against the stump of a cypress tree. A child of six or seven shook himself loose from his mother's grasp and ran up to Romaine, offering her a look at something in his open palm. Romaine leaned down and saw it was a baby alligator, snapping at the air with its tiny razor-sharp teeth.

Romaine and Mary went to confer with the king. The si-manoles played cards and tossed dice. The Muskogees placed bets as Jeremy of Savannah and Moses Brown arm-wrestled and leg-wrestled and head-wrestled and finally, exhausted, thumb wrestled. Henry, the best shot among them, polished the muskets and checked his teeth in the shine. James studied the communal kitchen and was impressed by its tidy efficiency.

That night, well fed and surrounded by swamp, even Ellison relaxed and fell into a deep, dreamless sleep. Romaine made her way to where the creek fed into the river and found a log to serve as an altar. She knelt in the sand to pray.

We have faith in you, Mary of Nazareth. We have faith in one another. We have faith in victory.

It was the prayer from Trou Coffy, at the start of the up-rising.

We have faith in you, Mary of Nazareth.

It was the prayer she said every night since then.

We have faith in one another.

It was the prayer that, since the betrayal at Léogâne, received no answer.

We have faith in victory.

Until now.

It was faint, barely a quiver in her bones. But the feeling was unmistakable: this prayer had a listener. Was it the Virgin Mary? If it was, she was very far away. But she was most certainly there. Romaine could feel her straining to hear.

We have an army of runaways, we have ships, we have the Muskogees by our side. She pressed her forehead against the log to keep from leaping up. *Where have you been? We are ready for your return.* Romaine prayed as hard as she had ever prayed. *We have faith in you Mary of Nazareth.*

A disturbance in the air prompted Romaine to open her eyes. In the darkness it took her a moment to locate the bird as it glided silently down to the water's edge. It was a heron of a sort Romaine had never seen before, tinged in blue with a wisp of beard falling from its neck. It tucked its wings and regarded the Prophetess, waiting for her to continue her prayer.

We have faith in one another.

The heron listened.

We have faith in victory.

The heron heard.

The next morning, with the maroons of Congaree Swamp leading the way, the simanoles and Muskogees set out downriver. They arrived at the first rice plantation not long after the break of dawn. Through the morning fog, white columns shimmered around the side and front of the owner's house.

Romaine turned to Elliot. "Are they up?" Her hair was bound up in her white turban. The crystals sat patiently in the folds of the cloth, ready to reflect the sun.

Elliot knelt and put his hands to the ground, as if trying to draw an answer up from the soil. "Awake, yes. Not yet in the fields."

Mary rode up with fresh horses. The one she'd selected for herself was the largest one, a black-coated animal with intelligent eyes and thick, powerful hindquarters. "Wait until you see them hesitate," Romaine instructed Mary. "If you bring in the cavalry too early, you lose your persuasiveness."

Mary smiled and bared her teeth. "Be assured, we will be persuasive."

Romaine turned to the firestarters. "Set the fires and fall back immediately. Work fast." The firestarters adjusted the packs on their backs, stuffed with bundles of longleaf pine needles. At Romaine's nod, they sprinted ahead and disappeared, crouched low in the brush.

The drummers tapped the tips of their fingers lightly on their drumheads, impatient to start. Romaine turned back to gauge the readiness of the rest of the army. Large red pennants hung from a dozen poles, marking the head of each column. The warriors wore their own swaths of red cloth as sashes or headdresses or simply tied around their waists. A sea of eyes stared intently at Romaine, waiting for a signal. Romaine waited until she smelled smoke, then raised her arms, palms up. A shout rose from the crowd. The drums took up the shouts, beating out a rhythm.

Romaine shook the reins and trotted her horse towards the plantation house. The wind brushed against her face and, behind her, she felt the surging energy of the army as they ran to keep pace.

The morning mist dissipated as they burst through, and, in an instant, the plantation house came into focus. Its perimeter glowed red, the handiwork of the firestarters. Every five feet, a burning bundle sent up a spout of flame. Plumes of grey smoke showed where the fire had already caught hold of wood. The sight of the plantation house on its way to ashes sent a wave of joy crashing through the army. A group burst past Romaine and veered off the path, intent on being the first into the house.

A hundred yards beyond the plantation house were two neat rows of one-room buildings. This was where they would find victory or defeat: by how many of those enslaved declared themselves free and joined the army.

Romaine was past the plantation house when she heard the first gun fired. It was immediately answered by six, seven, eight blasts, and the Prophetess knew the master was shot dead.

The drums grew louder, the beats of separate instruments finding their way to one another to merge, louder and louder, until they boomed in a deep and steady rhythm, without hurry. *Gather your things and come*, they seemed to be saying, *we have someplace else to be.*

Men and women opened their cabin doors and peered out into the dawn's early light. Elliot turned his horse into the lane separating the cabins. He trotted down and back and down again, shouting *freedom, freedom, freedom*! He pointed to the burning house. He pointed to the simanoles and warriors gathered in a mass behind Romaine. At Elliot's exhortation, some rushed out, others hung back. Among those who hung back, some looked towards the plantation house, thick with smoke. Some squinted their eyes and scrutinized the army, counting, assessing their weapons. Some seemed to be searching for someone in particular among the men and women emerging from the cabins, to know the decision of their lover or friend or brother. Someone caught a neighbor's worried look and passed it on across the lane. Hesitation spread from one person to the next. Elliot waved his pistol like a whip, furious, intent on driving them to their freedom.

Then there was a thudding of the earth that beat out beneath the drums, and all eyes widened and turned to look past Romaine. By their mouths gaping open, the Prophetess knew it was Mary behind her. Mary and her two hundred horsemen.

They galloped down the lane in two perfect columns. People leapt back to not be trampled. A toddler found himself trapped in the middle of the lane, eyes wide in wonder as the horsemen streamed around her. At the end of the lane, the columns split left and right, doubling back behind the row of cabins without breaking stride. The two columns galloped around to the open field between the army and the cabins and reformed as a single line. The horsemen turning their mounts to face the slave cabins. Romaine walked her horse up to join them as the horses tossed their beaded manes and pranced in place, frustrated at being held in formation.

An old woman stood outside the farthest cabin and threw up her hands, her face a laughing shout of triumph. In one hand she held a stick. If it had once been a cane, it was now a mighty staff. She waved it above her head and thrust it all around, yelling as she pointed. Romaine was too far away to hear her words, but the old woman's tone carried across the distance clear as a trumpet blast: the moment was now; there would be no other chance tomorrow; this was the glory of the coming of the Lord. She limped from one cabin to the next, yelling without cease. Anyone who hesitated she rousted with a slap of her stick.

They all enlisted, every one. The warriors tore strips off their red clothes and gave them over to the new recruits as armbands and headbands.

At the next plantation, the owner fled, a flash of white atop a chestnut bay. A clutch of Mary's cavalry gave chase but came back empty-handed. The next five plantations the army found to be abandoned by their owners. Where the plantation homes were built of wood, the firestarters did their work. Mary and her horsemen made their encouragements. They hitched up the abandoned wagons and loaded them heavy with ammunition, bolts of cloth, cakes of salt, casks of oil, bins of flour. Everyone came—even the children, even the lame—and now the new army was so swollen Romaine ordered a forward contingent to break off and move ahead, to keep the pace as morning turned to afternoon.

It was the hottest part of the day when they met their first meaningful resistance, at Belvidere plantation. A white man dressed in his Sunday best, the buttons of his waistcoat shining and his thin brown hair combed neatly back, stood at his doorway with a rifle at his shoulder and two muskets behind him. His pants bristled with pistols. His rifle shot whistled through the center of the army without hitting a soul. In the time it took him to toss aside the rifle and prime the musket, a group of simanoles were upon him. One wrestled away the gun and smashed the butt of it into the white man's face.

A volley of gunfire ripped through the front hall, and the five simanoles standing over the dead slave master suddenly sprang into a dance, staggering and spinning, until they each sank in their own way onto the floorboards. Moses Brown hit the ground first, three musket balls in his chest. Next to him was Jeremy from Savannah, who saw his mother's face as he fell, all the smudges wiped away, clear as the day she was sold away. But when he crashed to the floor he could see only the smashed half of the white man's face, and that of his friend Moses Brown, eyes turned to glass.

Romaine shouted for the others to fall back, and they retreated to the edge of the lawn to wait for another volley. When none came, Romaine ordered the house set afire. The firestarters darted in, drawing a few shots that landed harmlessly in the dirt. Romaine lined her troops up to wait. For a long while, nothing happened as the wood planks smoldered. Then one caught fire, and another, and in an instant there was a waist-high ring of fire around the house. The flames rose from plank to plank, until the entire house was ablaze. As the structure filled with smoke, shouts and screams from inside made clear it was a full house. Those who had abandoned the last five plantations, Romaine guessed, had come here to make a stand. Now they were trapped, being smoked out. Their terror radiated out with the flames. The first to emerge from the smoke were the owner's sons. They fired wildly as they ran out, and some of their shots found a mark. The man who stood in front of Romaine to shield her uttered a small oomph before he fell, blood spouting from his mouth even before his body hit the ground.

As the others ran out, they were cut down one after another by Henry, who sat on a boulder and calmly fired away, trading his discharged gun for a loaded one after each shot. There were occasional pauses, the occupants of the mansion knowing with each attempted escape they were doomed. Yet the heat of the fire became only greater, and when they could resist it no longer, they ran out and were killed.

Then there was a long pause. Henry kept his gun pointed at the door for as long as he could, until he tired and let the barrel drop. When a small figure finally darted out of the side door, Henry swung his gun around to sight it. Romaine yelled for Henry to hold his fire. Two of the warriors rushed to the man and seized him by his arms. They dragged him to Romaine.

"You are not one of them," Romaine said.

Beneath eyes opened wide in horror, the man moved his mouth but no words came out. His chin trembled. He managed a quavering, "Postal service."

"You were caught here on your way out of Charleston?" Romaine asked, almost gently. Something in the building exploded, and the grey smoke that billowed behind Romaine turned black.

The thin young man nodded yes.

"You will return to Charleston," Romaine said. She sounded utterly calm, as if she was talking to a child about the structure of a coffee bean. "You tell them—" Romaine searched for the word the whites called the Muskogee. She needed her message understood clearly. " Tell them the Creek have risen. You tell them the savage Creeks have been joined by maroons and runaways. Say it."

"The Creek have risen," the man said.

"And," Mary prompted. She pushed her pistol under the post rider's chin.

"Maroons and runaways," the man managed.

"Thousands," Romaine said.

"Thousands," the man repeated.

"They showed no mercy," Romaine said.

"No mercy." The post rider squeezed his eyes shut.

"The plantations are all in flames."

The man glanced at the burning house to confirm. A bonfire roared out from each of the upstairs windows. "It is all in flames."

"The slaves seek vengeance. Everyone was slaughtered," Romaine said.

"Slaughtered."

"They tore out the slave master's heart and ate it," Romaine said.

The post rider's face was a mess of tears, snot, and sweat.

"Ride directly to Charleston and find the mayor to give your message," Romaine said. "If you pause along the way and we catch you, we will peel your skin from your bones one strip at a time. It is pain impossible to bear. You will beg us for mercy. Will we give it?"

"No. You give no mercy."

"And."

The post master repeated the words the best he could, the task made harder by a sudden attack of hiccups. It took him three tries before he could say the message through without flaw. When she was finally satisfied, Romaine nodded to the warriors holding the man's arms. "Get him to his horse and see him safely off."

Chapter 17

Thirty miles to the east—past the city of Charleston and past its port—the *Black Dragon* slashed through waves against the horizon, its sails stretched taut by a strong and steady wind.

On deck, Captain Denmark handed his ornate pistols to the ship's surgeon, a white man.

"Stand up tall, man," Denmark said. "No one is going to believe you're a captain if you slouch like a drunk." Denmark took the surgeon's shoulders in his hands and bent them back, bringing the man to attention. "Now say it like there's no other possibility: *No need to check the holds, let's talk in my quarters.*"

As the surgeon practiced his lines, the nimble young boatswain tied a rope around his waist and lowered himself over the side of the ship. With a pot of paint and a remarkably steady hand, the boatswain turned the pirate ship *Black Dragon* into the slaver *Speedy Profit*. Nikola the Giant ran up the American flag as Denmark gave the surgeon a few more encouraging words. When the port of Charleston came into view, Denmark went into his bedchamber and closed the door behind him.

Through the door, Denmark heard Nikola's booming command to drop anchor. Then, after what seemed too long a delay, his ear pressed against the hinges, Denmark heard men entering his captain's quarters. Even muffled, he could hear the waver in the surgeon's voice. Denmark stopped breathing, certain the customs agent was looking askance at the surgeon and examining the details of the ship's manifold. Perhaps the agent was already asking how it could be that such a large shipment from Virginia would be sent without pre-advertisements of sale. Or why the crew wore such a strange assortment of clothing. But then Denmark heard the clank of coins being dumped onto the table and a pause. Denmark exhaled. If they were counting the money, then the day was won.

Sure enough, there was the sound of exiting and a few minutes later, the surgeon flung open the bedchamber door, his face radiant with relief and triumph.

"I didn't think he would take it," he said. "He probably would have taken half."

Denmark smiled at his loyal surgeon's success. "If you're going to offer a bribe, make it a fair one."

"He said the same thing," the surgeon marveled. "Two percent of the cargo value, he said, a business expense." The surgeon paused, and his eyes shifted to the left as he made a calculation in his head. "Wow. You people are valuable."

Denmark opened his hand for his pistols.

The surgeon hesitated—just barely, but enough for both men to notice—before handing them back.

Denmark tucked the pistols into their holsters and, seeing Nikola the Giant at the door, waved for him to enter. "Any sign?"

Nikola shook his head no as he interlaced his hands and cracked his knuckles. "Nothing yet, Captain. I go ashore for news."

"No, we wait," Denmark said. The Muskogee scout who found him in Port Royale a week ago had passed along a simple message: the plan he'd made with Romaine was intact but much accelerated. Romaine and Red Eagle were splitting the army into two. One would march down the Ashley River, the second down the Cooper, burning plantations and sweeping up recruits along the way. Denmark's charge was to wait until he saw, from the deck of his ship, smoke from inside the city itself before unleashing his pirates.

Nikola frowned and jammed a zucchini-sized finger into his ear, digging for a better argument to go ashore. "I go in quiet, no one will know. They may be close already but have no fire. What then? I should go."

"If they are close, we'll see the fire." The fire had been his friend when two years ago they'd sailed into the harbor of Le Cap Français and found it ablaze. When Denmark ran through Le Cap's streets that day, choking on smoke, buildings burst into flames as he approached. The fires marked his path forwards and he found Romaine. The fires were sure to guide him again this time. Denmark corrected himself. "*When* they are close. We will be ashore soon enough, Nikola."

Denmark turned his attention back to the surgeon, who was sulking in the corner. "Polish up your speculum and saw, doctor. You're going to be a busy man once the fighting starts." The surgeon brightened, buoyed by the promise he would soon be extracting bullets and severing limbs. He excused himself and rushed off to do as Denmark bid.

Giant Nikola persisted. "And if no smoke? We do nothing? We are at the docks!" Nikola waved the leg of lamb that was his hand at the warehouses that lined the waterfront. "Rice, Carolina gold you say, must be worth something. Cotton too. No work at all to sack one."

"We are not here for booty," Denmark said. He tried to suppress a smile but succeeded only halfway. The Giant's enthusiasm for mayhem was always good for the crew's fighting spirit. The big man was easy to spot in the chaos that followed boarding a ship, and the crew knew that all was well so long as the Giant was swinging away. At the first sign of fire, Denmark decided, he would send down the Giant, let him be the first one down the gangplank. For such moments, Nikola had a double bandolier of skulls he wore in a crisscross across his bare chest. What a fright that would be to the Charleston gentry. "Who's on watch, Nikola? Let's all get some rest. Our friends will soon be here to burn down this most godforsaken place."

Chapter 18

Storm clouds stacked in the southern sky, masses of dark grey that pushed up one against another until the sun was blotted out. The air turned suddenly cool. A bullfrog started its bellows, mistaking the darkness for the fall of night. At each plantation, the front ranks of the army were now greeted by men and women waving scythes and hoes and sharpened sticks in jubilant welcome, their former masters having fled the grounds. At each plantation their numbers swelled, sometimes by a few dozen, more often by the hundreds. Romaine considered pausing the march. If they moved too quickly, Red Eagle and Ote Emathla—who were leading the army of Muskogee warriors down the Ashley River—would miss the rendezvous.

But at each plantation the triumph drove the drummers to increase their cadence and the excitement from the newest recruits pushed them all onward. It was not until they were nearly to the edge of the city that exhaustion set in and the pace slowed. They were at a plantation with a grand mansion but no rice fields. Oddly, the cypress forest surrounding the building was intact and had not been cleared for planting. There was no welcoming party of would-be recruits. The silence that greeted them spooked the troops. Romaine felt the lull in energy and ordered a halt to the procession.

"We should not delay," Mary said, dismounting. Her horse dropped its head as she stroked its neck, and in an instant the animal dozed into sleep, too tired to nudge for water.

"If we don't stop we'll throw off the timing," Romaine responded. The Prophetess watched the procession pull off the river road onto the broad lane that led to the mansion. Majestic live oaks, dripping with Spanish moss, lined either side of the avenue and spread their limbs across. "Red Eagle needs to find enough boats to ferry his warriors across the Ashley. He's not going to swim across."

"He could," Mary said.

Romaine laughed. "The rest of his warriors, then. The river is wide." Romaine needed Mary to wait. If Mary insisted on riding her horsemen into the city tonight, the thousands now filling the field would follow her without question.

"They would swim if they knew we would be in the city in an hour."

"Everyone needs a rest."

"I don't." Mary frowned. "We are only giving them more time to prepare. You're the one preaching surprise."

"They're expecting us by now. It's the Muskogees who will be the surprise. And Denmark." Romaine felt a rush of affection for this young woman who always wanted to hurry ahead. How would her girls have turned out if providence had allowed them to live a few years more, to grow into young women? Romaine turned away, to keep Mary from seeing the tears welling up in her eyes. "Your horse needs to be watered. Everyone needs to get what sleep they can. We move out before first light."

Romaine, with Elliot and Henry flanking her, went to scout the mansion. It appeared empty, but there was no way to know what lay behind the curtains covering the windows. Halfway up the avenue, there was quick movement in the back of the portico that spanned the second floor. A figure rose and walked to the front railing. Henry raised his musket. When the figure did not respond, the trio continued their approach.

Elliot had not visited this plantation while he was

Governor Pinckney's driver. He offered up all he remembered from overhearing bits of gossip. "Two brothers. They made their money in the islands." Something else tickled his memory. "But they sold it." The sale had made an impression on Mrs. Pinckney for some reason. What was it?

Romaine strained to see through the shadow that the setting sun threw on the figure at the rail. "Who was the buyer?" The light shifted through the branches and lit up a flow of fabric, a peacock brocaded down its front in gold and silver thread.

"A woman." There was something else that had made Mrs. Pinckney grab her friend's arm in excitement as she recounted the sale. Elliot stopped and closed his eyes to help him remember. "East Indian."

The figure leaned over the railing, a drink in one hand and a pistol in the other.

Romaine stopped and stared at Elliot. "An East Indian woman rich enough to buy a mansion on the Ashley, huh?" Romaine laughed, her surprise suddenly gone.

Of course.

Romaine pushed the muzzle of Henry's gun towards the ground and quickened her pace. Somewhere behind her, the Virgin Mary was marching among them. Romaine felt her presence clear as a coming storm. Romaine raised both hands in greeting and yelled up at the portico.

"Captain Mai!"

The light shifted again and ricocheted off her glass eye. "Retired," she called down. They met at the front door and Mai peppered Romaine with questions.

"Denmark part of this? Where is he?"

"On his way, we hope."

"This horde of barbarians?"

"Our army."

"James?"

"Ready to cook a meal for them if you'll allow it."

"Shoes off. Do not tramp in dirt."

James complained about the lack of ingredients but brightened at the sight of Mai's spice rack. Rice, chicken, and sausage went into two massive kettle pots and soaked up a generous blend of spices that James hoped would make up for the lack of a good broth. He stirred—it was heavy work and constant—to keep the rice from burning—as Mai and Romaine talked behind him.

A small group of plantation owners from upriver, Mai reported, had galloped past her house earlier in the day. One peeled off to warn her of what was coming and encourage her to flee. She refused, this house and land being the sum total of all her profits from twenty years of trade deals. She was too old to start again. The white man called her stupid and left.

The food disappeared as quickly as it could be served. Romaine ordered the army to take their rest, knowing there would be little sleep among these newest soldiers. Spirits were too high. A group of men dragged in branches to start a bonfire in the middle of the avenue, but then it started to rain, and the prospect of a soaking drove the recruits into Mai's grand mansion. Within minutes, every bit of floor space was filled with men and women and children lying about, this way and that.

Romaine found a patch of space to place a straight-backed chair before a window in the front hall. She watched the rain as it fell in that peculiar coastal way, straight down in sheets through a swirling wind. Romaine watched and worried and, against her own orders, slept not at all.

The next morning, they found the road into the city empty. The guardhouse at the edge of town was also empty. Was it possible the mayor was going to turn over the city without a fight?

It was not.

Two streets inside Charleston's northern edge were the barracks. In the narrow lawn that lined its front, the town's police force crouched in wait behind a barricade of interlaced logs and planks. Two buildings stretched behind the police and their makeshift barrier. The long line of windows bristled with gun barrels. Romaine saw from their arrangement that they expected her to halt her troops and set up an opposing barricade, from which the two sides would trade volleys of musket shot. This being what they expected, she would do the opposite.

Romaine raised her sword and tipped it twice forward. With practiced ease and without breaking stride, the forward ranks of Romaine's army fixed bayonets into the barrels of their muskets. Jeremiah and Little Warrior tilted their banners and led the charge, running hard. They were more than halfway to the barricade before the first blast of gunfire erupted. A musket ball whistled through the air and found its way to Jeremiah's shoulder, shattering bone and sending the young man staggering. George, run from Sequatchie River, grabbed Jeremiah by the collar and hauled him back upright. The banner wavered, and George somehow grabbed that as well. A musket ball tore through the red fabric but too late— they were at their destination, the barricade. George planted the thin pole into the bramble as Jeremiah used his three good limbs to swing and kick through the flimsy fence.

There was a second round of gunfire, men from the barrack windows firing into the barricade. It felled friend and foe in equal numbers. A furious command from the police captain to cease fire was only half heeded. Another round of musket shot ripped into the mass of men fighting on the front lawn, then another, and by the time Romaine sent forward the second wave, as many white men lay bleeding from gunshot as from bayonets.

Romaine's second wave of fighters leapt over the bodies at the barricade and rushed on, pressing themselves against the wall of the barracks. Gun barrels swiveled to follow their mark but discovered the angle too sharp. George rolled away from the barricade and joined the fight at the barrack wall. From a window set chest high, a barrel of a gun probed the air. Instinctively, George reached over and grabbed it with both hands. With a ferocious yank, the gun came loose. After a moment of surprise, George shouted in triumph and turned the weapon around, pointing its lethal end into the barracks. The maneuver quickly spread down the length of the wall. Within the minute, blasts of shot were pounding the inside of the barracks.

From the window closest to the front door, a white arm emerged, waving a white flag.

At that moment, Red Eagle was half a mile away, where the Ashley River spilled into the harbor. The current was stronger than anticipated, and they were nearly a quarter mile past his intended landing point. Ote Emathla held on to Red Eagle's belt as he flung himself towards a tree branch, and together they pulled the flatboat hand over hand to the shore and lashed the boat to the trunk of the tree. Their passengers leapt ashore, silent as jaguars, red-painted war clubs in one hand, tomahawks in the other.

Of the dozen boats that set out from the far bank of the Ashley, Red Eagle's flatboat had landed the farthest downriver. He and Ote Emathla pushed through the brush that lined the riverbank, sweeping up warriors as they hurried north, hoping they were not too late. The sound of gunfire from Charleston's northern boundary had been brief, seeming to end even as it started. This could mean Romaine had secured a quick victory, but the brevity could also mean her troops had suffered a devastating defeat. Either way, the battle's final outcome would be determined by whomever controlled the powder magazine. That was Red Eagle's target. His fighters paused and looked to him for direction as brush gave way to an open field. In the center of the clearing was an imposing stone and brick building, four stories high.

"The Sugar House." Red Eagle knew of the place by reputation. Black people who carried no documents were held there to await their reclamation. It was also where masters who preferred not to administer their own lashes turned the task over to city officials. The whipping room displayed the selection from which they could choose: paddles, single-lash whips, cat-ó-nine-tails, and bluejays with their two heavy strands of knots.

Ote Emathla watched Red Eagle studying the building that stood between them and the powder magazine. The war chief put a hand on Red Eagle's arm. "No time. We have to get to the powder magazine."

"We need to signal Denmark." There was no smoke from where the gunfire had sounded. Nor would Red Eagle's band of warriors be able to set fire to the powder magazine. The building in front of them, the Sugar House, was four stories high and extended by a steeple of sorts that jutted up another two stories. The steeple opened to a turret that had a clear view of the harbor. It was the perfect place from which to send a smoke signal. "We will be quick about it," Red Eagle promised.

The Sugar House was designed to keep people in, not to keep them out. The red-bearded man at the front gate fired a single shot and fled. There was no other resistance. With the keys the guard dropped, Red Eagle went through the prison unlocking cells and opening manacles as Ote Emathla's warriors streamed around him, tearing the panels from the walls and carrying them up the winding steps to the turret that topped the building. They formed a towering teepee out of the wood and for kindling crumbled papers specifying *twenty lashes with the cat-o-nine, thirty with the paddle* and *seventy lashes total, reserve ten for my presence Tuesday am.*

It was a joy to set the monstrosity ablaze.

Then, true to his word, Red Eagle's battalion of warriors—now increased by a few dozen men and eight women rubbing their eyes at the rising sun, and wrists and ankles where iron had cut into flesh—swept out of the Sugar House as quickly as they had swept in. The contingent hurried inland through city streets lined with houses. Shutters slammed shut as the warriors passed by.

The powder magazine was much better fortified than the Sugar House. Perhaps the most important building in town, it was built in the style of a sea turtle, thick shelled and low to the ground. A guard stood before the heavy wood doors with his gun raised, the barrel sweeping back and forth in search of a target. Ote Emathla walked into the clearing and raised his arms, yelling to draw his fire. When the guard obliged, a pair of Muskogees warriors ran full speed at the man as he tried to reload, and, with a flying leap, one warrior grabbed the white man around the waist as the other wrapped a forearm around his face and drew a blade across his throat. The only sound in the clearing was the wet gurgling noise the guard produced as he tried to protest his death.

The magazine appeared, amazingly, to be without additional protection. Ote Emathla scowled, suspecting a trap. A sweep of the area confirmed there were no other guards, but Ote still scowled. The place was rigged, he suspected, to blow up upon being breeched. He had ropes looped to the latches on the front doors and ordered his warriors to take cover well back from the blast.

At his command, they pulled open the doors.

There was no explosion.

Inside the gaping entrance, there were barrels stacked upon barrels. The smell of gunpowder drifted out into the morning sky. Red Eagle looked at Ote Emathla and clapped him on the shoulder. The war chief was no longer scowling. He was almost smiling. Before them, the powder magazine was theirs for the taking. Behind them, flames flickered from the top of the Sugar House.

From atop the main mast, the barrelman yelled down "Captain!" and pointed at the smoke curling upwards from a location deep inside the city.

Denmark ran to the bow of the ship. Unable to see anything, he ran back to the mast and climbed up the rope ladder to the crow's nest. The thickness of the plume confirmed this was a fire intentionally set. Excitement surged through his entire body. Captain Denmark searched the ship's deck for his first mate. "Nikola! Nikola!"

Denmark's crew clamored up and out of the ship's hold into the brightness of the deck. They twirled their pistols. They grimaced at each other, contorting their faces into masks ever more frightful, until their growls turned into howls of laughter. They stamped their feet and yelled a nonsensical "Hoy! Hoy! Hoy!" waiting for Denmark to release them over the side of the ship. Denmark looked over his crew and grinned. He gestured towards the dock the way butlers in Great Britain announced the start of afternoon tea. Down the gangplank they streamed, pressing close behind the Giant Nikola. Two strands of skulls rattled across the Giant's bare chest as he barreled down the plank. His foot landed on the wharf and he let out a bellow of utmost delight.

Nikola led Denmark's pirates down the docks past the row of warehouses. Inside those warehouses, Nikola knew, the vast spaces were stuffed full of rice, some packed in barrels, others in enormous canvas sacks, all of it valuable. With great effort, Nikola resisted the urge to pause and sack the warehouses, and pushed instead onward to Bay Street. As the group turned the corner, the Exchange rose before them. This was where the trade in rice and Africans made white men rich. The building's majestic façade, smooth slabs of tan stone elegantly trimmed in white, greeted them with frank contempt.

Broad steps designed to accommodate public auctions rose from the cobblestone street upwards to the Exchange's triptych of arched entranceways. On the patio that stretched back from the top step, a crowd of white men milled around, gesticulating, eyes wide and talking over one another. These were the slave traders who had arrived earlier that morning to secure a good spot for the day's auction. Only an hour before, all had been calm, a normal day of business even as rumors of uprising drifted in from the river plantations.

But then word arrived, just moments ago, that the reality was much worse than the rumors. The gunshots they had assumed were the militia taking practice drills was in fact the militia being overrun at the barracks. At the sight of Nikola the Giant, the white men went still, chipmunks hoping to escape the talons of a hawk.

Too late.

Nikola roared at his prey. He bounded up the steps three at a time, a cutlass in each hand. The white men in his path yelped and scattered.

Denmark strode through the gaping front doors of the Exchange and went in search of the building's famous dungeon. The staircase leading down into the pit, Denmark knew from reports passed down the docks, was hidden behind a plain door that suggested a small closet rather than a cavernous torture chamber. He calmly pulled open door after door as his crew members rushed around him, chasing and cursing and firing off rounds of shot. A lead ball whisked past his ear. "Careful the ricochet," Denmark admonished. The next door he opened rewarded him with the smell of dank earth. Narrow stairs dropped away before him. A pale yellow light drifted up from below.

Denmark squared his shoulders and started down the

steps, fighting to ignore the dread that flooded his body. At the bottom of the stairs, he found a heavy oak door held closed by a thick crossbar. Denmark looked back up the stairs, hopeful Nikola might have followed him down, but there was only the rectangle of light from the hallway door. Turning his attention back, Denmark pulled on the crossbar. It slid easily off its brackets. He swung open the door.

The cavern was low and dark, the ceiling vaulted in the Islamic style. Beneath the undulating brick arcs, hundreds of people stood, lay, knelt, sat, and squatted in clusters and alone. Most ignored his entrance. Those who turned to look did so with indifference. In their midst was a single white man, neatly dressed and seated behind a desk. A lamp threw a circle of light around him as he worked, head down, marking figures on a broad ledger.

"You're early," he said, not looking up.

Denmark lifted his pistol, then hesitated. Did he want to waste a shot on a mere clerk? The man was no doubt just doing his job, keeping track of sales and purchases on auction day. Then again, there would be no auctions without clerks willing to do the counting. As Denmark wavered, the blast of a gun rang out. The clerk slumped over his papers, bits of his brain splattering across the ledger's neat lines.

Denmark turned to discover Nikola at the doorway. The big man's shot roused the room and a cacophony of voices suddenly filled the cavern as men and women scrambled to their feet. The clamor rising around him, Denmark lowered his pistol and quietly answered the dead clerk. "There will be no auction today."

Chapter 19

The Exchange, now suddenly and completely empty, had been constructed twenty-five years earlier to make more efficient the buying and selling of indigo, rice, and humans. It was now the wellspring of Charleston's wealth. But a few blocks away at the center of the city stood four institutions also of great importance to the fortunes of the white gentry: the Treasury, St. Michael's Episcopal Church, the Beef Market, and the grand stone building that had once been the statehouse and now served as the courthouse.

It was here at the intersection of Broad and Meeting Street that Mary's horsemen marched the police and militiamen who earlier in the day had surrendered at the barracks. The procession of white men tugged at the ropes that bound their hands and cursed up at their guards who towered over them on horseback. When Corporal Bailey pulled free of his bindings, the more courageous of his fellow captives raised their arms and shook the rope, cheering him on. Their burst of hope turned quickly to despair as a horseman trotted out and casually snatched the corporal up by the collar, returning him to the line.

As the parade crossed into the intersection, Mary—atop her horse—led the horsemen in turning left and then left again, encircling the procession and gathering the men into a cluster before the courthouse's white stone portico. Shadows peered down from the windows that lined the top floor. Among them, Mary guessed, were the mayor and members of the city council. She wanted to present them a good view of Charleston's police force and militiamen, now prisoners of war, shackled and bound.

It was at this moment that Denmark's pirates burst through the front gate of the Meat Market. A hundred muskets swung around to confront the commotion.

The Prophetess yelled "Hold!" before any shots were fired. Romaine searched for Denmark in the rough-looking throng. She rode over to greet him, jumping off her horse to embrace the captain. "You're the last one to the party."

"Red Eagle?" Denmark asked.

"Arrived half an hour ago."

"The dungeon in the Exchange was hard to find." Denmark looked over the crowd of white men crammed into the intersection. He raised a hand to greet Mary as she rode over to join them. "We emptied it. There's enough space there to hold all your captives. You're welcome."

Mary remained on her horse, leaning down to greet Denmark. "Thank you."

Behind her, Red Eagle made his way through the crowd. His path was cleared by the dozen Muskogee warriors and simanoles who flanked him on either side, muskets held at a menacing angle. Blood still dripped from the bayonets. Denmark raised an eyebrow at Red Eagle's fancy coat and sashes. "Going to a wedding, Chief?"

Red Eagle smiled and grabbed Denmark's hand in greeting. "Captain."

Romaine moved behind Red Eagle and put her hands on the young man's shoulders. "We're sending Red Eagle up to secure the surrender." Romaine nodded up towards the upper floors of the courthouse.

Nikola frowned. "We burn down the city. No surrender."

Denmark corrected Nikola. "This is not a single battle. We need a harbor city for the coming war. And for what comes after."

"We need to be sure they see all your fearsome pirates," Romaine said to Denmark.

"Oh, they can look more fearsome than this."

"Can they light some torches and wave them around when we go up to see the mayor?"

Denmark laughed and turned to Romaine. "You don't waste time."

"None to waste," Romaine responded. "Wish us luck, Captain."

On the third floor of the courthouse, the mayor waited at the edge of the staircase and made an offer even before Red Eagle and Romaine reached the top step. In consideration of the Carolinians' long association with the Muskogees in general and Red Eagle's esteemed family in particular, they were willing to grant amnesty to all Muskogees for their part in this attack. Further, the mayor was ready to ride to Columbia and seek authorization from the governor to appoint Red Eagle a major general in the state militia. The mayor was certain the commission would be granted. Whatever the title, he and the city council could guarantee compensation. The amount was so outrageously high the mayor whispered it into Red Eagle's ear.

Romaine interrupted the speech and walked the mayor to a window that looked over Meeting Street. "We have a counter offer." Romaine pointed to the street below. "Take a look."

The mayor stared instead up at Romaine's turban. "Are you the one who burned down my plantation?"

"The one and only. I am Romaine the Prophetess. All those you forced to labor are now under my command. They want payment for their years of toil."

"Preposterous!"

"You are not in a good position to call anything preposterous."

The mayor took a slow breath and worked hard to uncurl his lip. "How much do they want?"

"They don't intend to be repaid with coins. They want payment in blood. You had a most disfavored slave named Robert, I believe, at your plantation. He refused to work after you sold away his wife. You had to use a whip to motivate him." Romaine pointed down into the intersection at a thick-shouldered man sharpening the blade of a machete. "Many times. There he is."

A sweat broke out at the mayor's brow.

"The Prophetess shows no mercy, you might have heard."

The mayor nodded, barely.

"One word from me and every white person in this city will be dead. Starting with you." Romaine waited for the mayor to accept the truth of his statement. "But if you are wise enough to surrender the city, I will have my army stand down."

The mayor looked down at the intersection. The caravan of prisoners were being marched out of the intersection. He recognizd Corporal Bailey, escorted on either side, looking back over his shoulder, eyes wide in disbelief of his predicament.

Red Eagle stood on the other side of the mayor. "The dungeon of the Exchange is now empty—your police force is being taken there for safekeeping." Red Eagle waited for the words to sink in, then continued. "You should know the Sugar House has been emptied as well. The prisoners are now soldiers. There," Red Eagle pointed to the crowd amassed before St. Michael's Episcopal. "We also have control of the powder magazine." Again, Red Eagle paused, to give the mayor time to understand the situation. "And if you're hoping for rescue by sea, the harbor is in the hands of pirates friendly to our cause."

The mayor's face turned somehow whiter. "I need time to confer with the city council. We will need assurances…"

"One hour."

"Preposter…"

"Thirty minutes." Red Eagle pulled a pocket watch from the folds of his sash and showed the mayor the time.

"We'll wait here," Romaine said. "Oh, look, Robert is trying to get your attention."

Below, warriors and simanoles flowed in to fill the street. Denmark's pirates milled around, hoisting torches and singing. At the north side of Broad, the recent occupants of the Exchange dungeon mixed with those of the Sugar House. At the center of it all, Robert looked up at the courthouse windows and held up the now-sharpened machete, waving it slowly to and fro, the afternoon sun dancing off the edge of the blade.

In James's beautiful, flowing script, the surrender document specified, at the mayor's request, that his bestowal of Charleston to "the protection of the Muskogee nation" was made necessary by his "most Christian concern for human life." All who wished to remain in the city under Red Eagle were assured the continued possession of their material possessions, humans excepted. Those who wished to vacate the city had until sundown the following day to pack their possessions, humans excepted.

The mayor hesitated as he leaned over the table to sign the paper.

"You will be commended for saving thousands of lives," Red Eagle assured him.

The mayor's frown deepened. A drop of ink gathered at the nib of his quill. "You know those who lose their slaves need to be compensated for their loss."

"They can ask it," Red Eagle said.

"They will demand it. I tell you now so you cannot pretend it is a surprise."

Red Eagle did not respond.

The mayor looked up from the paper. "You are stealing their property. You will owe them a debt." He waited, expecting an acknowledgement.

Red Eagle did not give it to him. From the direction of the harbor, the muffled sound of an explosion drifted in through the window. The silence stretched on, and Red Eagle realized he was mimicking his mother. He felt a calm spread through his body. Sehoy would have waited in silence; he would wait in silence. How easy it was to know what to do. He needed only do as his mother would have done.

The mayor sighed and put his signature on the page. "You should pay the owners for their slaves." He put down the pen and straightened his back, then his coat. "I am offering this as advice. Pay them more than a fair price. You will not be able to govern people who feel so aggrieved."

Red Eagle took the mayor by the elbow and guided him towards the stairway. "Thank you for your wisdom." At the top step, the mayor seemed reluctant to go. His shoulders sagged like a half filled bag of rice. Red Eagle gave him a gentle push onward, and the white man gripped hard at the banister as he made his way down. The mayor's one plantation had, until the day before, been worked by three hundred people. Red Eagle made the calculation. It was enormous. He heard the familiar, vaguely exasperated voice of his mother. *No debt incurs for that which cannot be bought or sold.*

Red Eagle nearly laughed aloud. His mother was apparently as certain of herself from the next world as she was in this one. She disapproved of any payments for people. So he would make no such payment. But what of mansions and horses? Should he pay the Charleston whites for requisitioning their homes? Did it make a difference whether the material goods were bought with profits from slave labor? Should loyalty to Muskogee rule be a condition of recompense? Would it be simpler to force the departure of all white people? There was much to consider. And his tenure was only—Red Eagle glanced at his pocket watch—two minutes old.

When the mayor finally made his way to the landing, he had to step aside to let someone fly past him in the opposite direction. It was Little Warrior, racing up the stairs three steps a stride. The young scout's bare torso was slick with sweat. His head was bent forward at a determined angle. He had something to report.

When Little Warrior looked up, Red Eagle saw immediately that the report he was rushing up to deliver was not at all good news.

They convened in the judge's chambers. Denmark posted Nikola the Giant at the other side of the plain pine door, to act as sentry for the group as Little Warrior gave his report.

The Tennessee militia. They were, Little Warrior said, regaining his breath, joined by men from the Georgia militia. And Carolina.

How many?

Many. I could not count. Many.

Horses?

Little Warrior nodded.

Cannons?

Yes.

How far?

Wilson's Ferry.

Three days.

Maybe less.

Mary pulled a chair close to Ote Emathla while Romaine conferred with the king of the Congaree maroons and Little

Warrior, with Red Eagle translating. They came to an agreement and went as a group to James, who sat at the judge's bench with a sheet of paper spread before him. Pen in hand and brow furrowed in concentration, James did his best to turn the sudden rush of information into a diagram of their battle plan.

"This is thé narrowest point?" Romaine asked.

The king of the Congaree maroons confirmed that it was.

"There is no other approach?"

The king of the Congaree maroons folded his thin arms and vehemently shook his head. "This is the right place to build the line. The swamp here—" He poked a finger at the spot on the page James was busy drawing in little crosshatches—"is very good for us. It is as impassable a barrier as the river. The swamp and the river will squeeze them in—they will have to pass here."

Ote Emathla frowned and rubbed his jaw. "They can cross the river, as we did, can they not?"

Mary spoke up. "He won't. Anyone else who found Hickory Ground abandoned would have been done and let the militia go home. I'm sure he's hanged a few of his own men to force them on to Charleston. No, Jackson will not cross the river. He will attack head on." Catching the king's skeptical glance, she added, "I know Andrew Jackson. I know everything about that man. Knowing there's a line, he will attack it."

Romaine looked around and felt the room in agreement. "Let's build the line, then."

Listening hard to the discussion around him, James drew three ships in the Ashley River, doing his best to make the tiny little blobs of ink look ferocious. These were Denmark's pirate ships. They would hold the left flank. On the opposite end of the line, James drew tiny 'M's' inside the still drying marks that represented the cypress swamp. Here at the other side of the line would be the Congaree maroons, joined by a few dozen of the Muskogee's most experienced warriors. They would hold the right flank.

Placing the cannons required a heated discussion of whether the recoil mechanisms on the ships' twenty-four and eighteen-pounders could be rejiggered for use on land, and how long it might take to haul the dozen cannons stored in the powder magazine the seven miles to the line. James ended the argument by drawing in twelve little cannons along the line and fluttering his hand to move the discussion along.

Romaine wanted a trench. James drew a second line in front of the cannons to represent the trench. With the new recruits from the plantations and Charleston's grand mansions eager to do their part, Romaine believed there were enough shovels, pickaxes, and enthusiasm to dig a ditch four feet deep and twice as wide along the length of the line. By mounding the excavated earth into a low rampart, their position would be doubly protected.

The king of the maroons refolded his thin arms and again shook his head. The last two days of rain, he insisted, meant they would be digging into mud. The gooey mess would not form the kind of protective barrier they wanted. Shooting from knee deep in muck would be difficult. Firing cannons would be impossible. James glared at the king, having already drawn the ditch. The king stared back with confidence. He knew something about mud.

Nikola the Giant opened the door and poked his head into the room. "Cotton bales," he offered. "Set them into the mud."

All eyes turned to Nikola's big bald dome jutting in from the courtroom. Ote Emathla asked a question, and Red Eagle stretched his arms out wide to show the size of a bale. Romaine laughed. "Very good. But where will we get cotton bales?"

"The warehouses," Nikola said with relish. "I will sack the warehouses. They're stacked full of cotton bales."

"Cotton bales, then," Romaine said. She turned the discussion to placement on the line. The simanoles under Romaine's command would take the left side of the line, Ote Emathla's Muskogee warriors the right. As for strategy, they were facing off against the combined forces of the Tennessee militia and parts of the Georgia and Carolina militias. It was the simplest of military encounters. Their objective was to build their line and hold it against attack. Jackson's objective was to attack the line and break through it.

James leaned back and admired his handiwork. His rampart was bedecked end to end with carefully drawn muskets and cannons, the placement of the various contingents of fighters artfully indicated by his flowing script. The trench was a thick, impenetrable line across the page. The cypress swamp, a dense cluster of x's bedazzled with a pair of alligators, was clearly impassable. Little horses indicating Mary's horsemen were cleverly tucked away behind a conveniently located copse of trees. On the ships patrolling the river, the skull and crossbones fluttered from tall masts. "Perfect," James thought. He didn't realize he'd spoken aloud until Denmark, standing behind him, rested a hand on his shoulder and chuckled.

"Yes, battle plans do tend to look quite good," Denmark said. "Until the enemy arrives to spoil them."

Chapter 20

Three days later, the enemy arrived in the early morning, carrying with them a fog that spread over the field thick as milk. There were two shouts, unintelligible from such a distance, then nothing. Mary heard the whinny of horses but could not guess their numbers. Denmark wanted to move his ships upriver, but there was not a wisp of wind. The *Black Dragon* and its three sister ships sat like stones where they had been anchored the prior evening, next to the line, to unload cotton bales. Little Warrior begged to be let off the line to get a better look at how large a force was amassing before them, but Ote Emathla forbid it. Whatever is there will come, he said. Whatever we can do is done.

They waited.

The fog dissipated as the sun rose over the cypress trees and silhouettes started to emerge across the field, each smudge of grey holding a musket in the forward position of an army ready to march. Romaine looked through her field glass and counted a force of not even three hundred men. There must have been quite a rash of desertions in the last few days, and these were all who remained. They were about to be ordered by Jackson to run out onto an open field with not one tree or whit of cover. They would be cut down the moment they stepped into range of the muskets. The Prophetess said a quick prayer for these unfortunate souls and considered whether to allow them to surrender. Would these men consider the sparing of their lives an act of mercy or an act of weakness?

Then the sun brightened and burned off the rest of the fog, and what Romaine saw filled her with horror. This cluster of men she had taken to be Jackson's army was but a single battalion of something much larger, an enormous beast that sprawled to the left and right of the front cluster, then back and back and yet on back. There were men and guns, more than Romaine could count, but also wagons and horses and men on horses. And cannons. There was a full battery of cannons lined up in two staggered rows, giving the impression of a mouthful of dragon's teeth.

Romaine felt her distress start to spread down the line and turned her attention to quelling the feeling of despair. In the moments before battle, when their fates became bound to one another, each person, whatever their personality and reputation, was invariably swept up into the feelings around them. They would each fight as their neighbors did, whether with dread or with courage. Romaine knew this, and she knew as well there were few things more dreadful than waiting to defend against an attack from a much larger force. To save the line, Romaine knew she needed to make the opening move, and quickly.

From the fore deck of the *Black Dragon*, Denmark through his spyglass saw Romaine turn to him and raise her arm. She presented him her open palm, closed it into a fist, and swung it twice upriver. She wanted two cannon shots into their midst, to force them to either retreat or attack. Denmark was happy to oblige. He handed the spyglass to James.

"Two, center on," Denmark said to Nikola.

The Giant seemed disappointed. "Only two? We should open with a broadside." When boarding a ship, there was nothing as persuasive as a broadside to secure a quick surrender.

James raised the glass to his eye and whistled. "I would not have had enough ink to draw *that*."

Denmark shook his head at Nikola's question. "Jackson

must have all of Georgia with him. He is not here to surrender." The Giant did not move. Denmark turned and faced Nikola. "What?"

"You taking orders from a woman."

"Who is captain on this ship? *You* take orders from me. Two shots. Do you need me to calculate the angles, or can you do that yourself?"

Nikola offered a consolatory smile and touched two fingers to his forehead. "Already done, Captain. Two, then. They will be perfect."

They were, indeed, perfect. Red Eagle from his chestnut horse heard the *boom boom* of the ship's cannons as they fired and instinctively looked across the field to see where the cannonballs would land. He caught a glimpse of motion across the sky and from the sounds that carried across the field, Red Eagle guessed the balls had landed immediately behind the front line.

"They will pull back now," he said.

Beside him atop her battle horse, Mary disagreed. "They will attack." She stroked her horse's mane. In the boredom of waiting for the battle to start, she had plaited it into a braid. Now she unbraided it as they waited to see who was right.

"You cannot ride into the field," Red Eagle said.

"That is the fifth time you've told me that."

"Because the moment you see Andrew Jackson you will ride out into the field to try and kill him. I can see it in your eyes."

"Your warriors can shoot around me."

"You cannot ride into the field."

"Six times. Now you're irritating me." Mary's horse tossed its head, impatient. Mary was glad for a more kindred spirit. "Not you. Him. You, my dear, are perfect. We have a score to settle today."

"You are not the only one with a score to settle," Red Eagle said.

"So I will settle yours too," Mary said. "Two birds with one stone." A movement across the field caught her attention. "I was right. Here they come."

They came in a surge, running not at a sprint but also not too slowly, all in a clump, without structure or strategy. The field they ran onto was flat as a crepe. There was nothing taller than a molehill to hide behind. The men of the white militia seemed determined to suffer great losses. Or they were outrageously brave. Or perhaps they believed their opponents to be poorly armed and poor shots, and so did not fear them, did not hesitate to run across the open field, did not expect the terrible burst of gunfire that exploded all at once when they crossed the invisible line between out of range and within. Every fourth man dropped to the ground, struck by one ball or more, some wounded only slightly, others mortally so. It seemed impossible to be cut down so quickly, in such numbers. Those not struck by shot threw themselves to the ground, astonished.

Those able to turn and run, turned and ran.

Romaine gave the order to hold fire and was gratified to hear only two bursts of gun fire as her order was passed down the line. She did not want to waste powder. Jackson may have gathered an enormous force, but how foolish he was to send them helter skelter into a killing field. The white general's amateur move resulted in the loss of a quarter of his force, now strewn in gruesome heaps across the field. Romaine watched a man drag himself along the ground, both legs useless.

To Romaine's left, Henry made a startled noise. "Stupid," the sharpshooter muttered and raised his gun. Andrew Jackson's cavalry, it seemed, was racing onto the field. A cavalry charge in such circumstance was madness—even the worst shot on the line would be able to hit such large targets in the long approach to the line. Henry lowered his gun. He wasn't needed in this impending slaughter.

But then the cavalry did something unexpected. When

they reached the retreating mass of militiamen, the horses were pulled out of the charge and ridden in a long oval, the horsemen encircling the fleeing fighters the way sheep dogs circle their herd.

Romaine sensed that the tallest man among the riders was leading the maneuver. The man half standing in his saddle and shouting as he waved a pistol must be Andrew Jackson. Romaine grabbed her field glass and pointed it at the scene. When the tall man reappeared in the eyepiece, there was no question—this was the crag-faced devil exactly as Mary described him. A crooked nose split two sides of a face that did not match up, the eyes of a pickpocket were set deep under a forbidding brow. As Romaine watched, Jackson pulled his horse to a halt and confronted one of the militiamen. The red-haired, big-bellied man shouted at Jackson, pointing across the field at the line and then jabbing an accusatory finger up at Jackson. The field glass showed Jackson's mouth moving but could not amplify the sound. Whatever he said infuriated the redhead, who shouted again at Jackson and leapt up, trying to grab his commander's leg. Jackson kicked the man away and backed up his horse. When the man lunged again after Jackson, two other men rushed in and secured an arm each. They pulled hard to hold him back, and the redhead pulled just as hard to escape their grasp. The effort spread the man into the shape of a cross, still yelling, furious. From his horse, Jackson pointed his pistol at the man's belly. Romaine gasped as she realized Jackson had backed his horse up not to avoid a confrontation with his own troops but to get a better shot.

The pistol flashed, and the men holding on to their brother in arms jumped away. The complainant collapsed to the ground. Without hurry, Jackson pulled a second pistol from his saddle and shot a second man.

Now the retreat was completely halted, Jackson having succeeded in giving his panicked men a closer object to fear. Jackson and the militia regarded one another silently through the circle of Romaine's telescope. Then Jackson raised his left arm and pointed somewhere out of the field glass's narrow range of sight. Romaine swept the instrument across the field, and, at the exact moment the line of artillery came into view, the carriage carrying the first cannon shuddered, and Romaine watched a ball fly out of the cannon's muzzle. The booming sound of a cannon arrived after a half second lag, chased by a familiar whistle that grew louder and closer, and closer yet. Romaine dropped the telescope and grabbed the necks of whoever was on her left and right, pushing them down to the ground an instant before the cannon ball hit.

An enormous mass of dirt erupted at the point of impact, twenty feet in front of the trench. Even before the last of the sod completed its arc and returned to the earth, Denmark was at the gunwale of the *Black Dragon*, yelling across to his other ships. "Rolling fire! When ready!" The ships' cannons were already loaded and run out, so it took only an instant for the crew member tending the foremost cannon to fire the touch hole and send a ball blasting through the air. The team at the second cannon counted to three and sent their ball out chasing the first. And so it went down the line of Denmark's ships, the balls raining down one after another at or near Jackson's position. Some of the artillery teams were more accurate than the others, and their cannonballs produced dreadful screams as they thudded to the earth. But even the cannons set at too shallow or steep an angle of fire had their effect. The rolling fire ordered by Denmark was a trick of the trade, designed to make their targets feel as if there might never be a stop to the deadly hail of cannon balls.

As Denmark climbed the mast to secure a better view of the battle, he heard the thunderous roar of Jackson's cannons responding in kind. They fired all their cannons at once, it seemed, for there was a short burst of explosions and then no more. The captain hauled himself into the crow's nest and looked down. He saw at once the gaping wound to Ote Emathla's side of the line, a breach in the ramparts twenty feet across, made by what must have been a dozen cannonballs. Denmark could not help but admire the precision of Jackson's artillerymen. He saw as well that Jackson's men were now spread wide across the field and on the move. He made a quick calculation. "Rolling fire! Do not reload!"

The Giant Nikola looked up at Denmark and tilted his head to the side to ask why no reload? Denmark shouted down his answer and the Giant's face split between a smile and a grimace. They were going to go ashore.

Jackson turned his attention to the lieutenants of his cavalry. The general ordered a charge.

Denmark saw and shouted his alarm, knowing even as he cried out that there was no chance his voice would carry down to warn his friends. He scanned the line to find Romaine, hoping the Prophetess had her scope up and was seeing what he was seeing. But Romaine was rushing towards the gap in the ramparts with a battalion of troops, to fill in for those wounded or dead. "Affix your bayonets," Denmark muttered under his breath. If his shout would not reach their ears, perhaps his prayer would. "Have them affix their bayonets, Prophetess. Cavalry charge coming."

To Denmark's surprise, instead of rushing in to close the hole in the line, Romaine's battalion stopped short of the opening, and, on the other side, Ote Emathla's fighters drew back. It was as it they were inviting Jackson's cavalry through the gap.

They took the invitation. Thundering up the field, Jackson saw his chance to split the line and ordered the charge. The general dug his heels into his horse and charged past the militiamen as they lay on their stomachs firing away. The horses stumbled across the pockmarked earth but continued on. Nothing to stop them, the first of the white militia's horsemen sprinted through the gap and reached for their muskets.

The moment the last of Jackson's cavalry crossed behind the line, Romaine's fighters and Ote Emathla's ran towards each other, some hauling cotton bales, others throwing themselves into their new positions. Denmark marveled at their speed and discipline. When he realized what they were doing, he laughed. In an instant, the gap in the line was closed and it was now Jackson's forces that were split: the cavalry behind the line, everyone else before it.

Denmark caught a flash of movement at the far side of the line. Mary's horsemen were in a charge of their own, coming across to meet Jackson's cavalry. Denmark saw the front line of horsemen sight their pistols at a full gallop and rise up in their saddles. He did not have the time to stay and watch the outcome. Nikola's shore boat was already loaded, and Denmark had to jump to make it aboard.

Mary, at the head of the charge, leaned down low over her horse and urged him into race speed. She knew she should not ride too far in front, but it was impossible to contain herself. Jackson, the devil, was so close she could smell him. The horsemen behind her fired their pistols with deadly accuracy. Then, without pause and as a single beast, still charging, they holstered their guns and pulled free their red-tipped clubs. These they smashed across chests and skulls as the two lines of horsemen swarmed through one another. The force of Mary's blow to a bearded mouth tore her club from her hand. She rode to the edge of the melee and tried to reload her pistol but fumbled the powder horn and lost it to the ground. She screamed her frustration and galloped back into the fight, pulling from her boot a small knife. It was her last weapon.

The Muskogees and simanoles on the line paid no mind to the equine commotion behind them. Their attention was on the militia in front of them. On the left side of the line, Ote Emathla spotted the boats making the short trip across the water and ordered his fighters to reload and fire, reload and fire. A shout went up as Denmark and his pirates splashed ashore, swinging their cutlasses. A moment later, there was an answering shout on the right side of the line as the maroons swept out of the cypress swamps, muskets blazing. Jackson's men were now surrounded, caught in the pinchers of maroons and simanoles, Muskogees and pirates.

Clusters of militiamen turned in circles, searching for a way out. There was none. A white man stood and threw down his musket, reaching his empty hands to the sky. A moment later, another man did the same, then another. Denmark searched the field for anyone with the authority to surrender on behalf of the entire force. The man he was searching for was on the other side of the line, rallying the remains of the cavalry.

Andrew Jackson yelled at his lieutenant to reassemble, to act like men, to follow him. But then something caught the general's attention: a glint of light thrown by the crystals sewn into Romaine's turban.

Romaine had her eyes on the white men in the field offering their surrenders. Two turned to dozens, dozens almost immediately to hundreds, thrusting their empty hands up towards the sky. Romaine called for a halt in the shooting. She did not see Andrew Jackson turning his horse to charge at her.

Mary from atop her horse spotted Andrew Jackson. And immediately saw the danger to Romaine. "Prophetess!" Mary screamed. "Look up!"

Romaine did look up, but too late. The Prophetess looked up and saw the barrel of Jackson's pistol. She heard the sharp whistle of the incoming bullet the moment before it struck her. The shot that entered Romaine's body was a drop of lead, the size of a child's marble, but it felt to the Prophetess as if it was an enormous, invisible hand that swung down from the heavens and slapped her to the ground. So this was what it felt like to be shot. In her year of fighting in Saint-Domingue, hundreds of bullets had whizzed past her, some within inches, and she had emerged with not so much as a scratch. She had healed dozens of seemingly mortal wounds, building a reputation that brought her troops. The Prophetess will not let you die, they said to one another. As Romaine fell, she wondered whether she would be able to heal herself. Her head struck the ground very hard and a blazing pain flared in her shoulder.

The Prophetess watched the clouds drift across the sky. Her daughter Louise-Marie once asked whether the sky remained as blue the higher it climbed. Romaine wished to lie still a moment to consider the answer, but there in the near distance was Andrew Jackson wheeling his horse around. The legs of his horse made the turn and churned at the earth, carrying Jackson back towards Romaine, faster and faster. It was not only Jackson rushing towards her, but also, nestled in the barrel of the pistol that he held in his right hand, a bullet. This one was intended by Jackson to pierce her skull. Jackson's god, Romaine knew, would guide this one on the course the general intended.

Romaine struggled to gain her feet. She might be fated to die, but so long as she was alive it was her obligation to make the wishes of her enemies as hard as possible to fulfill. With enormous effort, Romaine managed to roll to her side, but now her good arm was wedged beneath her. She could not push herself up. Jackson was nearly upon her. Romaine had time for a final prayer to the Virgin. "Most beloved Mary," she said—

A black horse thundered by, charging head-on towards Jackson.

Mary rode low against the mane of her horse, full gallop. This horse, stolen by Red Eagle from the Jockey Club, was the fastest creature Mary had ever ridden. Its thick, powerful hindquarters were unsuited for multiday rides, or even for two-mile races, but for this—a mad quarter-mile sprint—it was magnificent. Mary had her knife but no plan. She knew only that this was Andrew Jackson before her, who had killed her sister as surely as if he had put a pistol shot between her eyes.

The two horses were fifty yards apart. Mary loosened her feet from the stirrups. Jackson's horse tried to veer away, but Jackson pulled it back in line. Both hands now on the reins, the general no longer pointed his pistol at the Prophetess. They were twenty yards apart. Mary pulled her right foot onto the saddle. Jackson raised his pistol, even though at such a close distance—ten yards now—he would not have time to get off a shot. Mary pulled herself into a crouch on the saddle and hung on one-handed to her horse's mane. Five yards. The animal knew what she wanted and obliged, angling in as if to collide with Jackson's mount.

Mary leapt. She slashed at the air and felt the knife make contact against Jackson's throat as she hurtled into him. The force of impact sent both of them crashing over the side of his horse. They hit the ground in a tangle of arms and legs, with Mary bearing the brunt of the fall. She felt the air get knocked out of her lungs. To her great fury, the air refused to return and she lay there on the ground open-mouthed and breathless as Jackson pushed himself away from her. Blood poured from a gash in his neck, yet he seemed unaffected by the wound. He reached behind his back.

His hand came back with a hunting knife.

Jackson flipped his hold on the knife into a reverse grip, the better to hammer the blade downward and rip back. The general raised himself up to his knees, the knife at the ready up by his ear. Mary did not blink. Jackson hesitated, recognizing Mary. His jockey. His slave. His runaway. His lost property. His lost profits. *His…*

Andrew Jackson's chest blew open. Mary squeezed her eyes shut at the splattering of blood and flesh. With great effort, her lungs finally sucked in a rush of air, and she rolled away as Jackson toppled forward.

By the way the body fell forward, Red Eagle knew his shot was good and Andrew Jackson was dead. A feeling of exaltation rose in his body. It had to struggle upwards through a heaviness in his gut that tried to block the way. In some other universe, Andrew Jackson was still alive. In some other universe, Red Eagle would never have met Mary or James or Denmark or Romaine. In some other universe, the age of revolution would close without completion.

But that was not this. In this universe, they would be victorious. His mother Sehoy would be remembered and respected and forever beloved. Red Eagle threw down his musket and ran as hard as he could to get to Mary.

Chapter 21

James made fourteen varieties of gombo for the victory celebration. It was nearly midnight when his fellow cooks hauled
the pots to the wharfs, the stars a fistful of salt flung across
the sky. These were now the wharfs of Chicora, the name the
Kiawahs called this place before it was Charles Town. A few
years to the future, when the revolution was to come complete, the new republic in Saint-Domingue would do the
same, calling itself by the Taino name Hayti. But that was
still in years to come. For now, James stood at the edge of the
festivities, his spatula cocked on his hip, keeping watch over
the doling out of rice and soup.

Cradling their bowls between their hands like hymnals,
the people found seats along benches and low stone walls.
Some stood on wagons or climbed atop posts. They slurped
at their wondrous soup, and James realized it was a mistake
to offer so many choices of gombo. The rising chatter among
the crowd was everyone asking their neighbors for a taste
of their bowl even as they tried to guard their own against
trespass.

Jeremiah and Ellison traded bowls, then nearly came to
blows when Ellison discovered he'd exchanged a half serving for a sludge of rice. Kwame intervened, spooning up a
chicken gizzard to mollify. Ote Emathla gave his bowl away
to Nikola the Giant, who downed it in a single slurp before
anyone could notice. Only Henry saw, his sharpshooter eyes
narrowing at the injustice.

Yours has crab? Look, I was on the line. Nicked by a musket ball right here—it's not much now but bled bad when it happened. Just one spoonful.

Fanny Goode's ancient face gave no quarter. She pulled her bowl in close and turned her back to the Congaree maroon's plea. Goode reconsidered as she ate. Was he even a maroon anymore, now that he was out of the swamps and back in town? Perhaps they were all maroons now, herself included, hiding in plain sight in this harbor town. *Their* town. The thought buoyed Goode. She turned back and offered what remained in her bowl to the man.

When the last lick of gombo was gone, the crowd pulled back to open a circle in the green along the waterfront. Red Eagle called for the start of the dancing. His warriors set their feet forward, soles gliding close to the ground, one foot never crossing the other. They moved with deliberate steps in a spiral to the clack of turtle shells and the beat of spoons against upturned bowls. Rebecca from among the simanoles recognized this was not a dance but a prayer and latched herself to the back of the spiral, calling others to join her. She clapped a syncopated rhythm against the turtle shell clack, and, as if granted permission, the beat of spoons broke into a dozen new cadences.

A bass drum sounded and took over the task of keeping time. Romaine, her right arm held close to her body in a cloth sling, felt the air shift around her. The dancers leaned their backs into the drum's easy heartbeat, arms suddenly free to lift up the melody of the song. The spiral grew dense with dancers, then thinned as some laid off to rest, then thickened again as a new song started. The dancers, Romaine saw, were forming a creature capable of continuing on through the night, through the next day, through however long it might take for their prayer to be heard.

Romaine wished to join the dance herself, but there was rice to be loaded if the *Black Dragon* was to sail in the morning. Those not dancing rushed to help. They hauled a treasury of the Rice Coast's finest product from the warehouses to the dock, lowering each bulging bag of Carolina gold carefully down into the dark recesses of the ship's belly. Romine was vastly pleased. There was no better offering to the rebels in Saint-Domingue. On an island with fields exhausted by the production of sugarcane and coffee, a shipment of rice was life itself. With such a gift, the rebellion in Saint-Domingue and this one on the main would soon be joined as one.

What form the combined forces would take, Romaine could only guess. Even before the last of the dead and wounded had been carried off the field of battle, Red Eagle had sent Little Warrior north, to let the Cherokee know their war chief Dragging Canoe's campaign against the Americans was revived. The young scout's instructions were to then travel yet farther north to find a young man among the Shawnee named Tecumseh. When Romaine asked Red Eagle whether he was reviving the Grand Confederacy of North and South, the new mayor of Chicora had smiled and agreed it was the right time for a revival. "But this time, all the way south to Cartagena," he'd said.

Romaine watched from the ship's deck as a trio of women wrestled with the final bag of rice. Laughing as they rearranged themselves to cross the narrow gangplank, the tallest of the three lost her balance, and the bag fell off her shoulders. The other two made a grab for the precious cargo but succeeded only in tearing the bag. Rice spilled out into the water. A small panic rose in Romaine's chest as she calculated how many soldiers on Saint-Domingue would go hungry.

The Prophetess waited until the last bag was safely in the hold before going to find Denmark. The captain was in his quarters, examining a nautical map. "The last time I took this route," he said without looking up, "we'd just picked up James in Philadelphia. He asked us to make a grocery stop in

Savannah. He wanted parsley. And pepper. We had pepper. He wanted *better* pepper."

"If you had not paused, perhaps you would have missed me in Le Cap," Romaine said.

Denmark straightened and cocked his head at Romaine. "I would have found you, Prophetess—there was no other possibility. This triumph is foreordained."

"Which triumph?"

"Of *liberté*. Over *libertad*."

"I'm sure you are right, Captain." Romaine liked Denmark's confidence, but she knew from personal experience even the most obvious of destinies could go askew. She glanced at the open door to Denmark's empty bedchamber. "James has not made up his mind?"

Denmark shook his head. "With James, nothing is foreordained."

The next morning, James went to the harbor with the rest of the town to bid the *Black Dragon* adieu. An old woman, one eye shut by age or violence, recognized him and grabbed him by the arm, pulling him through the crowd to the dock's edge. "Push over, it's gombo man!" she said, and they did, making room for James on the front row.

Barely aware of the hubbub around him, the great chef stood with his hands in his pockets and watched silently as Denmark prepared the ship to sail. From the quarterdeck, Captain Denmark called out to his crew, ordering the sails unfurled and the heaving lines loosed. The foresail caught the wind and pulled the schooner away from the dock. Denmark ordered the hatches battened and the anchor hauled home.

When the ship's stern cleared the farthest piling, Denmark appeared at the gunwale and looked back to the docks, searching for James across the water.

I will miss you until I return.

Yes, you will.

Denmark brought his right hand to his chest and tapped two beats against his own heart. The crowd around James leapt into the air and burst into cheers, believing the gesture was directed at them.

Someone jostled up against James and slipped their arm into his. It was Mary, with Red Eagle squeezing in next to her. Mary reached up on her tiptoes to give James a kiss on his cheek.

"You're good to stay."

James forced his mouth into a smile. "The stove on that ship—it's impossible to cook on."

The trio watched as the *Black Dragon* sailed off. The schooner was halfway across the harbor when it blasted out a twelve-gun salute. In the time it took the men mounding dirt into ramparts to scramble up the embankment, load the cannons, and respond in kind, the *Black Dragon* slipped around the harbor's lip and was gone, carrying Romaine the Prophetess home to Saint-Domingue.

A sharp, familiar fear gripped James, of leaving the known for something utterly new. He had done such a thing many times before, but this time even the name was new. *Chicora.* Under the command of Red Eagle who had never commanded anything more than a string of horses. Half the whites gone but the other half holed up in their mansions and cottages, simmering with resentment, waiting for rescue. Denmark's pirates on their way to Savannah. Romaine promising to return with fighters from Saint-Domingue, but did they not have a revolution of their own to fight?

James calmed himself by recalling his previous migrations. From Virginia to Paris. Philadelphia to Denmark's seas. Nuevo Orleans to Hickory Ground. He thought of Denmark in the sailmaker's loft, telling him the truth of his life, that he was not born to be a slave. He understood now that under those words there was another, more basic truth: no one ever is.

Yet there were those who believed otherwise, who believed profits were the essence of freedom, who believed humans and land could be bought and sold. Would Red Eagle be able to pacify the whites who remained in town and believed in the lash and the lie? Did Romaine the Prophetess have faith enough to bind together the uprisings here and on Saint-Domingue? How long did they have until the United States sent down their army to reclaim land they believed was theirs?

James knew such predictions were beyond his ken. But he did know one thing: that as sure as cream, properly whisked, rises into crème fraiche, the men and women crowded around him were the great hope of the most just God. James felt the heat of Mary's arm pressed against his. He felt the air of the future rushing into his lungs. James held the breath and let the taste settle in his mouth. It was earthy and rich, cool against his tongue. There was truffle in it, a bit of salt, iron, a sprig of mint. It was a taste both obvious and unexpected. James drew in another breath and tried to understand the blend of flavors. The parts of it were too complex for him to name, but the whole of it was simple. And magnificent. James let the breath seep into him and started a list of ingredients, wondering where in this town he might find a decent kitchen. He was ready to begin again.

Acknowledgments

To my parents, for your courage, wisdom, and unrelenting support, thank you.

To Tananarive Due, for teaching how a good story is a labor of respect, thank you.

To Karen Pittelman, for turning an olio of ideas and historical facts into that good story, thank you.

To Alta Starr and adrienne maree brown, for insisting the good story find a better home than my desk drawer, thank you.

And to Xochitl Bervera, love of my life, for your indomitable, revolutionary spirit, thank you, truly thank you.